BLADE, WE ARE GOING TO DIE HERE . . .

Blade, working by touch, gutted the huge woolly animal. He pulled the hot, steaming guts out and dumped them nearby, then picked up the shivering girl. "This is going to be bloody and messy," he told her, "but you will be warm."

By now Ooma was too cold, too near death, to care or to answer. She tried to cling to him, but her arms would not function. Blade put her into the hot cavern of the gutted animal and, wedging her as deeply into the carcass as he could, closed it about her. He fumbled for the entrails, found them, strung them out and used them to bind the two sides of the carcass together by looping the gut around the front and back legs. At least Ooma would be warm for tonight. He spoke to her down through the bloody slitted belly of the dead animal.

"How is it, girl? Snug enough now?"

"Warm, Blade. So warm. I think I will sleep now. It is like being in my mother's womb again."

Blade smiled, shook his head and went about the business of his own survival. He wedged himself back into a corner of the little makeshift cave, while wind and sleet moaned past the rock opening. Tomorrow, he would need all his strength . . .

THE RICHARD BLADE SERIES

LIBERATOR OF JEDD

The Richard Blade Series

by
Jeffrey Lord

PINNACLE BOOKS • NEW YORK CITY

Chapter 1

Lord Leighton was, at best, an indifferent speaker. For some reason which J was unable to fathom the old man had agreed to make the tiresome journey to Reading and address a seminar of Britain's leading brain surgeons gathered at the University. Later, when the confusion and danger was over, J was to guess that the old man had hoped to learn something about the human brain that he did not already know. What this could possibly be J could not surmise; the old fellow had already far surpassed the mortal brain by building a seventh generation computer—now waiting for Richard Blade in its guarded vault beneath the Tower of London—and so J put the rare expedition down to vanity, boredom and a desire to exchange chitchat with other scientific minds.

Lord L, J thought now, must get very weary of talking to J. For J was most definitely not a scientific brain. He was a prosaic and pragmatic man, a spy master when he had time to work at it. Which was not often these days. The truth was that J, caught up as he was in the computer experiments and Blade's dangerous forays into Dimension X, at times nearly forgot that he was head of MI6A.

Just now, as he squirmed on the hard seat and watched Lord L hem and haw and clear his throat, J was a little bored himself. Also tired and hungry. And worried about Richard Blade.

Lord Leighton clung to the lectern for support, rather like a frail old lion propping himself against a tree, and peered at his audience with hooded yellow eyes. His mane of white hair, thin and silky, haloed his pink scalp as though defying gravity.

"In such an electromechanism as the modern computer," he was saying, "we have at least succeeded in eliminating the danger of schizophrenia. We build computers to a complex schema, most complex, but when they *are* built they function exactly as intended. This certainly cannot be said of the human brain."

Lord L moved a bit, shifting his hold on the lectern to ease the omnipresent pain in his hump, and J felt a surge of pity and admiration for the old scientist. How did he ever manage to keep going?

For that matter how did Richard Blade manage to keep going? The boy had made four harrowing and desperate trips into Dimension X. In the morning he would go through the great computer again. His fifth time out. J sighed and shook his head, causing the man in the next seat to regard him curiously, and decided to reserve all his sympathy for Blade. The boy was tense. Nervous. Drinking a little too much and chasing far too many women. All symptoms of strain and fatigue, J thought, though Lord L did not agree.

"The chief difference," his Lordship was saying, "is that a computer, a cybernetic machine, is a unit, a single component, so to speak, and so it has the advantages and the integrity of such a unit. Man, on the other hand, really has three brains. The pity, and the source of most of our troubles, is that those three brains must function as *one* brain. This they find hard to do at times. And sometimes impossible. The three brains fight each other. And I think, though I admit to a great oversimplification here, that this is one of the reasons why man continues to war against man. In a world run by computers there would be no wars. Because to computers war would just not make *sense*."

J fidgeted and sneaked a glance at his watch. Some twenty minutes to go. Then, with any luck, they could catch the 10:47 back to London. J wondered what Dick Blade was doing at the moment. Probably something

6

much more sensible than listening to a crowd of elderly pundits discuss something that one didn't understand, in a jargon that was all but incomprehensible. J sighed again and shifted his lean nates on the hard chair. Yes. Blade was probably, in the parlance of youth today, making out.

"The oldest of our brains," said Lord L, "is reptilian. We have had it for billions of years. The second brain, engrafted onto the first is, of course, lower mammalian. The third brain, the latest to be melded to the first two, is also mammalian. But late mammalian. It is what makes man—man. Usually we call it the neo-cortex."

Lord L paused a moment, leered at the audience and added: "And that, gentlemen, is why we are always in so damned much trouble! That bloody neo-cortex of ours."

Titters. Then laughter. His Lordship, when the mood was on him, could sound more like a Cockney than a man born near Bow Bells, and his language could put a costermonger to shame.

J did not laugh. That bloody neo-cortex. Blade's neo-cortex that Lord L had been tinkering with for months now. Taking it apart and putting it together again. Scrambling the molecules and atoms and reassembling them in a manner that allowed Blade to wander into Dimension X. A dimension that no other man on this earth might see or know. Only Richard Blade.

J found himself shivering. He was sweating and it was almost cold in the hall. How long could Blade keep it up? How many times could he go into Dimension X and come back? Come back sane and whole?

Of a sudden J found that he was badly frightened. The terror of the thing, of what they were doing with Blade and the computer, descended on him like black dead weight for the first time.

He could only hope that Richard Blade did not feel the same. A frightened man would stand no chance whatever out in Dimension X.

Lord L hobbled around to the other side of the lectern and clung to it, sipping from a glass of water. "As you all know," he continued, "it was an Englishman, Charles

Babbage, who designed the first 'analytical engine' in 1820. He thought it out rather fully, as a matter of fact, though of course the technology of the time was not up to building it. And I might add that since 1820 a great many of us have not known whether to damn or praise Mr. Babbage."

More titters and laughter.

Lord L went into his peroration. He wound it up quickly, for which J was grateful. Only a quarter of an hour had been granted for questions. They might catch their train yet.

A tall balding man, young for this assembly, was asking a question.

"Do you think it possible, Lord Leighton, that we will ever learn to control human behavior by changing the pattern of the brain cells? Will the time come when we can restructure the cellular molecules, rearrange the constituent atoms? Completely change the electrochemistry of the brain?"

It seemed to J that Lord L, tottering by the lectern, looked directly at him. There was a wisp of smile on his Lordship's thin lips as he answered.

"I think that is very possible. I believe it is being done now, to a certain extent, on monkeys, by planting electrodes in the brain and controlling the subject by remote radio stimulation."

J felt an overwhelming desire to go to the men's room and vomit. He now understood why Lord L had made the trip to Reading. The sly old bastard was looking for a brain surgeon. He had plans, new plans, for Richard Blade. Just scrambling his brain cells and sending him into Dimension X was no longer enough. The scientist in Lord Leighton was taking over from the human being.

He was not normally a profane man, but now J let a string of obscenities race through his mind. It wasn't going to happen! Not while he was bloody well alive. Dick Blade was like a son to him and they were not going to butcher him. Rage overwhelmed J. He would see to it. He would blow the whole damned Project DX first.

8

Going back to London they had a first-class compartment to themselves. J wasted no time in voicing his suspicions. Lord L made no attempt at denial. The old man was arrogant and crusty and very much aware of his eminence as Britain's first scientist. As such he never stooped to lying.

"My dear J," the old man said, "there is no need to get all in a lather. It was a thought I had, a stray and tentative thought, nothing more. And of course we should have to have Blade's permission for any, er, any such brain surgery."

"I'll see that you don't get it," said J angrily. "I goddamned bloody well will see to it. The boy has done enough. Maybe too much. There are already personality changes in him that I don't like."

Lord L gave him a bland look, hooding his yellow eyes in the way he had. "I suppose so," he murmured. "Bound to be a few changes, my dear fellow, when your cortex has been restructured as many times as Blade's has. No help for it. But you overlook a point—such changes are not necessarily for the worse. I am quite as fond of Blade as you are, and I study him most carefully—though I admit I lack the emotional overload you carry—and so far I have seen nothing harmful, no cause for alarm."

J knew he was no match for this aging little hunchback. Lord L had a mind like a razor and he could slash you to bits with it. J set his jaw and retreated into stubbornness.

"I remind you, Leighton, that I am head of MI6A and that Blade is under my direct command. There will be no such operations as I am sure you have in mind. If necessary I will go directly to the Prime Minister. He was in the infantry. He will understand about combat fatigue."

His Lordship, when he found the going unpleasant, was given to non sequiturs. "In my war," he said mildly, "they called it shell shock."

J was shocked at his own reply. "I don't give a good tinker's fuck what you called it in your war. That boy has been into Dimension X four times and tomorrow he goes out again. All right. So be it. But when he comes back this

9

time, *if* he comes back, I am going to pull him out of Project DX. Blade has done his bit. You had better start looking around for a new boy."

Lord L smiled sweetly and leaned to tap J's knee. "I think we shall have to leave that up to Blade himself, J. And I also think that you know what his answer will be *if* it comes down to a question of country and duty. In any case it is all very much in the future. Now please do be quiet and let me think—I've a nasty little problem in quadruple feedback circuitry to solve."

His Lordship slumped in his seat, eased his hump, and began to scribble on the back of an old envelope.

J's first anger had faded. He now regarded the old man with his usual mixture of admiration and loathing. The cold-blooded old bastard was right, of course. Dick Blade would do anything that was asked of him. Meet any test, volunteer in the face of any danger, keep going out into Dimension X as long as he was needed. It was just the way Richard Blade was made.

J leaned back and tried to relax. The train was racing through a small village where a few lights still gleamed here and there. A crowd was spilling out of the local, laughing and shouting cheerful good nights.

J thought that he would call Blade as soon as he got back to his office. He would not be sleeping tonight anyway and there was work piled on his desk. He would just call and check to make sure that Blade was ready for the ordeal tomorrow. His fifth time through the computer into God only knew what.

Again he wondered what Blade was doing at the moment. He hoped it was something pleasant. Something very pleasant.

Chapter 2

Richard Blade was at the moment enjoying himself. Not many men, even fine swimmers and top-flight athletes, as Blade was, would have shared his enjoyment. He was half a mile from shore in the icy Channel. A raw mid-March wind was slicing off whitecaps and whipping up waves. The water was, as Viki complained, fit only for polar bears. But Blade found himself reveling in it.

Blade was naked but for a jockstrap. He floated and stared at the sullen dark sky, overcast and with no hint of stars or moon. A cold wave slapped at him viciously. Blade rolled through it and slid down into the trough. He was feeling better. The muzzy feeling from too many brandy and sodas had gone. He ran his teeth over his tongue and felt the thick coating. It had become a regular morning thing—the coated tongue. He was putting away too much booze. Far too much. He did not seem able to stop the drinking and he never got drunk. Weary at times, utterly weary, and with moments of desolation and despair that he had never known before, but never drunk. In a way it was a cheat.

And there was the little matter of satyriasis. Blade's smile was grim. His sexual appetite these days was excessive, to say the least. Not at all like the old Blade. Then he had been satisfied with one woman and very little booze. But that had been the *old* Blade. Before Dimension X. Before he had gone four times through the computer. He had had Zoe then and they had planned to be married. All this before Lord Leighton and the monstrous computer and Dimension X. And the Official Secrets Act

11

which precluded Blade from so much as hinting at his real job or the reasons for his long absences.

Zoe had left him and married another man.

Blade let a wave carry him toward the cove where Viki waited, a slim forlorn figure shivering in a British warm. She thought he was a little crazy. Blade went deep and swam powerfully beneath the turbulence, thinking that perhaps his latest girl was not too far off the mark.

Not that he had any real doubts about his sanity. He didn't. And he had never been in better physical shape. It was just that he knew, and admitted—and so must J and Lord L—that the brain-scrambling trips through the computer were affecting him. Looking at it dispassionately, Blade mused as his lungs began to pain, it would have been extremely odd if his brain had *not* suffered a few changes. It was to be expected. The important thing was not to panic—don't push the panic button. It was nothing he could not handle. He felt sure of that.

Viki—pronounced as though spelled with a C—Randolph was at the moment dancing in a West End musical. She had a speaking part—two lines—and considered her career well launched. She was a tall girl with an elfin face and gypsy eyes, slim legs and arms and a tiny waist, and surprisingly large cone-shaped breasts. Her real name was Poldalski and her father was a dustman in Putney. This latter Blade had ascertained more out of idle curiosity and boredom than anything else; he was not a snob and could not have cared less about the antecedents of his bed partners. It had been something to do, finding out all about Viki, and between trips into Dimension X he badly needed something to do. For with the advent of Project DX he was no longer permitted to work at his profession of secret agent. J might have allowed it, but Lord L was adamant. His Lordship had no intention of losing Blade to a bullet, knife, rope or poison.

He surfaced, blowing hard, and struck out for the cove in a fast racing crawl. Viki waved, and desire surged in him and despite the shockingly cold water he began to achieve tumescence. The hard bind of the jockstrap

12

caused him a slight discomfort. Nothing, he thought, to what Viki would presently feel. She had complained of soreness only that morning, after half an hour of his compulsive lovemaking.

Blade felt bottom and began walking in to shore. Yesterday morning, yesterday afternoon, twice last night and then that long bout this morning. Yes, my boy. Definitely you are afflicted with satyriasis. The Oxford Dictionary called it "insatiable venereal appetite in the male."

Ask Viki. For that matter, ask Hester or Stella or Babs or Pam or Evelyn or Doris.

Do you see, Lord Leighton, what your goddamned machine has done to a onetime English gentleman by name of Richard Blade?

Blade grinned and laughed aloud into the mad March wind that was tearing across the little beach. Why blame it on poor old Lord L and his computer? Maybe it was just his true nature emerging at last.

He left the water and stalked toward the waiting girl, droplets of salt water beading on his massive tanned body. To a sculptor's eye Blade would have seemed fashioned of brown concrete, with every muscle and tendon defined with the precision of a Praxiteles. So perfectly formed and proportioned was he that at first glance the eye was fooled. He appeared much taller than his six-foot-one and much heavier than his two hundred-ten pounds, and he had taken blues in all major sports at Oxford with an ease that suggested games for babies. Which, to Blade, they were. His physical prowess had been, quite often, a source of actual embarrassment to him. He did so easily what other well-endowed men could not do at all.

Viki Randolph had a whiney voice when she chose to use it, and she chose now.

"You were long enough," she accused. "I don't much like it, you know, being left to freeze on this bloody beach while you go pretending you're a seal or something."

Blade smiled and slapped her behind. He knew how to handle this type. He let his hand linger for a moment and

13

squeezed a buttock. Viki gave him a look and pulled away.

"You're pouting," he said, "and it does not become you, ducks. Come on, then. Back to the cottage and I'll see to it that you are well warmed up."

Viki watched him warily. Blade gave her a leer and a wink. She groaned. "Oh, no! Not again. Don't you ever think of anything except sex? Or *do* anything else?"

Just then Blade wanted a brandy and soda more than he wanted her. He watched as she gathered her belongings from a blanket, using a small flashlight to find cigarettes and purse and various oddments. The wind took on a shriller note and though he began to goose pimple he was not cold.

They started toward the path that led up the cliff to the cottage, Viki carrying the things in a pouch made of the blanket.

"I am a reasonable man," Blade said. "If you will tell me anything else that is as important, as interesting and as much fun as sex, I will give it due consideration and let you know if I agree. Now what could be fairer than that?"

She surprised him then. The whine left her voice as she said, "The trouble is, darling, that you treat me like any stupid totsy. Just another dumb showgirl. You don't really talk *to* me. You talk *at* me. And you're never serious, not even for a moment. You act as if it would be a waste of time to be serious with me, as though I wouldn't understand you. You're arrogant, Dick. Very arrogant. And you don't even know it."

Blade stalked on ahead. The path was difficult here, steep and switchbacking back and forth, with a fallaway of some 200 yards. It was the highest cliff on the Dorset coast and among the locals was known as Suicide Leap.

Viki was right, of course. He was on the arrogant side. Nature, birth, background and training had all conspired to make it so. Blade was aware of this venial sin and fought against it, not always with success. At the moment, just now, he was piqued and irritated. First because he

14

seemed to have misjudged Viki, or to have been badly fooled by her dumb showgirl mask, and second because he had no desire, need or intention of forsaking sex for philosophy and the finer aspects of life. He'd brought her down from London for one thing and one thing only—bed. And it was, by God, going to be bed, when and as often as he chose, and nothing else.

"Dick! Wait for me. I'm a girl, remember, not a great monster like you."

She was lagging far behind. He went back and picked her up and tossed her over his shoulder and began to climb again.

Viki panted in his ear. "You had a phone call while you were practicing to swim the Channel. I forgot cigarettes and had to go back and someone rang up while I was there."

Blade trotted easily up the steep incline. "Who?"

"Very mysterious. It was a man, but he wouldn't leave a name. He left a message for you."

"What?"

"To call J as soon as you got back to the cottage. That was all. Just to call J."

He nodded and stepped up his pace. What could J want? Everything was worked out, all plans made. Blade was due at Lord L's house in Prince's Gate for his final briefing at eight the next morning. Then on to the Tower of London and the trip through the computer into some new Dimension X. So? Some last-minute hitch? Blade shrugged. He would call J, of course, but in his own good time. Viki, warm and vibrant and bouncing on his big shoulders, had first claim.

Viki bit his ear. Then she thrust her tongue into it. Blade, who was lugging her along in the fireman's carry, moved a brawny hand up the inside of her pants-clad leg and gripped her firmly where she joined. She squirmed.

"Leave off that, Dick. For God's sake. Do you want to drive me crazy?"

"You started it, ducks. When a girl kisses a man's ear

15

like that it's like a green light flashing. And anyway, why play games—you know you love it. You want it as much as I do."

Silence. Blade trotted, easily. Viki joggled up and down on his shoulder, her spectacular breasts crushed against the back of his neck. He could feel them even through the thick coat.

She bit his ear again. "You're right, of course, you big bastard. I guess I am a bad lot. But only where you are concerned! That I will have you understand, Dick Blade. I don't act like this with—with every man I go out with. But with you I just don't know—I don't seem to have any willpower. All you have to do is touch me and I do anything you want. And I don't like it. I hate it. And I think I hate you."

"Good," said Blade. "Keep it that way and we'll get along very well." He squeezed again, manipulating her expertly, and she moaned and caught at his hand and tried to pull it away. Blade laughed.

When they reached the cottage he piled logs on a smoldering fire and took a fast shower to get the salt off him. He had a brandy and soda and debated whether to call J now or later. He decided on later.

Viki, sitting primly in a big leather chair near the fire, was reading an old copy of *Punch* as Blade moved restlessly about in his robe. She kept glancing at him over the magazine. She sat with her long legs tightly crossed. When he offered her a drink she refused it. Blade shrugged and made another for himself. It must, he told himself, be the last. He was due in London at eight and that meant an early start. It would be nice if he could sleep tonight—sleep as he had once slept, without the hideous nightmares that brought him awake screaming and covered with cold sweat. Sleep to knit up the raveled sleeve of care.

Sleep? Macbeth hath murdered sleep.

Macbeth hell! Lord L hath murdered sleep with his damned computer. Dimension X hath murdered sleep.

Logs were roaring in the fireplace now. Blade stood in

16

front of it, drink in hand, and stared into the blue-yellow flames. Viki had put down her magazine and was watching him intently. He ignored her. Outside the snug little cottage the wind hooted in derision.

In that moment Richard Blade knew what ailed him. Or rather he admitted it to himself—for the first time. He was afraid. There was nothing wrong with his brain and certainly not with his body. It was fear. Fear was the cankerworm eating away in his guts. And it was incredible. This sort of fear was beyond understanding. He had known fear before—as what man in his dangerous profession had not—but it was the healthy and necessary fear that kept a man alive. This present fear, the thing he now endured, was a slimy loathsome presence in his entrails.

Blade did not want to go up to London tomorrow. Blade did not want to go through the computer again. Blade did not again want to make the awesome and appalling journey into Dimension X.

Blade would do all those things. He would force himself to do them. It was unthinkable that he should not. Otherwise he would not have been Richard Blade.

Viki, back to her small, whiney voice again, said, "I'm hungry, Dick."

He was across the room in three strides and picked her up. He held her high over his head, as easily as a child holds a doll, and brushed her dark head against the timbered ceiling. His laugh filled the cottage and boomed over the March wind off the Channel.

"As my American friends say, ducks, I have got news for you. You are not hungry. Not for food. You are hungry for love. For sex. For a long and unstinted bout of sex that will never end. Never."

Viki struggled. She kicked him in the chest. "I am not," she moaned. "I'm not, Dick. Really. Please. I am terribly sore there. I don't want—"

He dropped her. She fell into his arms and he crushed her with one big arm and kissed her fiercely. "You do want," he told her.

Abruptly she stopped struggling and slid her sharp little

17

tongue into his mouth. She nodded and pulled away for a moment to say, "Yes, you awful beast. You make me want. God—I must be as crazy as you are."

Blade lifted her by the elbows and carried her to the fire. He kissed her again. Viki responded avidly, but said, "There is no tenderness in you, Dick. None at all. You are just rogue male, all of you. And I am mad for you. I don't understand any of it. Nor you. Nor me."

She was wearing a heavy cable-stitched sweater. As he searched under it, pulled it high and unfastened her brassiere, Blade admitted the accusation. It had not always been true. There had been a time—

To hell with that. One did not live in the past. Nor, in his profession, did one count on the future. There was only now.

The brassiere came loose. He lifted each perfect breast from its nylon sling. Soft milk-white marble brushed with flickering fire shadow. He caressed and kneaded and felt her go lax. Her knees sagged and he held her tight.

He pulled the sweater up over her dark cap of hair and tossed it away. The brassiere followed. Viki stood naked from the waist, her piquant face uplifted to his, the gypsy eyes narrowed and watching him. Her hands, small red-nailed talons, reached inside his robe and pounced. She sank against him and moaned.

"I can't, darling. I just can't. You are just too enormous. I told you— You have made me so sore now I can hardly walk. Please, Dick, can't we— I mean I—I know other ways. I'll make you happy. I promise."

Blade was not a selfish man. Much of his enormous success with women was due to his regard for their pleasure. He gave her a half smile and said, "But will I make *you* happy? That is the question, ducks."

Viki pulled his robe open and stared down. She would not look at him. It was either a trick of the firelight—or she was blushing.

"Oh, yes, darling. I will be quite happy. I really rather like to do it, you know."

She giggled suddenly. "You are the first one, man or

18

woman, that I have ever admitted that to."

"Your secret is safe with me," Blade said as he carried her to the bed. "And I want you to be happy, Viki. I really do. So if you like to do it you certainly shall do it."

He did not awaken until after two. The fire had expired. Viki was sleeping soundly beside him, her mouth open a bit. Blade pushed it shut with a gentle finger and rolled out of bed. The cottage was cold and the gale from the Channel was gathering strength. He got into his robe and went to the phone, resolutely passing the brandy bottle and the siphon. No more of that. He might be afraid of going into Dimension X again but he was no drunk. And no coward. No one would ever know of his fear but himself, and he would *keep* it to himself. He would handle it somehow. Because he must.

He got a trunk call through to the office in London. J answered on the third ring. He sounded tired, but his remonstrance was mild enough.

"You took your time about calling back, dear fellow. Delay in message?"

"No, sir. I was swimming in the Channel and then, well, sir, I had some other business to attend to. Then I fell asleep. Sorry."

"No real matter," J said. "It is just that I want you to stop past the office in the morning before you go on to Prince's Gate for the briefing. I want a chat with you. Understood?"

Mystified, Blade said that he understood. "That's all, sir?"

He heard J yawn in London. "That is all, my boy. And, er, no need to mention this little visit to Lord L. Also understood?"

Blade agreed. J said goodnight and hung up after suggesting that Blade get all the sleep he could.

Blade cradled the phone and stood for a moment staring at the pile of gray ashes in the fireplace. Viki snored softly. Blade glanced at the brandy bottle and shook his head. For the first time in weeks he didn't, really didn't, want a drink. Maybe that phase was over. Now if he could just get the slimy ice out of his guts whenever he thought of Dimension X.

He saw no point in going back to bed. He would not sleep again and it was better to stay awake and try to think this thing through. In the final analysis a man had to help himself—no one else could.

Blade rebuilt the fire, pulled up a chair and, smoking an infrequent pipe, stared into the flames and wondered where he would be this time tomorrow night? Would there be fire in this new Dimension X? Would they know the secret of flame?

What weapons? What dangers? What kind of men must he face—if they *were* men—and what sort of brains would they have? Cunning, cruel, complex or childish?

Viki snorted in her sleep and rolled over. Blade smiled. Who would have thought little Viki to be such an accomplished fellatrice? Blushing and shamed, or at least shamming it, and performing with an expertise that bespoke long experience. He smiled again and shook his head. How could you know, really know, about people? Anyone—even himself. People were robots wearing masks. They kept their real selves locked up in the vaults of their skulls. All the world ever saw was a reasonable facsimile. Even himself. Even Richard Blade. Who could ever guess about him? Guess at the unguessable.

He stood up and brushed his hand swiftly through the air. There. He had just invaded a dimension that he, nor any other living man with a normal brain, could not perceive or comprehend. This time tomorrow, with his brain cells restructured by the computer, he might well be wandering in that dimension. He alone of all the men in all the world.

In that moment Blade began to understand a little. And felt a growing relief. It was not so much fear—as fear—that plagued him. It was instead the terrible loneliness that he must bear. He examined the idea for several minutes and found that he was being honest with himself. The awful loneliness that he alone must bear. Just to be able to *tell* someone would help, but that he could not do. It was a burden that he must carry alone.

Even Lord Leighton and J could not share the load. They knew and yet they did not know. They had never been out there.

Blade laughed aloud. So be it. He was glad. Loneliness he could bear. Fear he could not. Not for long. It was good to know the true nature of his enemy. And now he could have a drink.

He poured himself a large brandy and drank it straight, then hurled the glass into the fireplace. And laughed again. He felt so much better, like a man let out of a prison cell.

Viki stirred at the sound of shattering glass. She peered from beneath the covers at him. "What is it, Dick? Are you getting drunk all by yourself?"

Blade went to tuck her in. He kissed her lightly and patted her shapely rump. "No, ducks. Now go back to sleep. I'll be getting you up at five and we've a long cold ride ahead."

"I still think you're mad," she said, and fell back into sleep.

Chapter 3

Blade, naked but for the loincloth, his body smeared with tar grease, sat in what he had come to think of as the "electric chair" and watched Lord Leighton tape the last shiny electrode to his inner calf. Lord L, in a long white surgeon's coat that covered his hump, seemed his usual cheerful and efficient self. Not exactly a benign type, the old man, but Blade had never thought of him as sinister. Nor did he now. J was upset and nervous over what he imagined Lord L's plans to be.

An hour earlier, in J's cramped office in Copra House in the city, Blade had listened to his chief's suspicions with growing incredulity. J came very near to making Lord L out to be a kind of Dr. Frankenstein.

"I tell you, Dick, he means to get a knife into your brain!" J tapped his pipe nervously on his teeth. "His Lordship isn't satisfied with things as they are, particularly with your memory retention. He won't be satisfied until he works out a means of direct communication with you while you are in Dimension X."

Blade, who had deposited Viki at her Belgravia apartment half an hour before, kissed her goodbye and given her fanny a last pat—and vowed never to see her again—was feeling very fit. Better than in weeks. Inaction and boredom were at an end. He had peered deep into his psyche and found the cause of his discontent—he was actually looking forward to the new foray into Dimension X. With certain reservations. He was a pitcher that did not intend going to the well forever. He intended, at the prop-

23

er time, to suggest that they find a new man and begin training him.

This was not the time. He said to J, "I thought my memory cells were functioning excellently. After all the work Lord L has done on them, all the hours I've spent under the chronos machine—and he never said anything to me! Never indicated that he was dissatisfied with the results."

"He wouldn't. Not to you." J began to pace his tiny office. "And he won't say anything, not until he is ready. That, I suspect, will be sometime after you get back from this trip through the computer."

"If I get back."

J nodded. "There is always that, of course. But when, if, you get back, then you had better be on your guard, Dick. You know how smarmy, how persuasive, the old man can be. Don't let him talk you into anything. Though even if he does, I—"

J broke off and jammed his pipe fiercely into his tobacco pouch. Blade waited.

"I am," J continued, "quite prepared to take steps. I will not allow him to tinker with your brain, Richard, in any surgical way. If you haven't the willpower to stand up to him, I, as your commanding officer, can and will forbid it."

Blade picked up his Burberry and slung it over his shoulder. It was a bleak and drizzling morning. "I think I can handle it," he assured J as he was leaving. "You should know that, sir. When, to your recollection, was the last time anyone made me do anything I didn't want to do?"

J did not appear reassured. "You don't know that old man as I have come to know him," he said bitterly. "He is a scientist, not a human being. He will stoop to anything—he'll play on your sense of duty, my boy, on your devotion to England."

"All that is a bit of old hat now," said Blade. "But I know what you mean. I'll be careful. You're not coming to the Tower?"

J sank into his swivel chair. "Not this time. No point to it, really. I just stand around outside and worry. I can do that here."

Blade left with J's usual blessings and luck and took a taxi to the Tower of London. Now, sitting in the chair in the glass booth, deep in the guts of the huge computer, bound like Gulliver with varicolored wires, he watched Lord Leighton fiddle with a series of knobs, toggles and buttons on a large gauge board. This was a new addition and Blade had never seen it before. In another segment of the gray computer housing was the familiar red button, set alone in its plaque and festooned by a hundred wires, that would send Blade into Dimension X.

By now Blade realized that things were different. Lord L was not following the usual routine. As a rule he wasted no time. Like a compassionate executioner who wished to spare his victim the terror of waiting, Lord L would smile, clap Blade on the back and press the button that sent him swirling away. But not this morning.

His Lordship was reading the gauges carefully and making minuscule notes in a large, ledger-like book. He seemed unaware of Blade's presence. He sidled back and forth in front of the instrument board, his polio-ruined legs causing him to lurch and sway like a white, fragile spider. He kept muttering to himself as he made entries in the book. Now and then he reached back to stroke the pain in his hump.

In the minutes of waiting, Richard Blade stumbled on another truth. If the hazardous computer experiments were affecting him, they were, in no less degree if in a different manner, also affecting Lord L and J. Neither man was the same as when this thing had started. Strain, fear, tension, guilt and responsibility all had taken their toll. Odd, Blade thought, that he had not seen it before. But then he had been concentrating on his own woes.

At last Lord L turned from the board and hobbled toward the chair where the naked, electrode-bound Blade waited.

Blade, as usual, was nervous. And when he was nervous

25

he was blunt. "What is it, sir? Something gone wrong?"

The old man did not answer at once. He stared at Blade with his yellow lion's eyes. Through the encompassing walls of the monster computer came, very faintly, the susurration of hundreds of lesser computers in the vast outerchambers. Monitored by men in white smocks who did not dream of what went on in this small inner sanctum.

"Not exactly wrong," said Lord L at last. He pointed at the gauge board. "It's just that I want to try something new, Richard, a new approach to our work, and I think you should know beforehand."

Blade looked deep into the yellow eyes. "Does J know about this?"

"No, my boy. J does not know about it. If he did he would only object to it. Make obstacles. And without cause. There is not the slightest danger—other than, er, the usual risks, of course."

"You had better explain it to me, sir. I'll decide about the risks."

"Of course, Richard. Of course."

Lord L flipped open his book and ran a finger beneath a line of what appeared to Blade to be ideograms. Beneath it was a cartouche with a mass of hieroglyphic symbols. Under this was a long column of mathematical abstractions. All Greek to Blade. He waited patiently.

"As you must know," Lord L said, "I have kept records of each experiment. Extremely detailed and minute records. It has long been in my mind that, if I could achieve a 'fix' on any particular setting, I could use it over and over again. That setting would always be valid and I could send you again and again into the *same* Dimension X. The advantages of this are obvious, Richard."

Blade nodded. He could see. One of the great disadvantages of Project DX and one over which the Prime Minister was grumbling—mindful of the millions of pounds being expended—was that they could never be sure into which Dimension X the computer would hurl Blade. In his first four trips out he had landed in a different dimension each time. The first three times it had not mattered greatly—he had found nothing of tangible value, nothing that could be exploited to enrich Home Dimension. But on his last expedition, into Sarma, he had found mountains of uranium. Enough, and cheap enough, to make England the leading atomic power in the world. All that was needed was a means of getting it back to Home Dimension, and at this moment in the Scottish Highlands a little band of top scientists was working on teleportation.

His Lordship, as though probing Blade's mind, nodded and showed his long teeth in a smile. "Yes, Richard, I know it is all very much in the future. But the Prime Minister is a practical man. He is a politician, not a scientist, and he has to make an accounting. He thinks it is time we began to show a profit. So with his permission, I might even say his urging, I am trying this new experiment. I am going to try to send you back into X Dimensions that you have visited before. I have selected Alb as the first and have set the computer accordingly."

Alb! Blade half smiled as he remembered the Princess Taleen. A saucy wench. Lovely and tawny skinned and a savage in lovemaking. It would be nice to see her again. Or would it? She was as dangerous as a barrel of dynamite.

"There is nothing of value in Alb," he said, and grinned. "Nothing to make the Prime Minister happy. Sarma would be more like it. The uranium."

Lord Leighton frowned impatiently. "I know, I know! You are missing the point, my dear boy. This is to be only a brief experiment at best. I will keep you in Alb for only a few moments, then bring you back. Because, if I can send you to Alb by choice, by predetermined setting, I can get you back any time I choose. I am sure of it."

Blade was not so sure. And he saw why Lord L had not confided in J. "You mean, sir, that this is in a very real sense a brand-new experiment and you offer no guarantees?" He gazed at the awesome loom of the giant computer. "This is not really the same computer, sir?"

Lord L jammed his book beneath his arm and clasped his fragile blue-veined hands on his white-smocked breast. He favored Blade with one of his best smiles. As J would have put it, he was being smarmy.

"When did you return from your last trip into Dimension X, my boy?"

"Six months ago." J had insisted on six-month intervals, time to find and assess any damage to Blade's brain tissue.

Lord L nodded. "Right. Six months. And during those six months I have been working every day, up to eighteen hours a day, on this machine. Of course it is not the same computer, Richard. How could it be? I don't intend it to be. Science can never stand still."

Blade blinked at the old man and pretended to think. Pretended because he already knew what he was going to do, what he must do—go through with it. Never mind that it was a totally new approach and dangerous as hell. What else could he do? Who else was there? It was, after all, his job. His duty.

He nodded curtly to Lord L. "Okay, sir. Let's see if you can put me back in Alb. Let's get on with it."

Lord L hobbled to the red button. He waved a hand. "Good boy. Good luck." He pressed the button.

Lights flashed on the instrument board. Gauges spun. Blade felt the slow itch of the current pulsing in his veins and arteries. Soon now there would be pain and more pain and then an exploding universe. He would be hurled, flung, not up or down or out, but into a new dimension. He would awaken as naked as a newborn babe in some strange land, and the fight for survival would begin. He would—

He became aware, and because of that very awareness, knew that something had gone wrong. There was pain, yes, but it was only the current clawing at him. Racking him, flowing through the conductors of his bones, twisting him. Pain. Blade wanted to scream and found his jaws locked. He was still in the chair, still in the glass booth, still in Home Dimension. Burning and yet not scorched. There was no smell of burning flesh. Long blue sparks flashed from his toes and fingers, and a crackling halo encircled his head. And now smoke.

Smoke. Dense, greasy brown, it poured into the tiny enclosure from the guts of the machine. Miniature lightning stroked back and forth across the room and in the forked luminescence Blade saw Lord L staggering toward the instrument board. The old man was bent double, coughing and shielding his eyes as he fumbled for switches and toggles and buttons.

Blade made a great effort to leave the chair. The current still bound him. He struggled and threshed about, pitting his great muscles against the current and the tiny wires that held him as if they had been chains.

Lord L pressed a final button. The current drained away. Blade snapped the wires, brushed aside the electrodes and was about to leave the chair when he stopped and stared.

Between himself and Lord Leighton was a spinning vortex of brown smoke. It moved and undulated, writhing, taking form and then it ceased to be smoke and became—

What? What was it? For one of the few times in his life Blade knew the heart-shocking thrill of pure physical terror. Not so much at the man who stood there, if it was a man, but at the manner of appearance. Blade hesitated, his hands braced on the chair arms, wary, and now responsive to the massive dose of adrenaline pumped into his system by fear.

The creature shared his fear. And acted. It let out a high snarl of rage and terror and rushed at Lord Leighton. In its right hand, raised to kill, was a crude stone axe. The old man cowered back against the gauge board, his hands raised to fend off the blow, his voice quavering in a shrill scream.

"Help, Richard! Help me. Get it!"

Blade left his feet eight feet behind the thing and brought it down in a flying tackle. Its legs were covered

29

with hair and it had a rancid animal smell. It was small, hardly half the size of Blade, but wiry and bulging with muscle. And as fast as a cat.

Lord L was screaming something that Blade could not make out. No time. The creature was on its feet and striking at him with the axe. Blade fended it off and got a wristhold and sent the axe flying across the room. The gaping mouth opened and long fangs slashed at Blade's throat. Blade held it off and struck with a tremendous right cross. He missed the jaw and jarred his hand and arm on an oversize skull.

A constant stream of furious sound came from the throat of the thing. Small deep-set eyes hated Blade. The thing screamed and slashed with long nails: "Orgggggghhhhh— Orggggggggg— Ohhrrrrggrrr."

Lord Leighton's voice, as from a far place, fell into recognizable words. "Be careful, Richard! For God's sake, be careful. Don't kill it! Don't hurt it! For God's sake, don't *kill it!*"

The sweating, struggling Blade had no time to appreciate the irony. He was too busy keeping whatever it was from killing *him*. Again and again he fought the fangs away from his throat and tried to get in a knockout blow, even a killing blow and to hell with his Lordship, but the creature was as fast and as slippery as a greased snake. It kept leaping at Blade, growling its Orggggggggg— orggggggggg—

Then Blade did what he should have done before. He stepped away. The thing stood gazing at him, hunched, long arms dangling, huge jaw thrust forward, looking at Blade in puzzlement and confusion.

Blade feinted with a left.

Orggggrgggggg— It sprang at him again.

Blade shifted his feet and brought the right in level and just right and with all his shoulder leverage behind it. His fist crashed home on the prognathic jaw. The man, animal, thing or creature slumped into a heap on the floor. Blade, panting and bleeding from a dozen scratches and cuts, stood looking down at it.

Lord Leighton leaped forward and caught Blade's arm. The old man was livid, sweating, shaking all over and in a mingled delirium of apprehension and delight. He literally danced round the supine figure on the rubberized floor of the computer room. The words came tumbling inchoate, hardly understandable.

"Don't hurt him—you mustn't hurt him—easy does it. A prize, Richard, a prize! Beyond my wildest dreams! A treasure—a veritable treasure. Must not harm it—by no means harm it— I— Something went wrong—something went wrong and—"

Blade wiped sweat from his eyes. "Yes, sir. Something sure as hell went wrong. What is it? Where did it come from? What are we going to do with it?"

Lord L ignored him. He was kneeling by the thing, examining the hairy body, stroking it like a baby with the colic.

"I don't know, Richard. Don't care. No time for all that now. But it must be from another dimension—a time lapse and possible parallel development and millions, maybe even billions of years. I—"

Lord Leighton came suddenly to his feet. He peered at Blade with his hooded eyes. "Top secret from now on, my boy. Absolute top security! No one must know about this. Absolutely no one. You understand that, my boy? Do you? An order, Richard, an absolute order."

"How about J?"

Lord L grimaced, hesitated, then with reluctance said, "Of course J. I suppose he must know. But no one else. Absolutely no one else. Now you wait here and watch it while I get a hypo and some drugs. I'll have to knock it out, I suppose. Keep it unconscious for a time. Have to. Otherwise it will only destroy itself or make us destroy it. That must not happen." He scuttled for the door. "I won't be a second."

Blade stared down at the thing on the floor. It was breathing heavily through large, flattened nostrils. There were flecks of foam around the mouth. It did not move.

31

Blade's hand and arm ached from the blow he had given it.

Blade sniffed at the burnt-out computer shell. He found that he could grin. The old boy had really fouled this one up. Six months of work gone up in smoke and the old man had conjured up some sort of a hairy demon from somewhere out there in limbo.

Blade shrugged. And laughed.

He touched the unconscious creature with his bare foot. The body hair was long and coarse and clotted with dirt and sweat, and the smell from it was fast overpowering the acridity of the smoke.

Blade was still chuckling when Lord L came back with a tray on which was a hypodermic needle and several small bottles containing a clear liquid. His Lordship gave him a reproving glance as he filled the needle and injected the brute thing on the floor.

"This is a very serious matter," said Lord L. "Not at all funny, Richard. We have probably made the greatest scientific discovery of all time. A serious matter, my boy. Very serious."

"Yes, sir," said Blade. "But now what, sir? Where do we go from here?"

Lord L glanced around as though he expected spies to leap from the shattered computer. "We shall have to be very careful and very cunning. And there is much hard work in store for us. All of us. I have already used my authority to clear the outer areas and seal us off. The first thing, Richard, is that you go and fetch J at once. Best not try to explain this matter to him. I will do that. Go now. Hurry."

Blade pointed out that he could not have explained the matter to J even had he wished. You cannot explain what you do not understand yourself.

Lord L ignored him. All he said was, "Go at once, please."

"Is it all right if I dress first, Lord Leighton?"

His Lordship did not hear.

Chapter 4

The next month was as frenetic as any Blade had experienced in his thirty years. Lord Leighton, always a martinet and a slavedriver, reached into some hidden reserve of energy and summoned a demonic fury that sorely tried Blade and J, both younger men. All three became master liars. Lord L, as chief Ananias, was a good teacher and was expert in twisting the truth into odd shapes. His Lordship's great fear, his chief nightmare, was that the world would find out about Ogar—as they had come to call the creature, from the snarling sounds he made—and wrest his prize from him before he could complete his studies.

J, who had a plan of his own, had a blazing battle with Lord L about this. J insisted that the Prime Minister be let in on the secret. His Lordship said no. J insisted.

"He must know," J said flatly. "For our protection and his. Else how do we explain the delay in Project DX? Be practical, Leighton! Our money is running out. The PM has to go before a committee and beg for more secret funds. He can't, and won't, do that unless he knows exactly what is going on."

J won that argument. It was the only one.

When the massive complex was excavated beneath the Tower someone had thought to include a single large cell, a modern dungeon, in the lowest sub-basement. It was to this cell that Blade carried the unconscious Ogar after Lord L summarily cleared the place of all personnel. It was there that Ogar slept his drugged sleep, fed intravenously, while Lord L did a detailed and loving Bertillon, crooning happily to himself as he made cranial measurements. When J rashly suggested that perhaps a professional anthropologist should be called in, the old man flew into a rage.

The Prime Minister came in the dead of night, spent half an hour viewing Ogar and listening to Lord L, and left in a state of shock, muttering to himself. His position, he told J later, was unique in every sense of the word. No politician had ever had to cope with a situation like this before.

The coming of Ogar did accomplish one other thing. For the time being, at least, it healed the growing breach between J and Lord Leighton. There was no more talk of brain surgery and, as they became less snappish, the two older men regained some of their former rapport. Even so, J, on the first day, could not refrain from jabbing the needle into Lord L.

With a malicious grin he quoted directly from the old man's computer speech at Reading University: ". . . we have at least succeeded in eliminating the danger of schizophrenia . . . when they are built, they function exactly as intended."

He received a cold glare from the hooded yellow eyes. "May I point out," said his Lordship, "that some of the greatest scientific discoveries have been made by accident. In any case I have already found the error and the computer will be rebuilt in a month or so. But that is not my chief concern at the moment. I have plans, great plans."

Both J and Blade left their apartments and moved into quarters far below the Tower computer complex. Here they were self-sufficient, with no need to venture outside. There was no elevator—it stopped on the level above —and the only way out or in was by a narrow stairway. This was guarded by a massive steel door that was kept locked. Above them the lesser computers were humming again, all personnel back at work, and the security had been redoubled.

The stone axe was shipped away, with elaborate

security precautions, for an appraisal by experts. Within three days the report was back and his Lordship shared it with them.

HAFT—this wood is unknown to us. Suggest may be some species of iron-wood believed extinct since Lower Palaeolithic Age. Workmanship suggests culture unknown to us.

AXE—this macrolith also a puzzler. We have seen nothing like it before. Main component is undoubtedly quartz, but with a mixture of greenstone, quartzite and cherty. This is impossible according to present knowledge, yet repeated tests prove it to be so. Possible that meld might be a result of intense heat, in which case heat would have to approach that of inner sun. Workmanship again suggests no culture known to us.

At the bottom of the report was a scribble. *Dear Leighton—what goes on here?*

The scribble made Lord L most unhappy.

"They're bound to start nosing around sooner or later," he told J and Blade.

"All the more reason to start cracking," rejoined J, who had his plan and was keeping it to himself for the moment. J was in a very good form and biding his time. For the moment the Prime Minister was appeased, if slightly dazed, and matters were going smoothly enough. J kept a steady pressure on the old man to see that the computer was rebuilt as rapidly as possible. This was not easy, but J did it. Left to his own designs, Lord L would have spent every waking hour by the cot on which Ogar still lay drugged.

At the end of the first week Lord Leighton summoned them to the cell and, as they stood around the cot on which Ogar slept, gave his first full report. Blade and J were too impressed to interrupt. The cell by this time was full of the body smell of the hairy creature on the cot.

Lord L, using a ruler as a pointer, poked and prodded and explained. You would have thought, as J said later in jest, that the old man had himself spawned the thing on the cot.

"Ogar," said Lord L, "is from another dimension. A

35

Dimension X. It is very important to remember that."

Blade, recalling the bloody struggle in the computer room, thought that he was hardly likely to forget it.

J said: "Do get on with it, Leighton, and do remember to whom you are speaking. Dick and I aren't scholars or intellects. Keep it simple."

His Lordship smiled. "I will try. But remember also that any statement I make, any description, is only an analogue and not an exact statement of fact.

"We know that in our own dimension, Home Dimension, our world," the old man continued, "that evolution develops along parallel lines, but at a slower or faster pace in remote and unconnected parts of the world. So, to get started at all, I must have a model, an abstract and theoretical model for guidance. I have chosen one. I have, *a priori*, chosen to think along the lines that Ogar here came from a dimension, a world, that is much like our own, but in a much earlier stage of development. Put it like this—when the computer malfunctioned and Ogar was snatched from his world, his dimension, he left behind a world similar to our own—half a million years ago."

J, practical man, and with the Prime Minister and committee to keep happy, relished this. Would there not, in such a dimension, be gold and oil and all the rest? Untold and untouched, wealth to be exploited by England when teleportation was perfected. It made a strong talking point.

Lord L tapped the creature's flattened skull with the ruler. "A puzzle," he admitted. "Not Pithecanthropus. Far short of Cro-Magnon, though he did walk upright in the, er, short time we saw him move of his own volition. The braincase is flat and the brow ridges very heavy. Yet the arms and legs are slim and well developed, the body protected by hair with an undercoat for additional protection from cold. That itself is totally unknown to us—a subhuman species with an undercoating of hair like some dogs have."

Blade said, with a faint smile, "What makes him smell like that, sir?"

J tried not to laugh. His Lordship scowled but answered the question.

"Pure animal odor. Ogar never took a bath in his life. Over the years a protective coating of dirt and grease build up. It would come in very handy in bad weather."

Ogar turned on the cot. Despite the heavy dosage of drugs he was given to tossing and turning and had several times fallen off the cot. Each time, Blade, the only one strong enough to lift him, had been summoned for the duty. And had taken a shower immediately to get the stink off him.

Now Ogar showed his teeth and snarled in his sleep. "Ogarrrrrr—rrrrrr—Ogarrrrrrrrrrr—"

"Having a bad dream," said Blade.

His Lordship tapped the hairy jaw. "Teeth much the same as ours, but larger and lacking any wisdom teeth. The canines are long and fang-like, as you can see."

Blade was still healing from the bites inflicted by Ogar in their brief scuffle.

Lord Leighton moved closer to the cot. He seized a handful of hair at the back of Ogar's neck and raised the head. He poked with the ruler at the nape of Ogar's neck. "The amazing thing is the foramen magnum. Identical with our own, or so close to being as makes no difference. So he walks upright and his brain stalk is vertical. Ogar, my dear fellows, is a human being. Or very close to being one. I only wish it were possible to work out a lineal descent pattern, a phylogeny, but that is impossible since he is not of our dimension."

His Lordship lectured them for two hours on Ogar. Blade was patient, abiding the smell and wondering what J was up to. That his chief was up to something Blade did not doubt—he had known J a long time and had come to know the meaning of that covert smile.

But it was Lord L who exploded the first bombshell. Two days later Blade awoke to the sound of jackhammers chipping away at stone. The sound was remote, in some far off sub-basement, but there was no mistaking the source. J, over breakfast, explained it.

"From our viewpoint," he said over the sausage and eggs, "the old boffin may have gone around the bend, but from his viewpoint it makes good sense. He is having a cave built for Ogar."

Blade halted his fork in upswing. "A cave?"

J speared the last sausage. "Yes, dear boy, a cave. Ogar is going to live in it when he comes out of the drug. So are you."

"So am I what?"

"Going to live in the cave," said J cheerfully. "With Ogar."

Blade dropped his knife and fork. "Like bloody hell I am!"

J nodded. "So right. You are. I am going to order you to do it. I'm sorry, Dick, but it has to be done. I have to humor him and I have to keep him working on the computer. He can finish repairing it in a week if I can keep him at it, but not if he gets a case of the sulks. You must be a good fellow and go along."

Blade groaned and choked back the obscenity he felt like voicing. "But why? Why in hell does he have to have a cave and why do I have to live in it with that—that whatever it is?"

J, though usually a taciturn and humorless man, was not without his moments. He said, "You mean Ogar? Our guest?"

Blade scowled at him. He tried to think of women. Tender-limbed, sweet-smelling, soft-breasted women. This monkish life was steadily taking its toll.

J shattered all that. "Lord L has deduced that Ogar, in his own dimension, lived in a cave. Probably he is right. So he is going to give Ogar a cave. And a fire—he is having special ventilation installed—and he is going to play tapes that simulate the night sounds Ogar must have been used to hearing. There will be meat, raw meat—he can hardly wait to see if Ogar eats it raw or cooks it—and of all this he is going to make moving pictures and sound tapes. In other words, he wants a record of Ogar living in his own natural environment. Or what Lord L thinks must have been his environment. It really isn't a bad idea, you know."

"It's a miserable idea," said Blade crossly. "That thing is dangerous, for God's sake. I should know."

J tutted that. He knew his Blade. "You're not afraid, Dick. Don't try to have me on. You're bored and restless and missing your totsies. But this thing you have got to do—it fits in exactly with my plans."

And J revealed his plan to Blade, who had to laugh. Lord L was in for a rude shock.

"Besides which," said J, "you will have a club and Ogar won't. You will be dressed in animal skin of some sort and Ogar will be, as usual, stark naked. That in itself should give you an overwhelming psychological advantage. Even a creature like Ogar is at a disadvantage without pants."

Blade left the table. He did not feel like eating.

A good-sized cave had been bored out of the bedrock. Noiseless ventilators kept a current of cool air moving through it. A small fire was built in the center of the cave, a crude jar of water provided, and Lord L installed his movie cameras and recording equipment in secret crannies. Ogar was still drugged in his cell.

Lord Leighton, waxing more ecstatic by the moment, talked incessantly as he puttered about making final arrangements.

"Ogar will be terrified when he comes out of the drug," he explained. "That will be the critical moment. And most interesting, too. I am counting on the night noises to keep him in the cave. If I am right he will not venture out of the cave at night. He will use the cave as a shelter and the fire as protection from the beasts. My guess is that he will remain very quiet and huddle by the fire."

"And if he doesn't, sir?"

The old man touched Blade's arm and smiled. "Then you will have to handle him, my dear boy. It is, after all, your job. You did it before. No, I anticipate no difficulty there."

Blade did not share his confidence. "Ogar is bound to

be hungry," he pointed out. "For meat. Probably raw meat. That just might make him forget his manners, sir. He might toss the script away." He did not think it necessary to add that he, Blade, represented 210 pounds of good firm meat on the hoof.

"Meat he shall have," said Lord L. "Fresh raw meat. I ordered a freshly killed beef yesterday. You, Richard, are going to offer him the meat as a gesture of friendship. Now let us go and fetch him."

Blade carried Ogar to the cave and stretched him out by the fire. Leighton was testing his tapes and the night noises began to filter into the cave. Blade, alone with the sleeping Ogar, felt a chill creep up his spine. It was all very realistic. And atavistic. The flickering firelight brought shadows alive. Ogar slept on, his brute face cushioned on a hairy forearm. In the darkness outside, the roars and bellows and death cries of great mammals and reptiles came from the tapes in eerie authenticity. For a moment time slid back and it was a million years ago and Richard Blade stood naked and alone in a primeval night.

The hours passed. They watched Ogar through cleverly placed peepholes. Blade, naked now but for a skin about his loins, and carrying a club, began to be caught up in the thing. In a rawhide pouch he carried several chunks of raw and slightly gamey meat. He waited patiently for the game to begin, his handsome face impassive, his great muscles relaxed.

J, watching Blade closely, marveled at the change in his top operative. He began to understand better why Blade had survived four trips into Dimension X. A faculty for absolute adaptation. Blade was like a chameleon in that. To look at him now, J thought with a sense of awe, he *is* living a million years ago. He *is* a caveman.

At last Ogar stirred. Lord Leighton made frantic signs. It had all been rehearsed beforehand and each man knew what to do. The old man flicked a switch and the night noises began. First a hideous bellowing, then a hissing, then sounds of deadly struggle and, at last, a high screech of triumph and a death groan.

40

Ogar opened his eyes. He rolled on his side, got to his knees and glared around the cave. He cocked his head to listen. He snarled, an ominous guttural chest sound, and showed his fangs. He fell to all fours and stared into the fire.

Blade, from a corner of his eyes, saw Lord L rubbing his hands together and grinning like an idiot. J watched in silence, without expression on his long horsey face.

Ogar was on his feet now, walking upright but with his shoulders hunched forward and his long arms dangling to his knees. He was plainly puzzled. He began to walk about the cave, examining it, all the time making sounds in his throat. Now and again he would pause and listen to the sounds from outside.

A pile of faggots had been placed in one corner of the cave. Ogar stared at them, snarled, then picked up several and placed them on the fire. The flames leaped higher. Ogar then began to search around on the floor of the cave. He was annoyed and angry. Several times he thumped his chest and growled.

The stone axe! Ogar was looking for his axe.

Lord L, unable to contain himself any longer, dying to share his triumph, sidled in beside Blade, whispering.

"I've got it. I do believe I've got it—or as close as is possible. Ogar is Australopithecine. Or what would correspond to austral-P in our scale and in our world. Six hundred thousand years ago! I—"

Blade put a finger to his lips. They shared the peephole. Ogar, even over all the hideous night sounds, appeared to have heard the whispering. He scampered to the far side of the fire and crouched there, fangs bared, his little eyes fixed on the cave entrance. His hands beat a slow tattoo on his chest, and from his throat came a steady snarling— Groooorrrr—rrrr—grrrr—

Lord Leighton touched Blade's arm and smiled.

"Better go in now, Richard. He's expecting you."

41

Chapter 5

Blade had planned it well, diagramming his every movement beforehand. If only Ogar would cooperate.

Ogar knew that Blade was coming long before he stepped into the cave. He retreated to the farthest corner of the cave and crouched, fangs bared, snarling softly in his throat. The slim, hairy body quivered with fear, but the great macrocephalic head wove back and forth, jutting and staring in defiance.

Blade stepped into the circle of firelight and stopped. He let the club hang lax in his right hand. He wanted Ogar to get a good look at it.

Ogar peered at him from small reddened eyes. The flattened brute head moved back and forth, back and forth. The splayed nostrils quivered and Ogar made a new sound as he scented the raw meat in Blade's pouch.

Blade tried to pitch his voice exactly right. He felt certain that he would get only one chance. If Ogar feared him too much he would attack. If Ogar felt contempt, thought he was strong enough to win, he would attack. A fine line must be drawn and in those first few seconds matters balanced on the razor's edge.

Blade tossed the club away. He patted his own chest gently and said, very softly, "Ogar— Ogar— Ogar— Ogar—" It was nonsense, but reassuring sounds must be made and Blade crooned as he would to a baby. He hummed, nearly sang, "Ogar— Ogar— Ogar— Ogar—"

Ogar remained in his corner. His glance followed the club, rested there for a moment, then came back to Blade. He snarled softly.

Blade made a slow motion of conciliation with his hand. He smiled. He kept talking all the while, a jumble of softly intoned nonsense words. After a moment of this he reached into the pouch and brought out a hunk of the raw meat. Ogar's nostrils quivered. Saliva dripped from the corners of his mouth.

Blade held the meat on high and waited. Ogar watched the piece of meat in Blade's hand. Blade kept talking, lulling, soothing, coaxing. And watching.

Suddenly Ogar held out a hand. He ceased to snarl. From his throat came a sound that was, quite possibly, a fully formed word. To Blade it sounded like—"Owwwnowwah." Ogar repeated the sound—"Owwwnowwah."

There was no mistaking the entreaty. Ogar was asking for the meat.

Blade smiled and nodded and tossed the meat through the air. Ogar caught it deftly, smelled it, growled and slouched to the pile of faggots. He selected a stick, the sharpest of the lot, and thrust it into the meat. He took it to the fire and poked it into the flames.

Blade, now as fascinated as Lord L, did not move. He crooned a soft little song in his throat.

Ogar was careful to keep the fire between himself and Blade. He left the meat in the fire barely long enough to sear it, then wolfed it down in two bites, tearing and rending the charred flesh. His little eyes never left Blade.

Blade tossed him another piece of meat. The process was repeated. This time Ogar made three bites of it, rubbed his belly and said something like—"Gooonah—nah—"

Blade nodded and smiled and said, "Gooo-nah —nah—"

Ogar looked puzzled. He cocked his head to one side, stared at Blade in a different manner, shook his head in some mysterious negation, scratched his chest hair vigorously, found something alive and popped it into his mouth. Then he settled on all fours by the fire and stared at Blade again.

Blade kept talking. And smiling. Ogar kept staring and

scratching. From outside the cave came a sudden terrible roaring. Ogar stared past Blade at the cave entrance. He clutched himself and rocked back and forth making whimpering sounds. Ogar was terrified of what was out there in the night. For the moment he appeared to have forgotten Blade, who was remembering what Lord L had said about Ogar's attention span.

"Probably not long," the old man had said. "Very likely that of a three- or four-year-old child."

Blade went into the next part of his act. He walked to the cave entrance. He shook his fist. He let out his very best bellow of defiance. It was a fine effort and he was rather proud of it. Let the current Tarzan match that!

When he glanced at Ogar again he was clapping his hairy, long-knuckled hands softly together and, Blade would have sworn, smiling, even laughing. The big mouth opened, fangs flashed, and there emerged a sound that was half hyena and half jackass.

"Arrhhh-ahh--ahhhhh-ahhhh-ahhh—"

Ogar was applauding.

Blade kept up the patter. "That's a good chap," he said sweetly. "A fine chap you are, too. I am glad to see that we are going to get along. We will, you know. We're going to be friends, Ogar, real bosom pals. And do you know, Ogar, you remind me of one of my old profs at Oxford. Professor Abernathy, I think. Yes, it was he. You are alike as two peas, you and the prof. Taught the classics, he did, and failed me once. Said I didn't know how to study properly. May have had something there, you know. Anyway I had to do the bloody course twice over."

Ogar was not listening. He was picking at his body hair again, searching for dessert.

Blade moved slowly toward the club. It lay about ten feet from where he stood. Ogar came instantly alert. He watched and the snarl began to build in his throat. Blade kept moving slowly toward the club.

"Nothing to be afraid of, old fellow. No need for alarm. I'm your friend, remember? I just want to prove it. You watch now, Ogar. You watch me very carefully."

45

Ogar was doing just that. As Blade stooped to pick up the club, Ogar growled and thumped his chest. Blade turned to show the club, to show that his intentions were pure, but Ogar was gone from the fire. He was back in his corner, terrified and blustering, snarling and raging and leaping up and down as he pounded his chest. Pure bluff, as Blade now understood. It would take a lot to make Ogar attack him now. Ogar was no fool. Blade had the club and Blade was the larger and stronger of the two. That sort of thing Ogar could understand. There should be no trouble now unless Blade did the attacking.

Blade did not forsake caution. He moved slowly, deliberately, smiling and talking all the time. He broke the club over his knee and tossed it into the fire. Ogar stopped snarling to stare.

Blade ignored him. He went to sit cross-legged by the fire. He took a chunk of meat from the pouch, found the same stick Ogar had dropped and poked the meat into the fire. Juice dripped. The smell filled the cave. Outside the horrendous noises continued.

Blade did, in fact, like his steaks on the red side. After letting it cool for a moment, he sank his strong white teeth into the meat and enjoyed it. He had not known he was so hungry. From a corner of his eye he watched Ogar.

Ogar was drooling again. He made word sounds and began to creep slowly toward the fire. Blade ignored him and went on eating. When the body smell told him that Ogar was close he looked up, smiled, reached into his pouch for a piece of meat and extended it across the fire. This time Ogar must take it from his hand.

Ogar was dubious. He stared at Blade and said, "Ruuurr—uuu—gruuuuu-unah—unah—"

Blade laughed and waved the meat back and forth. "That is exactly what I told the boys at the club, Ogar, but they wouldn't believe me. I am happy to see that you think as I do. As a matter of fact, old man, I seriously intend to propose you for membership. You are precisely what St. James Square needs. Liven matters up a bit, you know."

Ogar reached out a hand, then snatched it back. Blade

46

continued to dangle the meat enticingly. Ogar drooled and put out his hand again. Slowly it approached Blade's. Again Ogar hesitated. Then in one swift motion he snatched the meat from Blade's hand. For an instant their fingers touched. Blade experienced an odd shock, a tingling of energy, as though he had touched a cool and vibrant snake.

Ogar had forgotten him again. He found a new stick and seared his meat and gobbled it. He wiped his mouth on his hand and his hand in his body hair. Once again he began to search his body for such small edibles as might be present.

Blade watched all this. Lord Leighton, he thought, would be in paroxysms of delight. He was getting all this on tape and camera, getting it for posterity and the insurance of his own fame. As if that was necessary.

Blade thought of J's plan and his smile was grim. There would be one hell of a battle. Lord L was not a man to surrender a prize like Ogar without a death struggle.

Ogar chose that moment to defecate—literally in his tracks. He had been squatting by the fire, Blade apparently forgotten, and now he crouched and grunted and let fly. It was a spattering mess and the odor was horrible. Worse than Ogar's own.

When he had finished Ogar moved slightly and returned to his search for lice. The smell lingered. Blade made a face.

"Not so much on the toilet training, are you, old boy? Never heard of paper, for instance? Too bad. I'm afraid I shall have to think twice about having you up for the club after all. Wouldn't do just to let go in the bar, you know. Bad form. Terribly bad form."

Ogar, blissfully unaware of his social solecism, grunted and began to scratch his genitals with both hands. He gave Blade a toothy smile. Or so it seemed.

It was time to go. Blade got up and moved away from the fire. Ogar watched him. Blade smiled and patted his chest and, folding his hands alongside his head, yawned. Ogar blinked.

The animal noises continued from outside. Lord L was repeating the tapes now. Ogar did not move from the fire. To him it was dark out there and the only safety was in the cave by the fire. He watched Blade move toward the entrance.

Blade halted at the cave entrance and looked back. Ogar was on his feet. New sounds came from his throat. He extended a hand to Blade. Slowly Blade went back to the fire.

"Ahh nah guuu— nah—nah— gah guuuu nah guhh."

"I agree with you," said Blade, "but I really must say goodnight now. Goodnight, Ogar."

"Nah guh."

Ogar fell to his knees. He stared up at Blade for a moment, moving his hands back and forth. Then he laid his face against Blade's feet and made guttural sounds of obeisance. Blade smiled down and touched the hairy shoulder lightly. Ogar flinched and quivered but did not leap away. Blade gave him the last chunk of meat.

Godhood had just been conferred on him.

Chapter 6

During the next few days Blade lived almost continually with Ogar. He swiftly mastered the various rudimentary sounds that served Ogar for language and these, coupled with sign language—and here Ogar was very fast on the uptake—allowed them to converse after a fashion. Ogar was completely awed and subservient. Blade was the god who brought the meat.

Ogar did not appear to think it strange that it was always dark outside the cave and that the terrible night noises never ceased. This temporal discontinuity especially impressed Lord Leighton.

"No sense of time," his Lordship noted in his ledgers. "It follows that at his stage of development he does not foresee death for himself, does not understand it in other things. Death is a mystery to him, the more so because of his complete unawareness."

Then J, after a series of talks with the Prime Minister, sprang his surprise. Lord L was caught off guard.

J joined the issue over dinner one night, after leading the unwary old man into a cunning trap. Blade, over a steak nearly as raw as those he shared with Ogar, kept out of it as a good subordinate should.

J said: "The computer is repaired, then? We can send Richard into Dimension X any time we choose?"

Lord L, busy with his notes and barely pecking at his food, nodded vaguely. "Yes. I suppose so. But don't trouble me with that now, J. That can wait. At the moment Ogar is much more important than Dimension X."

J finished chewing and swallowed. Then, "Bear with me, Leighton. Now—can you achieve the same setting on the computer that you had when it backfired and Ogar came to us?"

His Lordship began to sense trouble. He put down his notes and glowered at J. "I suppose I can. What of it? What are you getting at, J?"

Blade stared down at his plate. He knew what J was getting at. He waited for the explosion.

It came. J socked it to the old man. "The Prime Minister wants Blade to go out at once. As soon as possible. Ogar is to go with him. Both of them through the computer and back to Ogar's dimension. I am sure that you will see the advantages of this—Dick will have a friend, a guide. For once he will not be going in cold. I—"

Lord Leighton's leonine eyes glittered down the table at J. "I see that you have been going behind my back. You have been conspiring against me, running to the PM with tales. I must say I am surprised, J. I expected better of you. But you've wasted your time. I am in command of this project. I and I alone. I will say when Blade goes into Dimension X—and that will be when I am ready, not before. And most certainly Ogar will not go with him. Lose Ogar now? Send him back to his own dimension? You must be out of your mind, J!"

J shook his head, in regret more than anger. "You're wrong, you know. On all counts. The Prime Minister runs the show. He holds the purse. Face reality, my dear Leighton. The Prime Minister wants results. Now. Practical results. Something to show the Committee on Secret Funds. Ogar's dimension is the answer—you yourself say that it must be very like our own was half a million years ago. Think, Leighton! Think of all that vast treasure. Untouched. Unspoiled. Oil, gold, coal, uranium, bauxite, copper—the list is endless. Diamonds lying around on the surface. And a laboratory, Leighton! A living, breathing, existing laboratory for Blade to study and report on. Against all that, Leighton, Ogar is of very little significance."

Lord L sat very still. He picked up his teacup, stared at it for a moment, then hurled it across the room to smash on a wall. "Of little significance, J? Ogar of *little* significance?"

The storm broke. Blade sat in silence and admiration. He had long known, and appreciated, the old man's command of billingsgate, but now his Lordship surpassed himself. He cursed J and the Prime Minister for five minutes and did not repeat himself once. J, like a clever old tree, bowed to the wind and was not broken. He gave Blade a saturnine smile, winked, and listened unperturbed to comments on his ancestry.

In the end Lord L went stomping off to see the Prime Minister. Hours later he returned, bitter and somewhat chastened, but unforgiving. J had won. Blade, and Ogar, were to go out first thing in the morning.

J had been sure of the outcome. After Lord L limped out, pale with rage and near to frothing, J said: "The boffins in Scotland are very near to a breakthrough on teleportation. A year. Two at the most. That means we will be able to achieve large-scale transport from X to Home Dimension. It bears very heavily with the PM. And with me, for that matter. I used it as a fulcrum to move him to my way of thinking."

He gazed fondly at Blade. "And it will be a great help, Dick. For once you won't be going into Dimension X as a total stranger. Ogar should be of immense value back in his own world."

Blade nodded slowly. The plan did have its advantages. What the disadvantages were, if any, he would have to wait and see.

"We'll have to drug Ogar tonight, then," J continued. "A light dosage. Enough to get him to the computer and through it before he wakes up. It's the only way."

So that night Ogar was treated to an especially delectable hunk of raw meat, saturated with a powerful sleeping potion. Ogar wolfed it down, rubbed his hairy belly, gibbered at Blade in appreciation—and soon dropped off into a deep slumber.

As dawn was breaking over London, Blade carried Ogar up the stairs, into the elevator and finally to the tiny room nestled in the penetralia of the gigantic computer. Lord L, who was not speaking to either of them, this time allowed J to enter the sanctum, something he had never permitted before. It was, J thought, an obverse gesture of contempt for all stupid and pragmatic minds. Lord L had not been persuaded by J's argument that if they could get Blade back from Dimension X they could also recover Ogar.

"It doesn't work that way," Leighton said tartly. "Blade's brain has been conditioned. Ogar's has not. It was sheer lucky chance that we got Ogar in the first place. No. Ogar will never come back."

His Lordship wasted no time. He set about his task as grimly as any executioner. He had devised a technique in half an hour, when he knew he must, and now he bound Blade and Ogar in a reticulation of wires and electrodes that practically made them one. Blade, sitting in the chair with Ogar clasped in his arms while J looked on uneasily, noticed an odd fact: he was hardly aware of Ogar's smell.

They were ready. Lord Leighton stepped to his instrument board and made a complicated series of adjustments. He had not spoken since they entered the compartment.

J cleared his throat. He was actually seeing it for the first time and he felt a renewed sense of the terror he had experienced in Reading. Sweat trickled down him and his knees felt quavery and there was an enormous painful lump in his stomach. Fear for Blade, and even for Ogar, lanced him. They were all mad, he told himself. Mad. And no help for it. None at all. Too late. Lord L, without warning, was pressing the red button.

A steady pillar of white flame began to build inside Blade. He was being scooped out, burnt hollow, eviscerated. His eyes left his skull and became separate entities attached to his body by long stalks. The ceiling slid down at him, about to crush him, then a rift appeared and he went soaring up and through the rift into blackness.

Not for long, the blackness. Blade went swirling through it on a long curving vector, the force and velocity of which were so complex that Blade, as he riddled the answer in neon chalk on a celestial blackboard, marveled at his own acumen.

The equation slipped away, torn from his bleeding brain by a mauve wind that blew between the spheres. Blade did a wingover, adjusted the fleshy rudder on his coccyx and became aware of a rude knocking on the tiny door in his belly.

A hairy little doll with a macrohead was demanding to be let in. A horrible stench sifted into the corridors of Blade's nostrils and drifted through him like decayed smoke.

Knock-knock-knock—the stinking little mannequin was demanding to be admitted into Blade's guts. Why not? Plenty of room. Was he not disemboweled? He reached down and opened the door of his belly and watched the small figure disappear within.

Immediately the pain began. Pain made more dreadful because Blade could not scream. His lungs were full of fetid smoke.

The universe screamed for him. One cosmic shriek of agony. The pain went on and on.

He was falling now, dropping into the midst of a bloody sun. Red incandescence licked at him. He was consumed. Ashes—ashes— Nothing—nothing—

Chapter 7

Blade, after four trips through the computer, had learned his lesson well—lie still. If you were fortunate enough to be under cover, stay there. Look and listen. Begin the adaptation to a hostile environment.

He was lying naked on marshy land, a sort of tundra that moved and quaked beneath his weight. But not so barren as tundra. Quite the opposite, in fact, for he lay in coarse grass that grew close-spaced and towered over him. This strange grass was a reddish-brown in color and the blades half a foot across; by looking straight up he could see the tops, some thirty feet high, and beyond them a fast darkening sky.

There was violent movement somewhere out in that sea of grass and great trumpeting sounds of combat, a violent threshing about, a final roaring and a death screech. Then the sound, unmistakable, of enormous cruel jaws and teeth devouring something. Blade huddled in his grassy niche, unmoving. The noises were very like those played on Lord L's tapes.

Ogar! Where was Ogar?

Blade's altered brain began to function at full capacity. Already, like the chameleon J had compared him to, Blade was beginning to adapt to this new Dimension X. But where was Ogar? Strange that they had been separated, but then you never knew what the computer would do. He rose cautiously and peered about. Suppose Ogar had gone to *another* Dimension X? Or that this dimension in which Blade now found himself was *not* that from which Ogar had come. In that case Ogar was not likely to be much of a help. More a liability.

It was growing darker. All about him, in the giant swamp grass, the feral sounds continued. It was feeding time. Life or death time. To Blade's left something vast went crashing and staggering through the grass. To his right a sound of slithering and a long, drawn-out hissing. Blade realized that unless he found some sort of shelter, some protection, he would not last through the night.

Where in hell was Ogar?

Blade was taken by surprise. The grass parted and Ogar rushed at him. He had found a stout stick somewhere and he aimed a terrible blow at Blade's head, his fangs flashing as he snarled deep in his throat. Blade had found Ogar. But godhood was dead. Ogar did not remember him.

Blade took the blow on his forearm. It hurt and numbed the arm, but the bone did not go. Blade caught the stick and wrenched it away from Ogar. Ogar snapped at Blade's throat with his long teeth. Blade hit him squarely between the eyes with his fist, a terrible blow that would have felled a horse. Ogar slumped into unconsciousness.

Blade recovered the heavy stick, then knelt beside Ogar. He was not too surprised. Ogar's brain was that of a man-thing of 600,000 years ago on Home-Dimension scale; his cortex was primitive, lacking the thousands of convolutions of Blade's own, and Blade had noted the short attention span. The trip through the computer had completely obliterated Ogar's memory, such as it was. Blade made a wry face. Now he had it all to do over again. He dug with his hands into the marshy earth and found water six inches down. He began splashing it into the brute face.

Ogar's eyes flickered and he gazed up at Blade. Blade moved back two paces and waved the stick in menace. Ogar cowered away. He was beaten. Might was right and Ogar understood that.

Blade loosed a string of the guttural sounds, grunts, snarls and sign language that he and Ogar had used back in Home Dimension. He pointed to his mouth and rubbed his belly. Ogar got it immediately. He rubbed his own belly and pointed away through the grass. Blade nodded and pointed in the same direction with the stick. He was relieved. At least he and Ogar could still communicate to a certain degree. And Ogar seemed to know where he was—they *had* landed back in Ogar's dimension.

Ogar, on all fours, was banging his head against Blade's feet. Restored to godhood. Blade tapped a hairy shoulder with the stick and pointed again. Ogar got to his feet, still cringing, and waved a long prehensile hand at Blade. He growled. "Come on then. Follow me." Blade supplied the words.

Ogar went slipping rapidly and skillfully through the grass jungle. The grass had sawtooth edges and Blade was cut in a dozen places before he learned to sidle through it as Ogar did. The creature moved swiftly and purposefully, and what few doubts Blade had had vanished. Ogar was on his home territory.

They reached an immense clearing in the grass. Here the tall-growing vegetation had been mashed flat, either by fighting or mating, or both, and near the center a spring welled and flowed and disappeared into the ground again. Ogar ran to the spring and threw himself flat and thrust his face into the water. Blade drank from his cupped hands. He was uneasy. This was obviously a watering place and, though the sounds in the grass jungle had died away for the time being, Blade did not want to linger.

Here in the clearing it was not so dark. Light still lingered in the sky, and somewhere beyond the grass the sun was lancing yellow and rose and mauve shafts of fire across this new world. Blade gripped his stick and waited for Ogar to finish drinking.

Ogar did not want to finish. Already his belly was swollen and still he kept drinking. Blade kicked him lightly and gestured with the stick and rubbed his belly with his free hand. Ogar grunted and left the spring reluc-

57

tantly. Blade pointed with the stick and did a little snarling of his own. Ogar got the message.

Ogar surprised Blade. He did not immediately lead the way out of the clearing. Instead he walked from one side of the clearing to the other and peered through the grass. Several times he did this, shielding his eyes with a hand, then suddenly he grunted and slapped his chest and beckoned to Blade.

When Blade joined him Ogar pointed through the grass. There was a path, well trodden and wide enough to provide a vista for some distance. At the end of the path—Blade judged the distance to be not more than a mile—there rose a line of dark cliffs. Blade stared. Smoke drifted above the clifftops and he thought he detected the red flicker of a fire. The cliffs must be Ogar's home. That meant food and shelter, fire, protection from the monsters of the night. Blade grinned at Ogar and prodded him gently with the stick. He pointed to the cliffs and smiled. Ogar made a happy sound and rubbed his belly.

As Blade followed Ogar along the path he was content enough. Things were working out as J had projected them. So far. Blade had a friend and a guide. He could get right to work looking for the mineral wealth that would keep the Prime Minister happy and Lord Leighton in funds.

For just those few moments Blade was careless, not quite as alert as he might have been, and it cost him dearly. Ogar was hurrying along, no doubt scenting the odor of seared meat long before Blade would, and he did not look back. He was fifty yards ahead of the big man when Blade stepped into the quicksand.

Blade stopped and reared back too late. Already he was in the stuff halfway to his waist. Blade let out a bellow and Ogar turned and came back. He had known about the quicksand and avoided it without thought. It would never occur to him to warn Blade.

Blade did not panic. He never did. But he was afraid. It was a nasty way to die. And, as Ogar returned and halted on the edge of the quicksand and gazed at him, Blade wondered if perhaps he had underestimated his hairy companion. For there was a certain look in Ogar's small red eyes.

Blade did not struggle. He was sinking fast enough as it was. He tried to turn, wrenching his muscular torso around, and gauged the distance to the path he had just left. Not more than four feet. No real danger with Ogar to help him.

Blade held out the stick. He made signs and sounds for Ogar to circle around the pool of quicksand and grab the stick and help Blade free himself. Ogar watched him and did not move.

Blade had a sinking feeling that he was no longer a god.

By now he was down nearly to his waist. It was like being caught in slimy wet concrete. Blade shouted at Ogar and made signs with the stick. Ogar began to search the ground around him for something.

Blade could not wait for Ogar. Could not trust Ogar. Whether or not the creature had led Blade into the quicksand deliberately, Ogar was now going to take advantage of the situation. Matters reversed themselves quickly in this Dimension X. Ogar was once again top dog.

Blade braced himself for a supreme effort. One end of the stick was sharp—if he could lurch back toward solid ground and manage to bury the point deep enough in the earth it would give him leverage of a sort. At best it wasn't much of a chance, but it was the only one he had. Ogar was gathering stones.

It occurred to Blade, even as he sweated and strained for his life, that this was an old game to Ogar and his people. They must kill game this way. Drive it into the quicksand and then stone it or beat it to death with clubs and axes.

The first stone bounced off Blade's ribs. It hurt. He glared at Ogar and bellowed and brandished the stick. Ogar flinched and retreated for a moment, then flung another stone that missed Blade and fell with a hollow plop into the quicksand. It was out of sight in a second.

There was a chill in Blade now and the faint wedge of panic. He fought it back. He would get out.

Ogar flung another stone. Blade was ready. He caught the stone and took aim and hurled it back with all his great strength. It caught Ogar in the pit of the belly. Ogar yelled and dropped his stones and clutched his stomach. He chattered obscenities at Blade.

Blade let his anger at Ogar fuel his final effort. He needed the extra incentive of his rage. He poised, raised the stick high over his head, summoned every muscle and lurched back for the path. He strained, grunting painfully, bone and sinew crackling, putting all his last reserve and hope into the lunge.

He fell short.

The sharp end of the stick dug into the bank of solid ground, slipped and skidded back into quicksand. Blade was chest down in the stuff now, his face barely raised, his arms outstretched, and the stick was driving down into quicksand, nothing but quicksand.

Blade groaned aloud. He had failed and it was an inglorious death for such a man as himself. There was still no panic in him, but fear clotted his guts and he cursed himself for a fool. To die so—in a stinking little patch of sand before his new adventure had fairly begun.

The sharp end of the stick hit something solid and held. Blade summoned new strength from somewhere and applied tremendous pressure. The stick bit deeper and deeper and held. It had reached solid ground where the path shelved out into the quicksand, which was shallow around the edges of the pool.

Blade began to drag himself back from death. Cautiously and very slowly. If he dislodged the stick again he was done for. The entire work fell on his forearms, shoulders and biceps. He gritted his teeth, tensed and staked his life on his muscles. Now—and again—and now!

Muscles corded and lumped, a slithering of blue serpents beneath the smooth-tanned hide. With an aching slowness Blade dragged himself out of the quicksand and onto solid ground. He glanced around. Ogar was gone. Gone to fetch others like himself. Cousins, members of his tribe or clan. Ogar had figured that out. Together they would bring larger stones and clubs and kill Blade.

Blade allowed himself a minute to catch his breath. Then he scraped most of the sand from his body, found the stick and pulled it out of the ground, circled the pool and took off in a long, swinging lope for the line of cliffs. The sun was gone now, all but a wraith of final afterglow, and along the base of the cliffs he could see the sparking of a dozen fires .

He had covered five hundred yards when he heard Ogar scream. He had not gone to get help in killing Blade. He had been watching from cover. Watching so intently that he had forgotten the menace all about him.

Blade was too late to be of any help. He watched, feeling sick, as the monstrous thing went through the rites, so obscenely ceremonial, nearly sacerdotal, of having its supper. Dining on Ogar. With Blade as a reluctant witness and fascinated against his will. Never, in all the dimensions he had visited, and certainly not in Home Dimension, had he seen anything like this.

The animal was not an anteater, yet it had a scarlet ribbon of tongue some twenty feet long. The tongue was rough and covered with tiny suction cups. The tongue was wrapped around Ogar, who could not scream because his bones were crushed and he was being swiftly drawn into a gaping maw. Instinct, automatic compassion, sent Blade starting forward. Then sense prevailed and he stopped. He could not fight this thing with only a pointed stick.

The thing's jaw was hinged. That hinge came unjointed now and the mouth gaped wider and the obscene tongue pulled Ogar in, whole and in one piece. The thing swallowed. Ogar made no sound as he disappeared. There was a lump in the thing's belly as it slithered around on great clawed feet and contemplated Blade.

Blade hoped Ogar had been already dead. Or, this

61

failing, that the stomach acids would kill him quickly.

The brute made no move to come at Blade. It huddled there, watching with cold, enormous eyes. To Blade it seemed part serpent, part crocodile, with scales and short, stumpy legs. He reckoned it at thirty feet long, including the scaled tail, and five feet high. It was very still. It watched him. Blade did not move.

The thing was like something out of mythology, a never-never product of man's imagination. Basilisk? Cockatrice? Gorgon?

Blade grimaced and watched it. He had no idea what it was, except that it sure as hell wasn't a product of his imagination. The problem was how to get past it and continue on the path to the cliffs. It would soon be totally dark. He dare not venture into the thick grass again. As it was, he had only the distant fires to guide him.

The problem was solved for him. Another of the things slid out of the grass and attacked without warning the one that had devoured Ogar. There was a tremendous sound of hissing as they locked tongues and went into a death struggle, rolling and clawing and butting at each other. They fought off into the tall grass. Blade ran.

Blade was badly shaken by what he had seen. He was not yet fully adjusted to this new world. That would come, as it always did, and he would take such things in his stride. But at the moment he still felt a strong and painful empathy for poor Ogar. It did not help much that such sudden death, and the manner of it, must be commonplace in Ogar's world. Blade's now. It was still a sickening way to die—as bad as quicksand.

Blade stepped up his pace. He did not look behind him, confident that he could outrun any of the huge, lumbering creatures frequenting the high grass. His salvation lay ahead in the fires and the caves.

Once a great furred head peered at him over the highest of the grass. Huge eyes glinted and the sound was a rumbling roar that tapered into a whine. Blade ran faster. At last he broke clear of the grass and was on barren ground, still marshy and springy beneath him. but free of obstruction. He could see the fires clearly now, dozens of them up and down the dark line of cliffs and scarcely a quarter of a mile off. Blade began to slow his pace. Time to reconnoiter. What manner of welcome, if any, lay ahead?

Chapter 8

Blade fell to his belly and begin to inch forward on all fours. He stopped to catch his breath, to make a survey, and chanced to look behind him. Something had followed him out of the grass.

It was too dark to make the creature out in detail, but his stomach did a flip-flop. It was a giant toad, horned and scaly, as big as a house. It hopped after Blade in twenty-foot leaps, stopping each time to nose at the spoor. Blade ran like a dog, on all fours, as fast as he could. When he looked back again the thing had stopped. It was afraid of the fires. Blade sighed with relief as it hopped back toward the grass jungle.

A faint stir of wind riffled from the cliffs toward Blade. It bore the faint but unmistakable stink he had come to associate with Ogar, but was now buffered with dung, smoke and the odor of roasting meat. Blade sniffed the latter in appreciation. He was near to starving. He crawled on. They were upwind and could not scent him.

He found cover behind a single slab up upended rock. It was tall and wide and stood on a natural boulder plinth —a dolmen, or cromlech, placed by Ogar's people for reasons beyond his understanding. Blade crouched behind the rearing stone and studied a group around the nearest fire. He counted ten of them. Four males asd six females. All naked. All covered with hair. All with small, slim bodies and huge heads. Ogar's people.

Two of the females were cooking meat on sticks held over the fire. Two of the remaining four women were nursing infants. The four males formed an outer circle between the females and the darkness. Each male, as he gnawed at a bone or a chunk of meat, kept a ceaseless vigil, staring into the darkness every few seconds and raising and dilating his nostrils to sniff at the wind. Blade willed the wind to hold steady, not to veer or back around. He wanted, and needed, the element of surprise.

His only weapon was the stick. Each of the males around the fire had a club or a stone axe ready to his hand. Blade pondered. He could not go back into the tall grass. Death was certain there. He was cold and hungry, naked, lacking in everything but a superb brain, matchless physique and all the guts he needed at any given moment.

Plus a smattering of Ogar's crude language. It should be enough. Blade took a deep breath and stood up. He tossed the stick away. It was useless as a weapon and it might frighten them.

Smiling, his hands held high and in conciliation, Blade stalked into the circle of firelight. There was a dead hush, a vacuum of sound. Twenty eyes stared in surprise and terror.

Blade took swift advantage of the silence. He remembered Ogar's exact sound as he rubbed his belly and asked for meat. Blade repeated it sow.

"Owwwnowwah—owwwnowwah—"

There was a great scrabbling rush—grunts and chattering and shrill cries of terror. The females snatched at their babies and ran. The men ran after them, forgetting their weapons. All vanished into the darkness toward the cliff. All but one—a young male who stopped and turned and snarled defiance at Blade. Blade took a step toward him and held out his hand. The male lost his nerve and fled after the others. Blade stood alone by the fire.

This did not discontent him. He had made friendly overtures and had been rebuffed and no doubt it was for the best. He set about consolidating his position. He piled new wood on the fire, selected a stone axe and a club and settled down by the blaze. One of the females had dropped a small haunch of meat into the fire where it lay sizzling

66

and emitting delectable smells. Blade fished it out and, after scorching his fingers, brushed off dirt and ashes and burnt his mouth as he tore into it. He chewed and grinned and knew that he was making slobbering sounds and did not care. Meat had never tasted so good. As he satisfied his hunger his confidence grew—he was making the adjustment so necessary to staying alive in this new Dimension X. The worst was over. The chances were now an even fifty-fifty that he would survive.

They were watching him from out there in the darkness. On two sides. The man-things from their caves in the foot of the cliff, the beast-things from the tall grass. The man-things were silent; the beasts roared and snarled and bellowed their hate and fear of the fire that kept them back. Blade stuffed himself on meat until his belly was swollen, wiped his greasy mouth, yawned and wished he could sleep. Impossible. He would never wake up.

He began to explore within the circle of firelight. He found a skin that would fit about his loins and another that would serve as a short cloak. He grunted and then smiled at himself—he must have sounded very like the late Ogar then. But he was pleased. Clothes, even raw, half-scraped skins, did make a difference. He busied himself, keeping his club and stone axe close at hand, and with a sharp, hand-worked flint he slit holes and made crude fasteners of wood and some creeper vine he found. He ate more meat and found himself thirsty and no help for it. No water. He would just have to thirst.

The supply of firewood, with care, would last until dawn. He fed the flames stingily and crouched near them, drowsing, yearning to sleep and not daring. And yet he must have dozed for a few seconds, for when his head snapped up and he came alert again she was there.

She came in silent abjection, on her hands and knees, crawling into view of the cliff side of the fire. Just within the aura of light she stopped and gazed at Blade, dog-like in her fear and cringing subjection. Blade understood. This young female had been sent to appease him. Once more godhood was bestowed and she was the price they paid, the sacrifice to a huge, massively muscled, hairless thing that threatened them. Blade smiled at the female and made a beckoning motion. She crawled a few paces nearer the fire, her small eyes intent on his, in terror, and yet doing as she had been told by the old men of the tribe.

She was very young, Blade thought. Possibly not more than twelve or thirteen, but already mature in body. A life span in this dimension would not be long.

The girlchild-thing—for so the thought of her—lacked some of the brutishness of feature common to Ogar and the others. Her body was supple, slim, fully revealed. Her body hair was lighter in color and not so thick as that of the males. Her legs were short and somewhat bowed, her waist small and her breasts, nearly hairless, were firm and plump with rigid out-thrusting nipples half an inch long. Her jaw and teeth, though out-jutting, lacked the prognathism of the males. Her skull was not so flattened, her frontal ridges less prominent. Blade thought of Lord L and smiled. By any gnathic index the old man would have had to list her as near to human.

Had he been longer in this particular Dimension X, and spent more time in the company of these creatures, Blade might well have accepted what she now offered. Offered in fear and trembling and, so he began to discern, some peculiar animal lust of her own. For there came a change in the glances she gave him and in the soft sounds she made deep in her throat. Nothing subtle.

The female halted just on the other side of the fire. She stared at Blade for a moment, then touched her breasts with her hands. She growled softly and he read both playfulness and desire into the sound. Most of her fear vanished. The smell of her came rank and acrid across the flames. She showed her teeth and chattered something at him. Blade did not move.

He was mindful that she might be a decoy, sent to lull him while the males crept up to brain him, and he searched the shadows beyond the fire. Nothing. He doubted they had the mental capacity for such a scheme. He went on watching her.

The lady was growing impatient. Blade choked back a laugh. By now she was puzzled and feeling slighted and beginning to dimly comprehend that the god-thing had no intention of becoming a lover. She growled at him. She lay on her back and clutched her breasts. She spread her legs wide, then raised her knees and stared through them at Blade.

Blade chuckled. He was not, he reckoned, cutting much of a figure in her eyes. It was evident that her awe of him was fast turning to contempt. And the watchers, especially the males, must be puzzled. This young female must be by far the most toothsome in the tribe—and the god would have none of her. Blade could only hope they would not become outraged and attack.

She tired of the game. She lowered her legs and glowered at Blade in reproach. A woman spurned. Blade smiled and patted his belly. He selected a tender bit of meat and tossed it to her. She gobbled it, her eyes never leaving his face, and her small fangs flashed in what she must have meant as a smile of enticement. Blade tossed her more meat.

"Not tonight," he said gently. "Thanks, but no thanks. I just don't think we could make it together. Your in-laws, for one thing. Just too many of them—and they would all want to live with us. Sorry, honey, but it wouldn't work out."

He went on crooning nonsense. The female cocked her head at him, flashed her teeth again and seemed to shake her head. Off in the grass something roared and Blade glanced in that direction. When he looked back she had gone.

For the rest of the night Blade fought off sleep. The sun rose on a deserted world wrapped in gauzy white mist. The grass jungle was silent and the caves scattered along the base of the cliff, dark holes in the gray basalt, were as quiet as tombs. Blade knew they were there—watching him. The word had spread. He counted a score of fires, smoldering black embers now, up and down the line of cliffs. But never a sign of them.

Blade, selecting a club and the heaviest of the stone ax-es, began exploring up and down the line of the cliff. He passed dozens of caves without detecting a stir of life. He was tempted to venture into one of the caves but decided against it.

As it turned out he found what he wanted without risk-ing the caves—a firepot, crudely fashioned of red clay and pierced for carrying by a vine sling, and a large collection of flints of varied sizes and uses. There were pebble tools and choppers and scrapers, axe heads, and even some punches and needles of bone. Blade made a pouch of skin and took what he needed. And found a prize second only to the firepot—a finely made knife of flint, double-bladed and with a tang properly chipped away and only waiting for a haft. He thanked the unknown genius who had made the knife. With it and the firepot he was in business.

Blade made a sling for the firepot, brushed aside ashes to find glowing embers, and half filled the pot. He covered the embers with a thin layer of ash, added sheets of dry bark to his pouch for tinder and began to seek a way up the cliffs. There was no question of going back into the grass jungle. It was quiet now, the towering green stalks moving only with the wind, but he knew what lurked in there. He thought of Ogar and made a sour face. It had to be up the cliffs.

The climb was easy. He found a series of crude footholds chiseled into the cliff face. Here and there wooden pegs had been pounded in. Half an hour later Blade stood on the rim of the cliffs. Before him, undulat-ing and steadily rising, was a vast plain. Vegetation was sparse and the plain was creased and crisscrossed by dry stream beds. Water might turn out to be a problem. There had been none by the fires. Blade shrugged his big shoul-ders and began to walk.

The plain was like an uptilted washboard. It dipped and rose, but the inclination was always upward. As he climbed out of one deep rill he saw a dark shadow on the horizon, stretching in either direction as far as he could see. After another hour of toiling across the plain he saw that the shadow was in reality the fringe of a forest, a dense black woods. As he drew nearer and the forest dissolved into individual trees, he noted that it slashed across the plain in an exact line, a ruler-straight edge. It might have been laid out by a surveyor.

Blade halted to rest as he reached the forest. He squatted, gnawing a meaty bone, and let his glance rove up and down the line of immense trees. The view was not reassuring. The day had turned leaden as the sun was obscured by thick clouds. There would be rain before nightfall and, in the gloom, the forest crouched like some black beast awaiting a foolhardy traveler. Nothing seemed to move in there. There was not even the flit or chittering of birds and the pall of silence did nothing to cheer the big man. It was unnatural and a bit frightening—the only sounds were those of the wind and his own breathing.

He tossed away the bone and began to explore up and down the edge of the forest, seeking a path. None was to be found. Blade cursed himself for hesitating, yet continued to linger on the plain. Here he was fairly safe. Once into the dark wilderness he might encounter death behind any tree. Yet venture into the primeval gloom he must. There was no other way to go.

Blade checked his weapons and crude equipment, made sure he still had fire and plunged in. There was no path, but he found an opening between the giant boles of oak and beech and variant conifers, and began to walk again. The terrain still slanted upward, but the grade was less and the going easier.

Immediately he was in a darkling twilight. Had the sun been out he might have been walking in aqueous light, stained green by a canopy of interlocking branches a hundred feet overhead; as it was, the gloom was near to Stygian and several times, as he slid between the massive boles—some a good thirty feet around—he had to feel his way.

There were creepers everywhere, binding the forest together, as thick around as Blade's own biceps. It was like trying to walk through a net of stout rope. Blade

71

swore and hacked with his stone axe, often got ensnared and cut his way out with the flint knife, and, as night began to fall, he reckoned that he had come perhaps two miles. If that.

He fought his way through a mass of tall, vile-smelling weeds into a small clearing, the first open spot he had seen, and prepared to camp for the night. There was much to do. He was famished and his supply of meat was gone; he had not yet found water and there was the question of wood for his fire.

Things began to go better. He found plenty of deadfall for the fire and, while gathering the wood, heard a stream purling and tracked it down. The water was sweet and cold and Blade, filthy with sweat and dirt and covered with burrs and ticks, cut and bruised in a score of places, plunged into the stream and had a bath along with his drink. As he went back to build his fire he felt better. He wondered where his next meal was coming from. He was famished.

As he was blowing on the embers in the firepot, readying them for the tinder, he sensed something behind him. Something had come out of the forest and was in the clearing just behind him. Bade put the firepot down and reached stealthily for the flint knife, wishing now that he had taken time to make a haft for it. The tang gave an uncertain grip.

The thing moved closer. He heard it and he smelled it. An animal smell of hide, fur? Blade whirled about.

It was a rabbit! More like an English hare, but like none he had ever seen before. It was the size of a Saint Bernard. Its ears were enormous, the feet huge and splayed, and it was of a peculiar rat-like color. It stared at Blade, unafraid, out of wide, pinkish eyes. Blade halted and looked back at the animal. It hopped closer to him. Blade nodded and readied his knife, thanking the Fates for supplying him with so easy a dinner. This hare-like creature was curious. Totally without fear of him. It had never been hunted and had never seen a man.

It hopped closer and wrinkled its nose at Blade's odor.

72

He moved closer. It did not retreat. Blade sprang.

It was the easiest kill he had ever made, of man or beast. The giant hare squealed only once as he plunged the knife into the throat and drew it across. Blood gushed and soaked him. He smashed a great fist down on the head for good measure, then let it bleed itself out while he got on with his fire. In five minutes he had a good blaze going. Ten minutes later he had skinned, gutted and disjointed the hare. He seared a savory joint over the fire and wolfed it down. It was delicious.

Blade found more wood and built the fire up until he had a well-lit circle some forty feet in diameter. Inside the circle of light he piled a great reserve of wood. Fighting off sleep all the time, he selected a slim tree within his pale of light and began to hew away with his flint knife and axe. It was slow work, and tedious, but within a few hours he had wood enough for a bow and several arrows. They would be crude, and he must use vine for a bowstring, but they added enormously to his scant arsenal. He had flint for heads and they could be bound to the shafts with vine tendrils. He was at a loss for fletching—there were no birds in this damn forest.

By now sleep was winning—he could fight it off no longer. He stacked wood on the fire and, with axe and club in hand, made a cautious exploration just outside the circle of light. He found nothing. The forest brooded, as silent and empty as it had been in daytime. Apart from the giant hare he had seen no living creature. It should be safe to sleep, and sleep he must.

He lay down near the fire. Yawned. Struggled to think. Closed his eyes. Richard Blade fell crashing into oblivion.

Pain brought him gradually and reluctantly awake. Not one concentrated pain, not a wound nor a bite, but rather a series of small pains adding up to agony. And there was sound—a sucking sound. A drinking sound. Along with the pain and the sucking, his body was covered with an intolerable itch. He was aflame with itch, going mad with it. He came fully awake and dug his nails into his crotch and upper legs, scratching furiously. His fingers touched something unspeakably slimy and he snatched them away. In the dying firelight he stared at them. They were covered with blood. His blood.

Only then, as he came fully awake to horror, did he realize what had happened. He was covered with leeches! Enormous leeches. Swollen, bloated slugs, hundreds of them, sucking and sucking away at his life.

Blade screamed harshly and leaped to his feet. He staggered and nearly fell, weak and reeling, and knew that he had awakened only just in time. The pain was a blessing. Another few minutes and the leeches would have bled him to death.

Still they clung in their hundreds. Blade pulled them off and flung them away. He crushed them with nasty bladder-popping sounds. He had gotten over the worst shock and he fought back revulsion and frenzy and went about the grim business of extermination. It was not easy. They were a solid wriggling and sucking mass on his back, from his anus to his shoulders, and he could not get at them. They writhed around his groin and in his pubic hair.

Blade, near to fainting from loss of blood, reeled to the fire and plucked out a brand and began to sear his body with it. It worked. He did not feel the bite of flame in the blessed relief of being rid of the leeches. In any case, the burns would be superficial.

When he was free of them, though scorched here and there, he mustered his strength and went around stomping as many of the things as he could find. He was amazed to see them, once deprived of their host, screw themselves into the ground like worms. Earth leeches! For one grim and angry moment Blade wished that J and Lord L might be here to share in *this* adventure.

His body inflamed, covered with thousands of tiny bites, Blade staggered to the brook and lay down in the cold rushing water, unmindful of any greater danger. He lay in the water for a long time, feeling some of his strength come back, knowing that he would be all right in a day or so. But he would have to eat—and eat—and eat. There was plenty of the hare left and he could make broth

74

in the firepot. Meantime he could finish his bow and arrows, make a spear and prepare for whatever new ordeals lay ahead. That there would *be* ordeals he never doubted. By now he had learned that life, and survival, in any Dimension X were chancy and that the odds were always against him. This particular Dimension X was not any different.

One thing he was positive about—he would build himself a platform in a tree and he would sleep there.

Chapter 9

Blade made a stick calendar and notched the days on it. His crude bow worked well enough at short range and he fletched his arrows with the obovate leaves of a tree he could not name. He made a spear and hardened the point in fire. He killed two more of the giant hares and an iguanalike creature, a miniature dragon whose belly flesh —the only part he could eat—tasted like chicken. In three days of trekking through the interminable dark forest he did not see a single bird. There was always the silence, vast and brooding, broken only by the sound of his passage, of his footsteps on the springy undermass of needles and leaves and rotten vines.

He built large fires every night and slept in trees, binding himself into a crotch or fork with vines so he would not tumble down.

Always the terrain rose in a gradual slant. A rough calculation told him that he had climbed some three thousand feet since leaving the cliff rim.

On the morning of the fourth day he was awakened by a harsh cawing, similar to that of crows in H-Dimension, but louder and more abrasive. He stretched and groaned as he cut away the vines binding him—there was *no* comfortable way to sleep in a tree—and searched for the source of the strange noises.

Birds!

Gulls. Or gull-like, for they were huge and had transparent leathery wings and cruel hooked beaks. One of them was carrying a fair-sized fish in its beak. They circled over him, apparently aware of his presence and not liking it, raucous in their disapproval. Blade thumbed his nose at them and cooked breakfast. Thoughtfully. Gulls meant a fairly large body of water. That could mean people, of some sort, and that meant danger. That day he traveled with more caution than usual.

About mid-afternoon he came to a path. Long disused, overgrown, faintly traced, but definitely a path. His caution increased. He lay in the brush for half an hour before venturing onto the path and stepping up his pace. The going was infinitely easier.

The path dipped suddenly into a long, narrow and dark ravine. As he traversed it, noting that it was his first descent since the trip began, he also noticed that the forest was beginning to thin out. When he emerged from the ravine, climbing again, the path made an abrupt right-angle turn and he saw the barrow, or tumulus, about a mile ahead. And saw what stood atop it.

The gulls had long since left him. Blade approached the high mound, covered with weeds and grass, with an arrow notched to his bow and his spear and knife ready. For this barrow, and the towering stone figure atop it, was definitely the work of men. Intelligent men. Engineering men. At a hundred yards he paused and contemplated it.

The idol, or statue, was some two hundred feet high. The great pillars of the legs, of cunningly worked stone, stood wide astride and the stone arms were crossed on the gigantic chest. The body faced Blade; the head looked away from him.

He made a wide circle around the mound and the idol, moving quietly and on the alert, and got into position to see the face of the thing. A chill traced down his spine. The stone visage still bore traces of paint, scarlet and blue, and the great empty eyes glared at him. It was a grotesque, a combination of skull and devil mask and something else he could not identify—an eerie and terrifying ethos of its own. Blade did not like the thing, nor his own reaction to it. He shook his fist at it and moved in closer. With each step the silence of centuries closed in on him, silence that was palpable, had weight and substance.

Blade strode between the colossal legs. In one foot, near the big toe, was a black rectangle. A door. Blade slung his bow over his shoulder and, with his knife and spear ready, stepped into semidarkness. He paused, waiting for his eyes to adjust, and sniffed about. After a moment he relaxed. Nothing but the musty, dusty smell of slow decay. There was nothing here. Nothing but the rotten detritus of the years.

The inside of the foot was a chamber of brick—the stonework was only facing—from which the mortar had fallen in great chunks. In the heel was another door leading to a flight of twisting stone steps that climbed steeply upward. Blade started to climb.

On the first landing he found the first skeleton. Bones so rotted by time that when he touched a thighbone it crumbled to dust at his touch. Blade contemplated the thing. His association with Lord Leighton had been long enough—and Blade was a good student when he chose—to inform him that these bones had once been a human being as he knew them. The skull was that of modern man.

"What happened?"

Blade asked the question as he edged around the bones and began to climb again. There were four more such landings before he reached the top, and on each was a skeleton. Just bones. No weapons, no jewelry or adornments, only bones.

He reached the top landing. A door led into the inner skull of the idol. It had been of wood, so rotted now that when he approached, the slight vibration caused the wood to turn to powder and fall away. He gazed into the chamber beyond, at the stone altar.

Atop the altar were two skeletons, bones now linked in their long death. He did not need to be an expert to know that the slighter set of bones had belonged to a woman and the larger bones over her were those of a man. In what weird, perhaps sexual, ceremony had they died so? He shrugged and went about his exploring.

Scattered about the chamber were three more altars, smaller and in the form of lecterns. On each one was a massive book of yellowed parchment or vellum bound in hide. He touched a page and it vanished in powder. He bent to scan the strange cuneiform scribble, so faded that only by looking at it slantwise and using the light refraction could he discern traces of ink. At last he turned away. This mystery he would never solve.

Once again the crying of the gulls startled him. Blade went to one of the hollow eyes and peered out. Nothing. He went to the other eye and saw it: a lake. A greenish-blue soupbowl of a lake, not more than two miles away. The birds were circling over it, crying, and now and again diving for fish. Blade paid no attention to the birds. There were huts in the lake. Thatched and wattled huts on stilts, each with a landing platform built around it. Gray smoke curled from several of the huts. Women, bare-breasted and wearing skins to cover their genitals, worked at various chores. One was pounding a clublike stick into a large bowl. Pestle and mortar. Grain. Flour. Blade nodded. These lake people were certainly a cut above Ogar's tribe, though far down the scale from the men who had built the idol from which he now spied. And they were dangerous.

Blade spent the remainder of the afternoon, while the light lasted, studying the lake village. He did not like what he saw.

The lake people, from what he could see at his far vantage, were not true men. Lord L would have labeled them apemen. Pithecanthropus. Yet they walked like men, had weapons of stone and wood, used fire and had built the stilted huts in the lake. They built round, cuplike boats of withes and mud and used them to scuttle between the huts and the shore. And they were cultivators! Around the edges of the lake was a narrow littoral of cultivated fields extending to the edge of the forest. Perhaps half a mile.

The lake people used slaves in the fields. And scarecrows to keep the gulls away from the crops. Blade did not at first grasp the nature of the scarecrows, nor feel any particular pity for the slaves. When he did understand it he decided, then and there, to stay well away from the lake. These were a cruel and brutish people. More intelligent than Ogar, hence more to be feared.

More than once that day he wished for a pair of powerful binoculars. His own vision was superhuman—as near to 10-10 as is possible—but he fretted at details he sensed he was missing. Yet by concentrating on the strip of plowed land closest to him he managed well enough. And redoubled his determination not to go near the lake.

Half the slaves working in that near field were women. Some old, some young, all naked and all being whipped incessantly by apemen overseers. The male slaves were whipped only infrequently or not at all. This in itself puzzled Blade, but still more puzzling was the fact that the slaves were definitely of a higher species. They were devoid of body hair, smooth-skinned and well formed—true men—and yet they were in slavery to the shambling apeman. Lord L, when he emptied Blade's memory file at the end of this journey, would be surprised. The higher species, then, did not always triumph.

The scarecrows were the dead bodies of slaves. The watching Blade saw one of the grisly things come into being. A female slave faltered at her work, stumbled and fell, and an apeman immediately began to beat her. She could not get up. Another apeman joined the first and began to use his knout, the heavy whip the apemen carried. Blade made a wry face. He expected such horrors in Dimension X, yet it was not a pretty thing to watch. What followed was worse.

The apemen stopped beating the slave. One bent over her and made signs to indicate she was dead. The other apeman dropped his whip and fell on her still-warm flesh, attacking her sexually. When he had finished, the other apeman did the same. Blade cursed them, then chided himself. He had not yet adapted fully enough if his emotions could be so involved. He must do better, adapt more and faster. Home Dimension rules did not apply out here.

The body of the female slave was dragged to a post set

81

in the ground and tied to it with withes. This task completed, the apemen went back to beating their female charges. Only now and then did a male slave receive a blow.

About this time Blade noticed one of the female slaves, young and, insofar as he could make out at the distance, quite pretty, quietly edging away from the other slaves. Step by step, yard by yard, she sidled toward the bordering forest. Blade, and he had to grin at himself for it, found he was holding his breath and wishing her luck.

Had the apemen overseers not been so engrossed in their maltreatment of the dead woman, the girl would never have had a chance. As it was she was discovered while she was still a hundred yards from the forest. One of the apemen saw her, let out a guttural scream of rage and bounded toward her. The young female slave screamed in turn and began to run.

The apeman was faster. He covered the ground in ludicrous fashion, awkward and with a leaping and lunging gait, but he covered it. The girl ran with her mouth open, screaming in terror, her slim legs and arms pumping, knowing what awaited her if caught.

Blade found Blade excitedly talking to Blade: "Come on—come on, girl! Run, damn it. Run!"

She was doing her best, but the ground was rough, recently gouged with sharp plowsticks, and she fell. The apeman screamed in angry triumph and struck at her with his knout. She rolled to her feet, eluded the blows and took off again for the forest. Blade felt his heart beat as fast as her own.

Another apeman, with the angle in his favor, was trying to cut her off before she could get into the forest. He lunged at her and, as she pulled away, Blade saw blood crimson her naked shoulder and breast. The apeman lunged again, and again she eluded him, still running, still trying.

Blade felt his heart swell within him. He wanted her to make it. How he wanted her to make it!

The slave reached the dark sanctuary of the forest and

82

plunged in. But Blade shook his head gloomily. For a moment there he had thought she had a chance, but in the tangled forest, impeded by trees and creeper vines and undergrowth, the apemen would surely overtake her. They were burly brutes, as strong as gorillas, and better equipped to make their way in such a wilderness.

Blade was wrong. He stared as the apemen stopped short of the forest's edge. They peered into the trees and made signs and chattered to each other, but they did not venture any closer to the trees. Slowly, making gestures of hate and rage, they backed off. Blade smiled and understood, at least in part. The apemen were afraid of the forest. Deathly afraid of it. Taboo!

He wished the young slave well, though he did not think highly of her chances. The forest had its own terrors. He studied the dark vista where she had entered. Not a twig stirred.

While the light lasted he watched the apemen. As the sun sank from view the slaves, male and female, were rounded up and herded into basket boats and transferred to a stilt hut larger than the rest. Men and women were shoved into the hut together, guards posted, and food brought by other male slaves who appeared to be trustees. Blade watched one of these trustees, his chores dispatched, return in a boat to one of the huts and be greeted there by an apewoman. So that was it. There was a shortage of apemen and the male slaves, under certain conditions, were acceptable as mates. He pondered this as he prepared for sleep. No matter the dimension—sex always found a way.

Blade slept in the skull chamber that night, soundly and undisturbed, and as the gulls began their hoarse crying with the first light he was on his way. He made a wide circle around the lake, staying deep in the forest, finding water where he could and noting that the terrain once again began to slant upward.

The forest began to thicken again. The giant hares on which he had been depending for food suddenly vanished. All that day he did not see one of the creatures. He still

83

had a pouch full of meat and did not worry too much—especially as he found a natural salt lick, a saline spring bubbling from a rock and evaporating to leave coarse salt lying on the ground. Blade concealed himself in a thicket and waited patiently.

The wait was long, but in the end he was not disappointed. He was careful to remain downwind and, after three hours, a tiny deer left cover and timidly approached the salt lick. Blade, who was in truth getting a bit tired of hare, watched with great interest. The creature was not much bigger than a large cat, with a dun hide and darkish yellow rosettes. The ears were mule-like, it had no antlers and, instead of hooves, it had three toes on each foot. Blade cared nothing for all this. What did the flesh taste like? he wondered.

When the deer had had its fill of salt and left, Blade followed it at a distance. He soon found tracks, well worn, beaten smooth over the years by the little three-toed beasts. He came suddenly on a herd of them grazing off to one side. They bounded out of sight in an instant, but Blade did not mind. Their traces were everywhere. His food problem was solved for the immediate future.

It was an hour before sunset when he first knew he was being followed.

Had it not been for the eternal brooding silence he would have missed it. He paused for a breather or, as he admitted, a loafing period, for he had by now fully recovered his strength and replaced the blood drained by the leeches. But it was his habit, while in Dimension X, to pause every now and then and conceal himself to watch and listen.

The sound came from somewhere behind him, on the deer trace, and it was very faint and did not come again. Whoever had made the sound was nearly as expert as Blade himself at moving through the forest. Yet a stone had been dislodged. It rolled and struck another stone. That was all Blade needed.

Whether or not he was in view of the follower he had no way of knowing. He presumed that he was and feigned ignorance. He continued on his way, halting now and then to study the deer tracks while listening and studying his back trail without appearing to. Nothing. The sound did not come again. Yet he was still being followed. The watcher was still there.

As night fell he built his fire. He made snares of vines and saplings and placed them up and down the path with great ostentation, wanting the spy to see them. As full darkness closed down, Blade left his fire and, vanishing like a shadow into the shadows, constructed two larger snares on either side of the path. He put himself in the watcher's place and knew that he would not approach along the path; he would circle out into the forest and come in from the side.

He cooked his meat longer than usual that night, holding it out of the fire so the faint breeze would carry the savory smell to the unknown lurker. He built two more smaller fires, each at a point where the trace led into the clearing and left it. He kept his weapons with him and was careful not to sit with his back to the forest. And he waited.

Hours passed. Blade pretended to doze between his fires, his hands never far from his weapons. Then it came.

First the snapping crackle of the bent young tree he had used as a spring, a whistling sibilance as it was triggered. A muffled scream. Blade snatched a torch from the edge of the fire and ran toward the sound, spear under his arm and stone knife in his hand. He had caught something.

She was well and fairly caught. The thick vine clutched her by shapely ankles as she dangled five feet off the ground, head down. Naked. It was the female slave whom he had watched escape from the apemen. Blade held the torch high and moved in for a closer inspection. She screamed at him, spat and, as helpless as she was, tried to claw his face with her nails. Blade moved back a pace or two. The girl was as wild as any animal. And terrified out of her wits. Now that Blade had her he did not know exactly what to do with her.

For the moment he did nothing. He stared at her,

neither smiling nor scowling, feigning more bewilderment than he actually felt. She had escaped, she was traveling—ergo, she must be going someplace, must have a destination. She was of this Dimension X, as poor Ogar had been, so perhaps she could take his place as a guide and mentor. If he could tame her and gain her trust.

He continued to stare, saying nothing. The girl stopped her struggles and stared back at him. In her wild disheveled way, upside down and stark naked—a fact of which she did not seem aware—she was beautiful. Her teeth were white and even, lovely even when she snarled at him, and he could visualize what her mass of thick, dark hair might be like when it was clean and free of burrs and leaves. She was young, certainly in her teens, and here again he could see beauty beneath the matted grime that now caked her regular features. Her eyes, narrowed at him and glittering green in the torchlight, were well spaced under luxuriant dark brows. Her superb breasts, even as she dangled in this undignified position, did not droop or flop. They were as round and firm and plump as partridges on the wing, with only the tiny red nipples flaccid and inert. Her body, deep-tanned by constant exposure to the sun, was smooth and hairless.

At that moment the breeze backed around a point or so. Blade stepped back a pace and sniffed at it—her odor was that of musky female secretions, natural, not subject to the lavage of H-Dimension antiseptics. He sniffed again and felt desire rise in him. And knew that he was, at last, fully adapted to this particular X-Dimension.

The caught girl said, "Who are you? Why did you trap me like this? You are not one of them."

Blade gave her a tentative smile. "I'm not? Who is *them*?"

She frowned and stabbed her finger in the direction they had come from that day. "Them. The hairy people. The beastmen. You are certainly not one of them. And you are not one of us."

He smiled again and advanced a pace. She showed her teeth but did not attempt to claw him with her nails.

"Who," said Blade, "is us? Who are you?"

For a long moment, she studied him. Her snarl faded and became a half smile, a cautious smile. "You really do not know?"

He was patient. "If I knew I would not have to ask."

Her smile grew. "Cut me down then and I will tell you. But I find it very strange that you do not know a Jedd when you see one. We have lived in this country as long as the world has been. Now you come, a stranger such as I have never seen before, and say that you have never heard of us. But cut me down first. Your snare is hurting my legs."

Blade pondered it. She was only a girl, a naked girl without a weapon. There was no possible danger. He severed the vine and let her fall to the ground, all the while conscious that beneath his scanty loincloth of animal skin he was excited. He had adapted, all right! He was surging with want of her, with raw animal lust for her body. In a cooler moment he would have known and admitted the cause—Lord L's megavitamin therapy—but now he only wanted to penetrate her, then and there, and send his seed bursting into her.

He might have fallen atop her then and there, forced her, willing or not, had she not been too quick for him. She broke her fall with her hands, did a swift somersault, and had the caught vine nearly off her feet before he divined her intentions and sprang. She had one foot out of the loop and was running when he caught the end of the trailing vine and tripped her up. She fell with a crash into matted undergrowth and twisted to meet him, once again spitting and fighting like a wildcat. He hauled her rudely back by the leg. She raked his big chest with nails like talons. Blade, his ardor blunted for the time being, lost patience and clouted her alongside the head. Not too hard.

While she was unconscious he bound her with vines, then carried her back to the fires and dumped her on the ground. She was still out cold. Blade went back to roasting his supper, seemingly indifferent but watching her from a corner of his eye. When her eyes flickered open he gave

her a few moments to recover, then he began to speak
without looking directly at her.

"I will speak first," he told her. "Then you will speak. I
am master here and so it shall be while we remain
together. That is understood?"

She nodded sulkily. "That is understood. You are
master."

"Good. What is your name?"

"I am called Ooma."

"I see. Ooma. You said you were a Jedd—what is a
Jedd? What does the word mean?"

She stared at the meat he was roasting. She licked her
lips and dribble ran from the corners of her well-shaped
mouth. "I starve. I will not talk until I am fed. You have
meat. Give me some. I have not had meat in all the year I
was a captive of the beastmen."

Blade gave her a hard look. He dangled a piece of meat
before her, then ate it slowly while she watched and
drooled. Her eyes hated him.

"You will talk first, Ooma. Then you will have meat.
Or you will not talk and shall have nothing at all." Blade
shrugged his big shoulders and smiled at her. "I do not
care if you eat. It is nothing to me. I have plenty."

She struggled against the vines binding her. Beneath the
facial grime she was crimson with rage. Blade calmly
speared a new hunk of meat and began to roast it.

Ooma said, "You are master. I will talk. But if you do
not keep your promise and give me meat I will wait until
you sleep and kill you. I promise it."

He smiled sweetly at her. "And I promise you meat. I
do not break my word. You will find that out, my girl.
Now—what is a Jedd?"

"I am a Jedd. Jedd means mountain. And we are called
Jedds because we are mountain people. Our Empress, a
very old woman who is dying now, is the Jeddock."

"Ah," said Richard Blade softly, "an Empress? Tell me
about that—tell me about the Jeddock."

This, he thought, was more like it. Ooma could lead

88

him out of the forest to something resembling civilization as he knew and understood it. Mountain people. An Empress. He listened with great attention, careful not to miss a word. When she had finished he untied her hands and gave her meat. She tore at it with cries of pleasure, gobbling and stuffing herself while the succulent juices dribbled down her chin. When she could eat no more she lay back, rubbing her belly and belching, and watching him with a new look in her green eyes.

"Who are you?" she demanded. "I have told you of myself and my people—what of you and your people? You are bigger and much stronger than the men of Jedd and much more handsome. You must come from a far place to be so different. Tell me."

Blade would as lief remained silent, evaluating the information she had given him, but he needed her and wanted to keep her happy. He told his story, sticking as close to truth as was possible under the circumstances and keeping it simple. Ooma was not likely to grasp much about Home Dimension.

He pointed through a break in the trees at a full moon. Blood red and exactly at the zenith. "I come from another world, Ooma. Not that one, but a world much like it. I came by magic, in the time it takes you to draw a breath, though the distance in days of travel is more than all the leaves on all the trees in this forest. Do you understand?"

"No." She scowled at him. "You lie to me. And you do not yet tell me your name, *if* you have one."

"I do not lie," he said calmly. "I have magic of my own, which I may show you if we remain friends. As for my name—it is Blade. That is what you will call me—Blade. Blade master. Try it, Ooma. See how it sounds."

She frowned at him and showed her white teeth, but slowly she pronounced the words: "B-la-de mas-ter. Blade master."

He nodded. "That is it. It has a good sound on your lips."

89

"I do not like it. It has a sharp and cruel sound. And I do not think I like you, even though you gave me meat. You look at me strangely and it frightens me. I know what is in your mind, Blade master, and it shall not be. I will never give myself to you."

She had a way of getting to the crux of things. Blade smiled. Though he still lusted for her, he had himself under control now. It would be criminally foolish to hurt or offend this child. He needed her more than she needed him, though perhaps she did not realize it. He tried to placate her. Without surrendering his dominance.

"You will not take that tone with me," he said severely. "Listen. Do not fear me. I will not harm you. I will never touch you unless you wish to be touched. I want only for us to be friends, to help each other. You will guide me and answer all my questions and in return I shall take you safely back to your people." He indicated the brooding dark forest encompassing them. "You will never get back to your Jedds alone, Ooma. There are too many dangers."

For a moment, she gnawed at her red underlip with sparkling teeth, then nodded. "You are right. I will need you to get past the Api. *If* we get past them. They will probably kill and eat you and make a whore-slave of me, but I do not worry about that now. It is still four days' march before we reach the Api. So for now I will be your friend. You agree to this, Blade master?"

"Of course I agree. Have I not said I want to be friends!?"

"Then untie me. One friend does not keep another friend bound hand and foot. Or do they so in this world you say you come from?"

Blade chuckled. It was logical enough. "No," he admitted. "In my world real friends trust each other." No use mentioning that real friends were hard to come by and most friendship mere feigning. Things *might* be different in Dimension X, though he doubted it. He had discovered, at times to his sorrow and peril, that there were certain constants in *all* dimensions. This thought he could safely leave to the philosophers who might one day study Lord

L's records. Blade had two objectives—survive and return.

He patted her sleek brown shoulder as he cut the vines binding her legs. "You are right, Ooma. I admit it and I set you free. And you need not be afraid of—"

She was faster than any cat. She had doubled and redoubled a length of vine into a heavy cord. She slashed him across the eyes with it. He instinctively fell back and in that instant she was gone out of the firelight and into the forest. Her mocking laugh floated back to him.

"Goodbye, Blade master. One think I know—they breed fools in your strange world."

He rubbed the welt over his eyes and cursed her briefly, then began to laugh at himself. She was right. He was a fool. She had conned him but good. It was what he got for underestimating her. The Jedd brain, it would appear, was as good as his own, if not so sophisticated.

At that moment there sounded, from far off in the depths of that immensity of forest, a high-pitched shriek, an animalistic gibber, that curdled Blade's blood and prickled the hairs on his body. The awful sound was like nothing he had ever heard before, not even on Lord Leighton's tapes. There was terror and triumph in it and blood and death and the surging vibrato of life. Blade crouched by his fires and stared in the direction whence the sound came. Miles away. No direct threat to him. He smiled then, a covert smile and sly, and prepared for sleep. They would see.

He pretended sleep, his weapons close to his hand. And listened. Half an hour passed. An hour. Then a faint sound in the undergrowth. He grinned.

"B-la-de master?" An echoing sigh on the breeze. Perhaps only a trick of the breeze and he was hearing what he expected, and wanted, to hear.

But it came again. "Blade master. I am sorry. Ooma is sorry. I wish to come back to the fires."

Blade turned over and yawned loudly. "Come back? Why? I thought you liked it out there in the forest all alone."

"I do not like it."

He patted a yawn to conceal a smile. "But I thought you were afraid of me?"

Silence. Then—"I am. But I am more afraid out here by myself. Let me return. I—I will let you do anything you wish. To me."

Blade pillowed his head on his arms and emitted a mock snore. "I do not wish to do anything to you, Ooma. Not now. I have found that we are not friends and I cannot trust you. Goodnight."

Long silence. He could hear her moving in the thick bushes.

"I beg you, Blade master. I beg. I am cold and frightened. I want to come by the fires."

"Then come," he snapped, "but do not bother me. I wish to sleep."

Feigning sleep, he watched her through slitted eyes. She came slowly out of the forest and crouched by the largest of the fires. As she warmed herself she watched him intently. Blade made no sign or sound. She began to search her sleek young body, carefully removing burrs and bits of twig and matted leaf. She smoothed and rubbed her body with her hands, cleaning it as thoroughly as possible. Blade felt his loins begin a renewed stirring. Could it be?

Ooma went to the pile of wood Blade had collected and began to search through it. He was about to warn her against using up too much wood, but kept his silence. She was not tending the fires. He watched with growing interest as she broke off a branch into a short length, stripped it of tendrils and began to use it as a comb. Squatting on her heels and casting an occasional glance in his direction, Ooma began to pull the makeshift comb again and again through her tangled dark hair with a coarse rasping sound. She grimaced and shook her head as the rude comb encountered an especially hopeless tangle.

By now Blade was in an acute state of readiness and had the control not to do anything about it. He thought he now understood what was going to happen. Let her come to him.

Ooma left off combing and began to squeeze and caress her plump little breasts. When her nipples were erect she wet a finger in her mouth and moistened them again and again until they glowed dark pink in the dim firelight. She then combed out her pubic hair with her fingers, very carefully, and toyed briefly with herself there. Then she came toward Blade. He still feigned sleep, but a sardonic part of his mind was putting himself in the place of Lord L, when that old man made his notes: Jedd females indulge in extensive foreplay to ready themselves for coitus. At times this foreplay is carried so far as nearly to constitute autoeroticism. Yes, his Lordship would put it all down in his tight, sparse handwriting, with no hint of lubricity. He was an old man. He was also a scientist.

Blade was neither.

Ooma nestled close to him from behind, slipping in until their bodies, his huge one and her small one, fitted like two spoons. He felt her breasts velvety and firm against his back, the nipples rigid and like warm little needles boring into his flesh. She breathed in his ear.

"Blade master? Do you sleep, Blade master?"

He grunted. "I do not sleep. As you well know. How could I sleep at a time like this? But I do not understand—you have changed your mind about many things, it would appear. Why is this, Ooma?"

She laughed softly and sank her fine small teeth gently into his ear. "I have been thinking. All the time I was frightened out there in the forest I was thinking. You were right and I was wrong. We *will* be friends and I *will* trust you."

"And," said Blade with some malice, "there was that cry. That sound in the forest. Or perhaps you did not hear it, Ooma?"

He felt a tremor run through the body pressed so close to his. "I heard it, Blade master. It was the cry of the Api. They hunt at night and it is rare for them to come this far from their own land, but when food is scarce they will. But I would not speak of the Api. They are far away and

93

no danger to us tonight. Tonight, at this moment, it is something else that I want."

Her hand came slyly around and found him and he heard her gasp. "Blade master! You are a giant there. There is none in Jedd, no Jedd male, who has anything like *this.*" Ooma gave *this* a tug and a rapid manipulation. Blade stifled a groan of pleasure. Already he was having difficulty with his breathing, his heart was trying to pound out of his chest, and he fought back the urge to consummate then and there. Go warily. He did not, in possessing her body, want to lose her allegiance and friendship. What was now transpiring, about to happen, was sheer, brute sex, animal lust on both their parts. It would die as the fires would die, leaving ashes, and there would still be tomorrow to face. He needed Ooma. For far more than sexual relief.

Ooma had none of Blade's reservations. The more she caressed him the more her ardor grew. Her voice went high-pitched and her breath sobbed and whistled in her throat. She licked his body with her moist tongue and murmured words he did not understand. She stroked his swollen testicles with her fingers, performed a brief, but avid, fellatio, and then dug her hands into his hair and pulled him down atop her. She guided him into the sleek, wet, tight and rough-walled grotto. Blade was huge and Ooma small and the fricative sum was an unbearable agony of pleasure. It seemed to Blade, trying to prolong the blissful pain, that Ooma spent incessantly without ever losing her grip on him. Her muscular control was beyond anything he had ever experienced; she squeezed him and milked him and, when he could struggle no longer, she took the final gush of his sperm with a high-ringing cry of pleasure that skewered the forest night.

Blade lay on top of her, sweating and panting, still twitching and mindless, fighting his way back from the little death. It had been sex such as few men were privileged to know—barbaric and primitive sex with a unity, a wholeness, a lack of inhibition that even Richard Blade did not often come by. He was grateful. He was also wrung out, depleted, wasted and weary. His massive body was a cocoon nurturing an ennui and death-longing beyond all measure or telling. The past was blotted out, the present did not exist, the future would never be. The great lie of living was over. He could rest now. Sleep now—rest now—die now—

He knew his danger and fought back. He rolled off Ooma, who was already sleeping. So simple, so easy to do it like that. Sex, satisfaction and sleep. The three esses.

He jabbed himself with the stone knife to keep awake and bring him back to reality. He made a tour of the camp, halting long in shadow to listen and peer, and saw no danger. Finally, sleep overpowering him, he bedded down in the shadows away from the fading fires. Thus an intruder would be apt to attack Ooma first, so giving Blade a chance at him from behind.

... as quiet, except and warm. His muscles too were ... from the night's ... hunt and now slowly relaxed as ... sleep ... wang. The rest of the world out the cabin ... had ... ease, he knew he would ... later. The first faint light was gray. He could rest now, sleep now until ... now the sun ...

He ... any danger and caught it ... He rolled on ... Coita who was already sleeping, so close, so easy to ... in the ... his aspiration and sleep. He then cated. He pulled himself with the utmost will to keep awake and bring him back to reality. He made a note of the camp before long to show ... to Coita and ... He ... set it off the camp overlooking the ... to side-town in the distance away ... Coita, yes. This would ... if ... there would be another ... attack. One must stop giving Coita a chance at protection before ...

Chapter 10

Ooma turned out to be a chatterbox. When she was not using her tongue for his, and her, sexual gratification—every night after dinner and before sleep—she talked incessantly. Blade fell into the habit of listening in silence. Now and again he would grunt in assent, or snarl in dissent, and on the latter occasions she would fall silent for a time. Never for long. Blade learned a great deal in those four days, but there were times when he almost wished the beastmen overseers had caught her.

He spent much of his time in deep thought, pondering, trying to fully grasp a concept slowly building in his mind. It came slowly, with much painful groping, for Blade was no scholar, no intellectual and certainly not a scientist. He was a highly intelligent man of action, gifted with a fine brain and a superb body, but he was uneasy with the novel precept slowly burgeoning within him. Lord Leighton would have welcomed the challenge; Blade was baffled and unsure.

He had, of course, read Lamarck and Darwin at Oxford. After the computer experiments began he, at Lord L's behest, did some refresher reading. It was this that enabled him to spot the salient difference in the present X-Dimension, the thing that set it apart from those he had visited before, and also made it so akin to Home Dimension and yet so vastly different.

Blade was witnessing the evolutionary process in microcosm.

First he had been struck by the symbolism—the way

the terrain kept rising. He had come out of the swamps, scaled the cliffs and had been climbing ever since. Flora and fauna were changing. The lake people were a cut above the cave people and the girl, Ooma, of the mountain-dwelling Jedds, far superior to both.

Blade had walked through vast stages of time, as reckoned by H-Dimension standards, in a few days. Less than a week. Evolution was encapsulated. It was like wandering through a cross-section of an evolutionary model. In this dimension cultures and civilizations, true men and submen, reptiles and mammals, were developed not along parallel lines, far separated in time and space, *but in contiguity*. Jam-packed together. Impinging on each other, yet not merging, each with a sharply etched phylogeny of its own.

But if the slant of the terrain was always upward, the ontological line was not. Ooma was proof of that. Her remote ancestors—about whom she was somewhat vague—had built the mammoth idol in which Blade spent the night and from which he had spied on the lake people and seen Ooma escape.

They were bathing together in a limpid pool, warmed by hot springs merging with a slow-trickling cold brook. They scrubbed each other with brushes made of leaves and twigs, and she showed him how to scour his body with fine white sand. Blade watched with some amazement as Ooma cleansed herself and a new girl appeared. He had known she was beautiful. Until now he had not suspected how beautiful.

Blade's libido, as always of late—blame it on the computer and brain restructuring—was enormous and unmanageable. He was not an easy man to embarrass—and in this strange Eden there was no false modesty—yet for once he found himself feeling sheepish. As he watched Ooma make her careful toilet he began to achieve an enormous erection. Helpless, he watched his flesh dilate, grow and grow until it jutted as hard and firm as a steelyard. Ooma saw it, her eyes widened and she began to laugh. Blade managed a faint grin.

Ooma shook her head. "This is not a time for love, Blade master. In darkness, and after food, is better. Can you not control your monster?"

Blade admitted that he couldn't.

"Then let me try." Ooma giggled and flashed her white teeth. "It frightens me."

She scooped cold water on Blade. No result. She found a twig and whipped him with it. Gibraltar stood firm. Ooma frowned down at the offender.

"It persists. I do not know what more I can do, Blade master."

"I do," said Blade.

She shook her head again. "No. I do not really want to now. And it is written in the Books of Birkbegn that sex is only sanctified after the sun has set."

The Books of Birkbegn! Blade remembered the rotting vellum in the idol chamber. And pushed it from his mind. Later. At the moment he was not interested in Birkbegn, whoever or whatever he, or she, had been. Very slowly, with a tenderness he thought he had forgotten, he pulled Ooma into his arms. He kissed her softly and stroked her dark hair. With his lips against hers he murmured, "I do not command now, Ooma. I ask."

She pulled away a little, craning to stare up into his eyes. In her green eyes was a flicker of something he had not seen there before—though he had seen it often enough in the eyes of other women. Many times he had seen it—in various dimensions and in Home Dimension. Love. Devotion. Submission. Ooma had changed. For her, sex now had a new meaning, new values. Ooma was in love with him.

Blade put the thought away for consideration at a more convenient time. Just now he itched with desire. And knew that it was more than desire.

Still she demurred, though she stroked his face with her fingers. "I am clean at last, Blade master. If we lie in the grass or on the earth I will be dirty again. And there are the Books of Birkbegn. I—"

He could wait no longer. He was being consumed. He

99

pulled her closer, kissed her avidly and muttered, "We will do it here, standing in our bath. The flowing water will carry away the sin and Birkbegn will forgive us. I must, Ooma, I must. Do not make me order you."

She clung to him, limp and phocine, her wet hide gleaming, her damp breasts squashed flat against Blade's massive chest. She let her knees sag, spread herself for him, then gave a little upward leap and locked her legs behind his back. Blade plunged and she emitted a groan of mingled pain and pleasure.

It was short and incredibly sweet, and when Blade collapsed he took her beneath the water with him, down to where the springs were nearly boiling hot. When they surfaced, sputtering and laughing, both realized, with no words spoken, that things had changed between them.

That night they camped near the Api country. Ooma spoke not of the Api, for she had already warned him of what might befall them, but of the great idol and the Books of Birkbegn.

"I will tell you," she confided, "as it was told to me by my father, and my grandfather, and *his* father and grandfather, and by all the old men who have lived since the beginning of time and life. Since the egg was hatched."

"The egg?"

She poked him with a stick she held. This night they had no fire and had eaten cold meat. Blade fashioned a cunningly contrived lean-to that blended in with the forest. They spoke in whispers. This was Api country.

Ooma poked him again and leaned close. "Do not interrupt me, Blade, or I will never get it told."

He, in his new softness for her—a thing he did not quite understand as yet—had decreed that she no longer need call him master. And, though he hastily pointed out that it did not mean they were equals, the girl did not seem to care either way.

She whispered: "I will tell it in the *exact* words I had from my father, for I know no others. And I may forget some of it, for my memory is not good." Here she gave

100

him an impish smile. "But you will not know the difference."

Blade grinned and pulled her head onto his big shoulder. "No. I will not know the difference. And I will not hear it, either, unless you get on with it. I am sleepy. You are much like the women in the world I come from—you talk all around the point and seldom get to it."

She nuzzled against him and said, a bit pettishly, "I do not want to hear about the women in your world. I will tell you of mine:

"In the beginning there was only the Occ, the great bird of the Universe that filled all creation. The Occ dwelt alone in all space, or so it thought, for it did not know that there was space beyond space. Then one day, suddenly out of the space beyond space, there came another bird. It had no name. It was very tiny and it built a nest on the back of the huge Occ. The Occ did not object, or kill it, because the Occ was lonely in forever time and forever space. The tiny bird and the Occ became friends and the Occ was not lonely any more.

"One day the little bird told Occ something that made the big bird very sad. The smaller bird was going to die. The Occ wept and there was water in the world. The little bird laughed at this and the Occ was dismayed until the bird explained that now its task was lighter—one fourth of its task was accomplished. The poor Occ did not understand and continued to weep and weep until there was *too* much water in the world. To stop the Occ from weeping the little bird decided that it was time to die, though it had not wished to die so soon, and it explained to the Occ what would happen and what the Occ must do."

It was a weird cosmogony, the sleepy Blade thought, but at the same time it had a quasifamiliar strain. He held her closer and fought off sleep. When he came to the land of the Jedds all this might come in handy.

"When the tiny bird died, it explained to the sorrowing Occ, the large bird was to tear it into three parts and eat it. It was to have been four parts, but now that the Occ

101

had wept and brought forth water there was need for only three.

"At this sad news the Occ began to weep again and the little bird, fearful that even space beyond space would be flooded away, died at once. Each part had a voice of its own and issued commands to the Occ.

" 'I am fire,' said the first part. 'Eat me.' And the Occ obeyed.

" 'I am earth,' said the second part. 'Eat me.' And the Occ did so.

" 'I am air,' said the third part. 'Eat me.' And the Occ ate the third and last part of what had been the tiny bird.

"At once the Occ became very sick. It flapped and fluttered and groaned in great pain. This went on and on and the Occ thought it was dying. It could not vomit and could not void; nothing, it seemed, would ever rid the great bird of its agony.

"Then in one great convulsion it gave birth to an egg called the World. But the egg was fouled, vile, dirty with the excreta and voidings of the Occ. The Occ wept again in memory of its little friend and the egg of the World was cleansed. And for a little time the Occ nested atop the egg it had hatched and was content, until a voice from the space beyond space called to it and gave commands. The Occ was to leave the egg and fly into the space beyond space and there, after a long journey, it would find a vast fire. It was to fly into the fire and be destroyed. And this the Occ did, leaving behind it the egg."

Ooma poked Blade with the stick. "Are you asleep, then?"

He kissed her. "No. I was listening. It was all very interesting. But what of the Books of Birkbegn?"

Ooma pouted a bit. "All I have told you was *written* in the Books of Birkbegn. Birkbegn was the first man, he who evolved from the egg, the father of all the Jedd tribe. All this *was* written in the Books, by Birkbegn and his sons, and once it was read. But now it must be told, because the writing has faded and been forgotten. No Jedd can read the Books now. The tale is told at night around

102

the fires, along with the stories, all true, of how great the Jedds were and of how they alone ruled the egg of the World."

Blade yawned. "What happened?"

Ooma stroked his face as she prepared for sleep. "Who can know all the answers—except that the Jedds did not live by the Books of Birkbegn and suffered, were punished for their evil ways. More than that I do not know for, to tell the truth, I did not always listen closely when the old men spoke. I had other and more interesting things to do and I did them. I would creep away from the fire and do them."

"I'll bet," murmured Blade. Jedd females, he thought, must come to puberty very young by HD standards. Possibly nine or ten years old.

Ooma wormed her tongue into his ear. "I have decided that I do not wish to sleep right now. First we will—"

"You are insatiable," said Blade. "In fact, I am beginning to think you are a nympho."

She crushed her mouth against his and began to stroke his more sensitive parts. As dead beat as he was, Blade responded instantly. She squealed softly in delight and began the usual oral foreplay, talking all the while.

"This," said she, "is a proper time and place. It is dark and we have eaten and soon we will sleep."

"I hope," he said feebly. "And I also hope you leave me some strength to fight the Api, if I must fight them."

"Tomorrow we will worry about the Api," said the practical Ooma. "For now it is no sin and I will have it. Be still. Do not move. I, Ooma, will do everything."

Which she did.

In the morning, after a plunge in the brook and breakfast, they continued on their way. Blade, as he listened to Ooma's chatter, grew somber and looked to his weapons. He did not like what she told him of the Api.

For one thing, he did not know just how much credence to place in her reporting—for Ooma was a feckless little creature. This he had to acknowledge despite his growing fondness for her. So, as they finally left the forest behind

103

and plunged into a narrow falling and winding defile—once again descending, the significance of which did not escape Blade—he listened and made mental notes and took nothing for granted. He became aware of a coldness along his spine. The Api sounded formidable in the extreme—Blade might very well reach the end of his trek long before he reached the mountains and the Jedds. But then death was always a possibility in any Dimension X.

If Ooma was frightened she did not show it. She was matter-of-fact.

"If the Api slay you," she explained, "they will take me captive and use me as a common woman for all of them. Unless you kill me first, or I can kill myself."

He shot her a glance. "Do you want to die? Are the Api so bad that death would be better than being taken and used by them?"

For a moment she pondered this, frowning. "I do not really know. I am very young and the Jedds live long. I am fond of life and all it offers, and now that you have come to me, Blade, it will be even harder to die. But the Api! They are hairy monsters, though very intelligent, and their ways are not those of the Jedds. I suppose I *would* be better off dead."

Surely a strange child. Blade eyed her. "But you are not really sure?"

Again a fatalistic little shrug. "It does not really make much difference, Blade. *If* you lose and *if* I am taken prisoner and used by them, I will not live long anyway. They are brutes, much too large for a Jedd woman —which is exactly why they take so much pleasure in Jedd women—and I would be ripped apart after a little time. I would not like to die that way—no, Blade, I think that if I see you are losing I will manage to kill myself. If you would give me your little stone knife it would be easier. It is hard to kill yourself without a weapon."

Blade gave her the stone knife, thinking that in any case it would be of little use against the Api. Ooma fashioned a sheath of bark and bound it to her thigh with vines. At Blade's suggestion that she make a kilt and a bra of the same material—he thinking that if her breasts and pubic area were covered the Api might not be so aroused—she only stared at him and said with disdain that out here clothing was of no importance. Only in the land of the Jedds, her own people, did covering oneself matter. Among the primitives, beastmen and the Api, clothes had no significance.

Blade let it go.

The defile ended and widened onto a plain. Far across the plain, shining in the sun, reared the serrate tips of a vast mountain range. The wind sweeping toward them over the plain bore the chill tang of ice and snow.

Ooma gave a little cry of joyous recognition. She pointed toward the far-off mountains. "That is where my people dwell. Once past the first mountains there is a valley where they have lived all the years since being driven from this land in the time before knowing. Oh, Blade, you must win today! I want to see my home again."

He hardly heard her. He was examining a large stone hut that stood on the plain some three hundred yards from the mouth of the ravine. It was flat-topped, with a mortared wall around all four sides that he guessed had been built to catch and hold rain. Water must be scarce on this plain.

At the moment Blade was more interested in the lookout on the roof. It was his first view of an Api and he did not like it. He let out his breath in a slow whistle of dismay. The thing was about eight feet tall and appeared to be a cross between a gorilla and a baboon. The face was snouty, dog-like, and the body a massive and hairy block of bulging muscle. Blade blinked and stared again. The lookout was wearing a horned helmet and a swordbelt—nothing else. And it was peering over the plain at Blade, studying him under a raised forepaw. Just as intently as Blade was studying it.

The Api vanished suddenly through a trap in the roof. The stone hut brooded on the plain. Blade looked at the girl.

"So that is an Api?" He kept his voice calm and steady, making no outward sign of the trepidation he felt. What a brute! And he with only a spear and makeshift bow and arrows. He was on the verge of asking for his knife back, then decided against it. Ooma might very well need the knife to kill herself.

A coil of dark, greasy smoke was rising from the hut now. Ooma pointed to it.

"They signal. This is only the first outpost of the Api. There are others, many more, guarding the pass leading into the mountains. But they are not important. It is here, Blade, that we will live or die."

Blade had been watching the door of the hut. He counted them as they emerged and lined up in military fashion. Ten of them. Nine in the single rank and one leader. All wearing the horned helmets and the swordbelts. Blade's lips quirked in dour amusement as he watched the leader dress and order his men like any squadleader back in Home Dimension. The commands came drifting across the plain, borne on the wind, and Blade perked his ears. The voice was that of a woman or, at best, an emasculate! High-pitched, shrill, a near falsetto. He looked askance at the girl.

"Are they women, these Api?" She had mentioned nothing of this.

Ooma, who had gone a bit pale, shook her head. "No. How I wish they were. Or that they had females of their own. But they do not—all Api are males, which is why they are so few now, and all children born of women taken by them are always males. And always Api. Oh, Blade, I begin to be much afraid. If I spoke bravely before it was a lie. They will slay you and make me their group whore—for I will not have the courage to kill myself."

She snatched at his hand. "Come. We can still escape back into the forest. They will not pursue us. Their duty is only to guard this plain."

Blade pushed her away. "Too late for that now. Trust me and obey me. Exactly. Stay back and keep silent. Not one word. You understand?"

Her voice quavered. "Yes, Blade."

"See that you do. And trust me. I will deal with these Api."

The leader of the Api gave a high-pitched command. The line wheeled and began to march toward Blade. The maneuver was executed with grace and precision, the leader marching four paces in front. Blade leaned on his spear and, with a coolness he did not really feel, watched them come. He curled his mouth into a sneer, a grimace of disdain, as if the Api were scum and he the lord and master. How else to play it? Bluff it must be. Bluff and brass. Cold nerve. And when the time for killing came?

He must wait and see.

Chapter 11

The leader of the Api halted his men twenty paces from Blade. He ignored the big man leaning so indolently on his spear and sneering, and addressed the rank again. On his command, the Api drew their swords and presented them in salute. Faint hope stirred in Blade—they were so correct and formal. Maybe he would not have to fight for his life, and the girl's, after all. Of this notion he was soon disabused.

The leader Api barked a last command at his troops. "Rest. Remain as you are until further orders from me. It should not take long to settle this little matter. And remember, all of you, that as the ranking officer, and in command here, I will have the woman first."

After four trips through the computer Blade had thought his capacity for amazement exhausted. Now he found that this was not so—it *was* amazing to find gorillas with baboon faces speaking, making sense, executing fairly intricate military maneuvers. As the leader swaggered toward him Blade found himself thinking of an American word—goon. A word that had its genesis in gorilla and baboon. From that moment he began to think of these strange creatures as goons. Intelligent goons.

The leader stopped five paces from Blade. He had drawn his sword, but let it dangle carelessly at his side. Just as careless was his first glance at Blade. He hardly deigned to notice the man. He was looking instead at Ooma, who had retreated to the mouth of the ravine and was crouching behind a boulder. Now, too late, she thought it better to conceal her nakedness.

Blade, always bold, said: "Your business is with me. Not with the woman. She is *my* woman. I will have that understood at once."

A look of surprise flashed across the baboon face. The deep-set eyes studied Blade again, this time with more care. Strong man that he was, inured to travail and danger, Blade felt a shock of apprehension as the little eyes studied him intently. Pale. Colorless. Albino eyes without the pinkish tint. Intelligent eyes lacking any hint of emotion. As cold as death itself.

Still the goon did not speak. The white eyes swept Blade up and down. The fang-like teeth flashed in a snarling laugh as the long baboon muzzle crinkled in amusement. Finally it spoke. The voice, though still high-pitched, a treble, had nothing feminine about it. It was loaded with menace.

"What manner of thing are you? Whence come you? What do you want and where do you go?"

Blade left off leaning on his spear. His eyes were as cold as the goon's when he replied: "I am called Blade. I am a man. That is enough for you to know of me. I want nothing of you except to pass by in peace. I go to the mountains yonder and I take the woman with me. That, I think, answers all your questions. If so, and by your leave, we will be on our way. It was most courteous of you to turn out a guard of honor for us."

And Richard Blade, cradling his spear in the crook of his elbow, standing tall with legs apart, put his hands on his hips and laughed at the leader of the goons.

For a moment doubt flickered in the pale, feral eyes. The goon put a paw to its hairy muzzle and stroked it. Slowly the sword came up until it was pointed straight at Blade. The weapon was long and pointed, double-edged, of wood cunningly inset with jagged flints to make a cruel edge. A terrible weapon, given the five to six hundred pounds of gorilla muscle behind it. Blade stood little chance against it. This he had known from the outset. Bluff was his best weapon.

110

Bluff was not going to work.

The goon leader was in no hurry. He gave Blade a deadly smile—the incisors were dog-like—and said, "You tell me your name is Blade, but what is that to me? My name is Porrex and what is that to you? You say you go to the mountain people, and yet I have had no word from the Jedds that they expect you. What of this, Blade?"

Blade scowled. "Nothing at all of it. The Jedds do *not* expect me. They know nothing of me. How could they? I come as a stranger from a far-off land. Yet it is to the Jedds that I will go—and nothing will stop me."

Once again doubt showed in the colorless eyes and the goon hesitated before answering. Blade remembered what Ooma had told him—the Api were mercenaries, though vastly independent ones and not to be trusted, and their normal duty was to guard the Jedd borders against raids by the beastmen. Often they did not attend to duty, but went off hunting and searching for women. The Api never had enough women to go around. It had been on just such an occasion, when the Api were lax in duty, that the beastmen, the lake people, had slipped through on a raid and captured Ooma and many other Jedds.

This Porrex was now deep in thought, but he did not think long. The pale eyes stared at Blade and he said, "You may be right. I, Porrex, will not try to stop you. What my superiors do at the pass station is another matter, but it does not concern me. You who call yourself Blade may pass. But you must leave the woman to us. The Jedds have been very stingy of late, and we in the outposts are always last when it comes to women."

Ooma had also explained that—now and then the Jedds gave women to the Api. Old women, or young women who had been condemned to die for some crime. Most of the latter, Ooma said, managed to kill themselves before they could be turned over to the goons.

Porrex was watching him narrowly. Blade smiled coldly and shook his head. "That I cannot do. I have told you— the woman is mine. She goes where I go."

The baboon snout tightened. The wooden sword flashed

111

in an arc. "Then she goes no further. Nor do you, Blade. I offered you your life and you refused. So be it. I will kill you and take the woman anyway. Wherever you come from, Blade, they must breed fools."

Blade backed off slowly, his spear poised. There was sickness in his gut and a vile, hot fluid in his mouth. His heart was racing. The spear was nothing but a fire-sharpened stick of brittle wood, his arrows crooked and untrustworthy, the bow a poor thing meant for the smallest game. Against six hundred pounds of gorilla-baboon they were useless. As he backed away, circling, the spear poised bravely enough, he doubted if the spear or arrows would even pierce that massive furred body.

And yet maybe—the eyes?

Something sharp jabbed him in the back. There was pain and he felt blood trickle on his flesh. Blade glanced around. He was ringed by the other nine goons. They made a small, tight circle, their swords out-thrust to pen him in, nine pairs of eyes glittering in malefic glee. Life was dull at a dreary outpost like this—a little bloodshed would be a change of pace. Plainly they would enjoy seeing Blade gutted. And there was, of course, the woman.

The goon that had jabbed Blade spoke harshly. "Next time, stranger, I will put my sword through you. There is no escape this way. Fight Porrex and die, but do it quickly. We have not had a woman for months."

The other Api guards laughed at that. One said, "Yes, get it over with. Kill him, Captain Porrex, and have done."

Another goon muttered, "And then let Porrex have done as quickly with the woman! I am content to cast lots for my place, but it had better not be like last time when the captain kept the woman to himself for two days and a night."

A third goon said, "Hah—I remember. And when finally she got to us she was no good—too near dead to move. It was like making love to a corpse."

With a high, chattering giggle, another of them said,

112

Latest U.S. Government
tests of all cigarettes
show True is
lower in both
tar and nicotine
than 98% of all other
cigarettes sold.

Think about it.
Shouldn't your next cigarette be True?

Regular: 12 mg. "tar", 0.7 mg. nicotine,
Menthol: 12 mg. "tar", 0.8 mg. nicotine, av. per cigarette, FTC Report Feb. '73.

Latest U.S. Government
tests of all menthol
cigarettes show
True is lower
in both tar and
nicotine than 98% of
all other menthols sold.

Think about it.
Shouldn't your next cigarette be True?

"Fool! She *was* a corpse by that time. I told you so, remember? But you—"

Porrex let out a roar of outraged command. "Be quiet, you scum. Mind your duty and your discipline and keep your mouths shut. The next man who speaks without permission gets no chance at the woman. Now—tighten the circle a bit. This is an agile fool, and a brave one, and I have no desire to chase him over half of Jedd before I kill him. Move in, I say!"

The circle tightened. Porrex, calm and unconcerned, kept his distance from Blade, of whom he seemed scarcely aware. The leader Api's attitude was that of a man who had a not too distasteful, but very boring, task to perform. Blade contemplated making a rush at the huge Api, pressing the fight, trying to catch his opponent by surprise and blind him before the battle was really joined.

He decided against it. He must let Porrex come to him. He must retreat constantly, slipping and avoiding, feinting and counterfeiting, judging and studying his foe and waiting for him to make a mistake. Blade, who knew his own prowess and could kill most men with his bare hands, was not at all sure he was going to get out of this. He was, after all, fighting a gorilla. A baboon-gorilla with an intelligence nearly as great as his own. Porrex weighed six hundred pounds and stood eight feet tall. Blade weighed two hundred-odd and was a little over six feet. His sweat ran cold and, deep within himself, Blade admitted that maybe this was it! His time to die.

Porrex leaped without warning and swung his sword at Blade's head. The Api was nimble for all his bulk, and Blade ducked just in time. The flint-edged sword missed him by inches. Porrex looked disappointed. Blade thrust with his spear at the massive hairy chest. Porrex grunted in surprise, his little eyes glaring down at the stick that had dared to puncture him. There was a faint trickle of blood. Porrex slapped at the spear with an enormous paw. The spearpoint snapped off, still embedded in Porrex's chest fur. He fumbled at it, pulled it out, snarled and flung the point at Blade.

113

Blade did not toss away the broken spear. He poked with it, trying to keep the giant off balance as he retreated and circled and retreated again. Whenever he got too close to the watching circle of Api he was jabbed in the back. The wounds were only superficial, but they bled copiously and Blade realized that in time the blood loss would weaken him. Already his lower trunk and his legs were covered with his own blood.

The area in which he had to maneuver was about the size of a boxing ring in Home Dimension. Blade, who was a superb boxer, now called on all his skill. He ducked and slipped and evaded and back-pedaled. He was constantly on the run, around and around the narrow circle. He began to breathe hard and now his streaming sweat was hot and stinging in the wounds. Still Porrex could not get in a killing blow. His sword had not yet touched Blade. It swooshed and swished and darted, hungrily seeking flesh, and Blade was never there. He was as evanescent as a shadow, always vacating a spot just before the sword arrived. Not by much, but enough. Once the flashing sword clipped hair from his head, and still Blade lived. And by now he had a plan.

There was no question of Porrex's tiring. The Api could fight all day at this pace. It was Blade who was tiring, who was sobbing for breath, whose legs were weary. The time was fast arriving when he must stop running and take the fight to Porrex, dare everything, put matters to the final test. Soon now. He had a plan and it might work—but even if it did work it might still be the death of him.

Blade began to let Porrex see how weary he was, how he was gasping for breath, how his legs were stiffening and turning to lead. Porrex grinned his baboon grin and shuffled after Blade, plodding and serene, confident of victory and only mildly puzzled as to why it was taking so long.

Blade wanted to lull the Api still further. He skipped away from a lunge of that terrible sword and notched one of his poorly made arrows to the bow. He aimed the arrow at Porrex and drew it back until the vine string was taut.

114

Several of the watching goons laughed. Porrex stopped his pursuit and cocked his head, his sword lowered, one paw akimbo. He also laughed.

"What sort of toy weapon is that, stranger? You intend to fight me, Porrex, with it? To kill me, perhaps, with a piece of wood and a string?"

Blade stalled desperately. He needed every precious second he could get to catch his breath and regain his strength. If Porrex charged him now and that terrible sword flickered, Blade knew he must die. He must have time.

"I will show you," he panted. He let the arrow fly at Porrex.

The shaft lodged in the huge paw that the Api raised to fend it off. Porrex snarled in annoyance and dropped his sword to pluck out the thing that was pin-pricking him. He placed a great splayed foot on the sword. His obvious contempt for Blade did not make him careless.

Blade moved in with every bit of speed, strength and concentration he possessed. Now or never. Live or die. In Home Dimension he had attended harsh schools and learned cruel tricks. He used one now.

Swift as a heartbeat Blade was within the circle of those massive furred arms. Porrex, though caught off guard, surprised, embraced him with a triumphant growl. His fangs probed for Blade's throat.

Blade counted on three seconds before he was crushed to death, squeezed and stamped out of shape like matter in a hydraulic press. He used his three seconds. He kept his forearms and elbows free and rammed his thumbs into the inner corners of the Api leader's eyes. Blade's nails had grown long and sharp. His thumbs were like steel meathooks gouging into the tender tissue. At just the proper instant Blade rolled his thumbs, hooking and pulling up and outward. Porrex screamed in agony and rage. He forgot Blade and tore at his bleeding sockets with his paws. Blade skipped nimbly back and held both his hands aloft for the other goons to see—the pulped, bloody,

115

grape-like mess that had been Porrex's eyes. The Api stared, shocked and unbelieving, and Blade counted on this lapse in comprehension.

Time was everything. Blade scooped up Porrex's sword, jabbed him with it and shouted insults. Porrex, his paws still fumbling at his bloody empty sockets, let out a roar and shambled toward the sound of Blade's voice. Blade retreated a step or two, taunting the goon leader, luring him on. He risked one glance at the other Api—they were still in shock, still not quite believing that this thing had really happened, still undecided what to do. He had, Blade reckoned, another few seconds.

He called mockingly to the groping Porrex. "Over here. This way, Porrex. Who is the fool now? Who is blind now? Come and kill me, Porrex, if you can."

Porrex let out a horrendous shriek of rage and pain and bafflement. He left off clawing at his eye sockets, raised his great arms in the air, two prongs of a terrible vise, and rushed at the sound of Blade's voice. Blade stood his ground. He shifted his feet deftly and extended the sword. Porrex ran squarely on it with all the driving force of his six hundred pounds. The Api stopped and reared back, ripping at the embedded sword with his paws, his screams stifled by the blood gushing from his throat. Blade lunged then, with all his might, and drove the sword on through the thick body and out the back.

Dying, Porrex still refused to topple. He very nearly wrenched the sword away from Blade. But he was weakening fast as the blood spurted in arterial fountains. Blade put a foot against the creature's chest and tugged the sword out. Porrex swayed, roared again, then toppled with a crash. Blade watched the ring of Api. They began to move in.

Fast now. Each minisecond that ticked away lessened his chances of bringing off the gamble. Blade put one foot on the still-twitching Porrex and brandished the blood-stained sword aloft. In a stentorian voice of authority he roared:

"Stop! I, Blade, command it. There will be no more

116

fighting, no more bloodshed. I have slain your leader and so I am now leader. And as your new leader I promise you this—women for all! Women and easier and more pleasant duty. I, Blade, promise you this. Take it and be content. Or fight me and die like Porrex."

So saying, calmly ignoring them, Blade turned his attention to the corpse of Porrex. The die was cast now. He either won or lost his gamble and the next few seconds would tell which it was to be. He began to hack off the head of the dead leader, apparently intent on his task, not deigning to cast a glance at the goons who crept closer and closer. But he heard them well enough, heard them muttering among themselves.

"Rush him. Kill him. He has killed our leader."

"No. Wait. Who are you to command? We are all equal now. And you heard what he said—women for all!"

"I do not believe. Where would *he* get women? He has only one woman, which he claims for himself. Are we fools, then? Take *his* woman. Kill him. Then we will share her equally."

"Hah. Yes! At least he has done us the favor of slaying Porrex, who would have kept her for himself until she was useless."

"I say no. Let us hear from him *how* he intends to get us women. And how he will make our duty more pleasant. We would be fools not to listen, and we can always kill him later."

"I am not so sure. You all saw what happened. He is bound to kill some of us before we can kill him. And if we are to have women I do not want to die yet. Let us talk."

Blade breathed easier. His bet had been that there was no natural leader among them. They were all followers, not leaders, and the dead Porrex had not been loved. Now he had a chance.

He severed the head from the body. He impaled it on his sword and held it aloft. The huge baboon head was heavy, the sword long and also heavy, and the muscles of Blade's biceps corded and writhed as he waved it back and forth.

"You make a wise choice," Blade told them. If he treated it as a *fait accompli* it might in fact become one, though hazards enough remained. "I will take this," he said, indicating the head, "as a passport into the land of the Jedds. You will send a signal to the next Api station, explaining everything and promising, in my name, that all shall have women and better living and working conditions. For, as I am leader here now, I shall also be leader among the Jedds. What I promise will come to pass. I swear it."

If you were going to lie and bluff, Blade had long ago learned, it was better to do it big, without stint. The big lie, the colossal bluff, had the better chance of succeeding.

Still they hesitated, snarling and muttering, unable to come to agreement. Blade plunged into a more elaborate and cunning lie, waxing sweetly reasonable and attempting to gauge the degree of their intelligence and attune the lie exactly to it.

He lowered the head, disengaged it from the swordpoint and moved it with his foot toward one of the Api. "Take that and find a bag for it. Wrap it carefully. Quickly now. Move!"

The goon hesitated, glanced at his companions, then picked up the head and carried it away toward the stone hut. The others watched him go in silence. Blade felt his heartbeat slow. He was going to make it. Yet he needed a clincher.

He began to clean the sword, jabbing it into the ground and talking all the while. "Think of it this way, Api. If you kill me you gain nothing. I will kill some of you. This you know. But if I go in peace, with the woman and without trouble, and come to Jedd and become leader there and keep my promise, then see how much you will have gained. Women for all! Is that not worth a chance? What can you lose even if I prove to be a liar?" Which he most assuredly was, a whopping great one. Blade had no intention, should he ever reach the Jedds and gain leadership, of sending women to these Api. He knew this. The Api did not. Blade kept at them, talking, using again and again the

118

key word—women—women—women.

It worked. The goons consulted among themselves. Blade, from a distance, saw them take some sort of a vote using a helmet and colored stones for box and ballots. While they were about this he made a furtive sign to Ooma, who had ventured a little way from her rocky cover. She hesitated to obey, plainly bored with hiding and curious about the turn of events, forgetting both her fear and her nakedness, and Blade cursed her softly. He mouthed at her—get back! Stay under cover.

Damn her! She was an intelligent child, but still a child. And she could very well get him killed yet—and herself well raped.

He let out a sigh of relief as she disappeared again behind her boulder. And breathed still easier when two of the Api guards came and told him: "Pass, Blade. Quickly. Six of us favor you, three do not. We will all stay in the hut until you are gone. And see that you keep your word, Blade. Send us women. Young women who have not been overmuch used."

It was, Blade realized, the universal plaint of soldiers. Even in this X-Dimension as in Home D. Send us women.

When the Api disappeared into the hut Blade went to Ooma and, in silence and pulling her along not too gently, made a wide circle around the hut and began to run toward the glistening mountains. He would not answer her questions and soon she was too much out of breath to ask them. Blade did not slacken his pace, nor allow her to rest, until they were over the horizon and out of sight of the guard hut.

He scooped a shallow hole with his broken spear and buried the head of Porrex. Ooma sulked because he would not let her unwrap the grisly object and have a look. Blade, as his anger faded, considered this new facet of her character and judged her leniently. She did not appear bloodthirsty or vindictive, only curious, and he supposed that captivity among the lake people had brutalized her.

Ooma did not sulk long. She tried to ease his displeasure in the only way she knew, but Blade would

119

have none of it. He hustled her on, saying there was no time for dalliance. Which was true. Too true. They were not out of danger yet. Blade had no thought of trying to talk, or fight, his way through another Api station. It had been a very near thing and he still could hardly believe his luck. He would not tempt Fate again.

As they rested he said, "We will keep along this course until dark, then we will leave it and swing wide and into the mountains. Do you know a path, a way through, that will bypass the Api guard stations?"

Ooma shook her head. "I know of none. There is only one pass leading into the valley of the Jedds. We must take it."

"No," said Blade. "We will not take it. I have a feeling about the Api—next time they will kill me and take you for their use. We were lucky this time. Next time there will be more of them and more intelligent and higher-ranking officers. I have a sense for these things and I smell death if we are again taken by the Api. We go around them."

A pale vestige of moon was hanging in the late afternoon sky. He pointed to it. "For a few hours we will have moonlight. It will give us a chance. There *must* be a way around the pass."

Ooma nestled against him and stroked his cheek. She nodded. "As you say, Blade master. You go and I will follow."

He gave her a sharp look. "You are not to call me master. We agreed on that. Call me Blade."

Her look was demure, her eyes tilted with suppressed laughter, her lips quirking at the corners. "That was when you were not angry with me, Blade. Now you are and I must call you master. Unless—"

Blade could not repress his own smile. "Unless what, you minx?"

She laughed and threw her arms about him and kissed him for a long time. "Unless you prove that you are no longer angry, Blade. Prove it now."

Blade wondered, as he set about proving it, if he would have the strength to climb mountains that night.

120

Chapter 12

Ooma had been right. There was no way around the pass.
So Blade made one. Made it with his strength and his guts
and his skills as a mountaineer—he had climbed every
major peak in Europe—and by lashing his superb body to
an effort beyond anything even he had attained before.
More than once he was on the verge of defeat but would
not surrender. His nerves frayed and his temper went and
he shouted obscenities and defiance at the mountain gods;
he staggered through snow and sleet and wind and clawed
his way over countless glaciers. He scaled crags that could
not be scaled and took chances that a mountain goat
would have disdained. This latter was no particular credit
to Blade—he had nothing to lose. He could not go back.
He could not stay in the mountains. It was forward or die.

After the first few hours he had to carry Ooma most of
the way. The girl, near to death from cold, soon ceased to
care if she lived or died. When the moonlight petered out
and he could not see to climb farther, Blade cast about for
a spot where they might have at least a chance of surviv-
ing until morning. He spotted two huge, black, uprearing
rocks that formed a crude cave and carried the girl toward
them. It was a decision that eventually saved them both.

The animal, whatever it was, had scented them long
before and was in hiding. But when Blade approached its
lair it charged with a high bellow. Blade barely had time
to drop Ooma and step aside. As it was, the creature
caught him a glancing blow with one of its great horns, a
blow that stunned Blade and sent him reeling near the

edge of the precipice. He recovered his footing in time, plucked the little stone knife from his belt and cagily moved away from the edge of the fallaway. He could not see the animal well, but it was food and it had fur or wool of some sort. He did not want it charging him again and going over the edge. For already Blade knew that this beast, whatever it might be, spelled the difference between life and death. Blade charged it. The animal came to meet him, snorting and stamping its front hooves in fury and fear.

The last of the moon had gone and Blade had to kill it in the dark. He met the charge with his own great shoulders, was knocked back, kept his footing and clung to one of the curved horns with one hand as he daggered with the stone knife. He got a terrible leverage and bent the horn over and flung the animal on its side. Then Blade, a berserk animal himself, making mindless sounds, leaped on it and used the stone knife with both hands. His hands were red and hot and steaming with blood and still he attacked. Again and again, over and over, he stabbed and ripped and tore with the stone knife. When his senses came back the animal had been dead for minutes. Blade stood over it, his legs trembling, gouts of blood congealing on him, and knew that for a moment he had been very near to madness. Fatigue, fear, nervous strain, constant alertness, the great hazards he had already faced—they were all beginning to take a deadly toll.

Blade let out a great shuddering breath and slumped in relaxation. He laughed into the black wind. It was like this in Dimension X. Always.

He groped his way back to where he had dropped Ooma. She lay huddled, knees up, shivering convulsively. "I am so cold, Blade. So c-c-cold. We are going to die here, I know. It would have been b-b-better to take our chances with the Api in the pass."

He laughed as he picked her up. "You are wrong, Ooma. We are not going to die and we would not be better off with the Api. I will have you warm in a few minutes."

She mistook his meaning and shook her head. "N-no,

Blade. Not even that can save me now. I am too cold. I will die. Jedds do not stand cold well."

Blade chuckled and carried her into the shallow cave that offered little but some shelter from the wind. He put her down and went back for the thing he had killed. It was totally dark now with no sign of stars or moon. The sky was a dark canopy pressing down on the mountain peaks, the wind a dank, cold sword seeking them out.

Blade, working by touch, gutted the huge woolly animal. He pulled the hot, steaming guts out and dumped them nearby, then picked up the shivering girl. "This is going to be bloody and messy," he told her, "but you will be warm."

By now Ooma was too cold, too near death, to care or to answer. She tried to cling to him, but her arms would not function. Blade put her into the hot cavern of the gutted animal and, wedging her as deeply into the carcass as he could, closed it about her. He fumbled for the entrails, found them, strung them out and used them to bind the two sides of the carcass together by looping the gut around the front and back legs. Ooma, at least, would be warm for tonight. He spoke to her down through the bloody slitted belly of the dead animal.

"How is it, girl? Snug enough now?"

"Warm, Blade. So warm. I think I will sleep now. It is like being in my mother's womb again."

Blade smiled, shook his head and went about the business of his own survival. He hacked off lengths of the entrails and forced himself to eat. He would need all his strength tomorrow. He wedged himself back into a corner of the little makeshift cave, then pulled the carcass, with Ooma inside it, over on top of him. Wind and sleet, cheated for the moment, moaned in constant threnody past the rock opening.

Richard Blade slept.

Two days later he and Ooma half slid, half fell, down the last rocky, shale-strewn incline and stood in a narrow ravine that led in turn into the lush valley of the Jedds.

It would be, Ooma said, some days yet before they came

123

to the city of her people. As they left the ravine and came into the valley proper, she pointed about and explained: "This land is old, nearly as old as the Idol of Birkbegn. When my people first came here, after being driven from their own land because they disobeyed the Books, they resolved to do better and so set about creating new and better lives for all the people. So it is written in the Books. Of course it did not last. The Jedds are an ill-fated people."

Blade, gazing far down the valley, felt a moment of regret that he would not be able to explore these ancient wonders. But his time was growing short—on the final descent into the valley he had been seized with that sudden sharp pain, the brain spasm, that told him Lord Leighton was groping with the computer. Any time now he could be snatched back to Home Dimension. Tomorrow, the day after, next week, next month. Or in the next minute.

He put an arm about Ooma's shoulders and gave her a hug. "The first thing we do," he said, "is to find water and clean ourselves. If we come on any of your people looking as we do now they will either kill us for demons or die of fright."

It was true. They were both covered with dirt and dried blood, and Ooma's hair was one great tangle. Blade had hacked the skin of the beast into two equal parts and made crude cloaks for them both, binding them around their waists with twists of gut. With the leftover scraps he made a pair of shoes of sorts for the girl—his own feet and legs were a mass of bruises, sores and still-oozing rock cuts. They were in truth sorry sights, both of them, but as Blade glanced back at the mountains he was not discontent. They were alive, with the barrier range and the Api behind them, and that in itself was miracle enough.

Over the valley, narrow and steep-sided and lushly rank with greenery out of control for centuries, there hung a great and perfect silence. Dry canals, choked with weeds, interlaced to make a great frond-choked net. Everywhere were deserted temples and desolate, leering images, some in the image of the Idol of Birkbegn, others merely grotesque. Ooma did not know their meaning or origin.

After some hours of walking, during which their thirst grew—the snow they had eaten in the mountains was gone—they at last found a temple which mirrored itself in a cool, steel-colored pond. It had no visible source and the water, when they plunged in, was icy cold. Blade guessed at springs on the bottom.

They drank and scrubbed and drank and scrubbed. Ooma made brushes of twigs and leaves and they washed each other. They flung away the raw skins. Ooma, a little to Blade's amusement, made a small prayer for the soul of the unknown animal that had saved them. Blade, by this time, had come to think of it as a Dimension-X version of a mountain sheep or goat.

Ooma was her old self again. This Blade knew when, being clean at last and their thirst slaked, she insisted on making love on an altar before one of the eroded idols. He held back for a moment, teasing her.

"You forget, girl. It is not yet dark and we have not yet eaten. It is against all the Jedd law and custom, so you told me. So it is written in the Books of Birkbegn." He grinned and pointed around with a finger. "You see what happens when you disobey the Books? All this desolation."

Ooma scowled at him and snatched at his penis, which was belying his words. "Do not tease me, Blade. It was *you* who begged me to break the laws, remember? And I did and I liked it. So I care not what happens now. Come, Blade, and carry me to the altar and we will celebrate being alive again. For we were all but dead and you know it."

When they had made love and both lay satiated and content beneath the vacant stare of a long-forgotten idol, Blade said at last: "How far do you reckon it from here to the city of your Jedds?"

Ooma stirred lazily in his arms. She was nearly asleep. There was no sun, but a warm gray haze lay like a blanket over the valley and the air was silky against their newly-scrubbed flesh. When she did not answer, Blade nudged her. "Come, girl. This is no time for sleep. We must be on our way. For one thing there is the matter of food—I like your valley and it is warm and peaceful here, but there is nothing to eat. Your little stomach may still be content, but mine is not." They had long ago eaten the last of the mountain beast, Blade taking the larger share since he needed it more and had had the burden of carrying Ooma over the most difficult trails.

"I seem to remember," said Ooma, "that as we come near to the city there are fruit trees and bushes. I think there will be no food before that." She yawned and stretched and bent quickly to kiss his now-shrunken organ. "I suppose you are right. We had better get on."

Blade was not listening. His ears, as near to perfect as a man's could be, caught a faint sound in the undergrowth about them. He said nothing, but stared over Ooma's head at the spot whence the sound came.

He was never sure, never positive beyond a doubt that he had seen and heard what he thought he had. Not even when, back in Home Dimension, Lord L taped Blade's automatic memory and played it back to him.

The sound was a faint hissing. The sight, if indeed it was there at all, was that of a brilliantly colored snake, long and sinuous and diamond-backed, slithering away into the greenery. Blade shook his head, blinked, and when he looked again the thing was gone. Or had it ever been?

Richard Blade and Ooma began the trek down the valley, walking hand in hand and as naked as when they came into the world. Of his weapons Blade had only the little stone knife left, and this he carried in his hand. Ooma assured him that in this wasteland there was no danger, not until they reached the city or encountered a Jedd scouting party. Then the peril might begin again. She did not know. She did not know how Blade would be received by her people.

Blade had his own ideas about that.

They came at last to a wild orchard where trees bore an apple-like fruit as large as watermelons. He slashed one

126

open and they devoured it eagerly, then another. The inner flesh was a soft and creamy pulp, reminding Blade of durian, the prickly-rind fruit he had eaten in Malaysia, yet without the bad odor. They both ate until their stomachs bulged.

Now there were clear streams of water tumbling into the valley from both sides, noisy falls that spilled ice cold water, and beside one of these, having drunk their fill, they fell asleep in each others arms.

Blade was first to awaken and he noticed the smell immediately. During their slumber a breeze had set through the valley and it carried to him, now, clouds of dirty gray smoke and the odor—of burning flesh? Human or animal?

Ooma was still sleeping peacefully and he did not disturb her. He felt a tenderness for the girl as he gazed at her, and ignored for the moment the smoke and the smell—knowing that both were a harbinger of trouble ahead and the end of this brief peace. She was lying curled up, her knees drawn up under her chin and her cheek cushioned on her two hands. In her thick, long hair were still the two wooden combs she had made. He smoothed her hair and she stirred and murmured something in her dreams. Ooma was, he thought watching her now in this caught moment of time, as lovely as any of the women he had ever known back in Home Dimension. Or, for that matter, in any Dimension X. And he had known many.

Brief memories, misty and fragmentary, drifted through his mind like a cleaner smoke than that now encompassing him. Taleen—Lali—Zulekia. Had he really known them all, made love to them all, left them all forever? Had they ever been anything but dreams, computer-induced fantasies?

Ooma smiled in her sleep. Blade in turn smiled and continued to stroke her hair. Renewed tenderness surged through him. In what dreamland did she wander? Through what maze and in what personal dimension? Through what reality was she struggling at the moment?

He felt the beginning of pain and rubbed a spot on his forehead just between his eyes. Reality—who could say

127

what it was? Not even the person who experienced it and—

Pain sprang at him like a tiger. His head was filled with white-hot sparks and expanding gases. Blade moaned and leaned forward, then fell over on his side. Lord L and the computer were reaching, searching, had found him. His last thought, as darkness swirled in with a rocket roaring, was that of resentment. Not yet. He was not yet ready to return.

A splash of icy water in his face brought him awake. Ooma was haunched down beside him, peering at him anxiously. She had made a gourd of one of the huge fruits and had carried water from a nearby spring. It was still half full.

"Blade? Blade master—do you live?" She raised the half gourd and was about to drench him again. Blade rolled away and sat up, sputtering.

"I am all right, Ooma. I merely slept, girl." He tried to carry it off with a grin. "Am I so dirty, then, so unclean that you must bathe me while I sleep?"

She put down the dipper and regarded him with narrowed eyes in which there lurked both suspicion and concern. "You were talking, Blade. Talking and screaming and crying in your sleep. A most strange sleep, I think. I was very frightened. It was as—as if your body remained here while your soul had gone far away. As if you had left me and would never return. I was," she repeated, "very frightened. I would not have you leave me, Blade. Ever."

He felt a twinge at the dog-like devotion in her dark eyes. He pulled her down beside him and held her tight. No use trying to explain the truth to Ooma, no use at all. Matters must take their course, as always. But the computer had almost had him that time, had nearly taken him back to Home Dimension. Lord Leighton was searching for him with a vengeance. Why was he so loath to go? Blade could not answer that.

They made love, slowly and with great pleasure, and not until it was over and they had caught their breath did

128

Blade mention the stinking smoke that by now was clogging the valley and hanging over them in a greasy brown-and-gray pall.

"They are burning corpses." Ooma explained at once. "Or so I think. In my life I have never seen it done, but I have heard the old people speak of it. It is like the Yellow Death, come again to plague the Jedds. It is said to appear once in the lifetime of every man, if he lives a true and normal span."

Blade listened carefully, silently, prompting her only when she faltered in the tale. She did not seem unduly concerned, and this he understood. Ooma was young and had never seen the Yellow Death, and so to her it meant little. Blade felt a bit differently—his prime mission was to survive and to return to Home Dimension with a report. This expedition, into a dimension so like his own, with the promise of vast treasure to be teleported one day—was especially important. Plague could kill him as surely as a knife or spear or sword.

Yet go into it he must. He and Ooma resumed their journey. She had never seen a victim of the Yellow Death, but could only tell him what she had heard. Blade, listening intently, could not escape the parallelism. He had read it all before in his history books.

The Yellow Death came suddenly and without warning. None knew whence it came and no Jedd was safe. First there were blinding headaches and a rash, then buboes—inflammations—in the armpits and groin, then bleeding from the nose and ears. All this was accompanied by a heavy jaundice that turned the victim a deep yellow color. Then death. Death always to manic laughter.

This last shook even Blade. He questioned her closely on it as they trekked deeper and deeper into the smoke.

Ooma, trotting along beside him and clinging to his arm, tried to answer all his questions. "Some call it the Laughing Death," she said, "but most call it the Yellow Death because that is how the elders have always called it. But it is true, or so I suppose, that all begin to laugh when death is near. They cannot stop laughing, nor can anyone else stop them."

"How long does it last, this laughter?"

Ooma shrugged her shapely naked shoulders. "I have not seen any of this, Blade, as I told you. But some laugh for hours, I have heard it said, and some for a few minutes. Some hardly at all. But of one thing I am sure, for I have heard it so often—the laughter means that death is near."

Blade did not feel at all like laughing. Yet, as they drew near to the first charnel pit, he found some personal comfort even in the Yellow Death. The Jedds, being struck by a plague of such proportions, were all the more apt to be disorganized, off guard, and this should make it easier for him to establish himself and take charge. For that was what he meant to do. He must become head man. This was a technique for survival that he had understood since his first trip into Dimension X. It was simple, stark and true—dominate or die.

They began to pass houses now, mostly small dwellings built of stone and mud with thatched roofs. Some of the houses had a yellow mark on the door. Blade did not need Ooma's explanation of this.

Beyond the first small cluster of houses they came upon the pit. It was twenty feet deep and about one hundred feet square. Already it was half filled with corpses of women, men and children. In the distance, toward the taller buildings of Jeddia, Blade saw strings of carts bearing more bodies.

For a time he and Ooma watched, standing well concealed in a grove of melon trees. Not that anyone paid them the slightest attention. The pit attendants—Ooma called them "corpseburners"—were too engaged to mind anyone's business but their own. Their method was simple—they took the corpses from the carts and distributed them about the pit, using every inch of space. They then sprinkled some kind of oil on the fresh bodies and set fire to them. Then the same thing again, over and over, the

130

corpseburners being careful to leave paths among the dead so they had room to move and work.

Blade studied the attendants carefully. They were big fellows, most of them, hairy and slovenly, and all wore the same uniform: long yellow breeches and a yellow vest that left their arms and chests bare. On their heads they wore a sort of yellow stocking cap. Blade began to form a plan.

Ooma, for the first time, began to show uneasiness. She tugged at his arm. "Come away, Blade. I do not like this. Come—we will go to the house of friends of mine who live not far from here. They will give us food and clothes—for now that we are in Jeddia we must have clothes. It is forbidden to go naked in the streets."

He noted that she was averting her eyes from the corpse pit. It was beginning to sink into the girl that she too was mortal. An unusual thing, Blade thought, for the very young.

They circled the walls of the city and came to a small house that stood on a hill within a forest of melon trees. Here Blade was introduced to two older women and an enormously fat man. The women were aunts of Ooma, and the fat man, called Mok, was, so far as Blade could ascertain, the lover of both. They accepted Blade as a matter of course and with no small amount of awe at his size and appearance. He was well fed and given a shirt and breeches of rough homespun cloth that, he gathered, was made from the bark of the melon trees. This he could believe, since the clothing chafed even his toughened skin unbearably. He was also given a pair of roughly tanned sandals.

Ooma and the aunts went off into seclusion and in half an hour Blade found that Mok was a drunkard and, like all drunks, was looking for someone with whom to share his liquor and troubles. Blade, itching horribly under the rough cloth, his sores and cuts troubling him, put a good face on and pulled up at the table and began to match Mok drink for drink. The ropy brown liquor, poured liberally from a huge clay jug, was a sort of hard cider brewed from

131

the apple-melons. The first swig nearly tore off the top of Blade's head and, though he did not let Mok see it, he was very near to spewing. Immediately his respect for Mok, at least as a toper, increased enormously. Blade set out to pump the man for every last snatch of information he might possess.

Chapter 13

"The old Empress lies dying," said Mok, pouring himself a cup of liquor. "In her tent on the pavilion in the lake she lies dying. For days now she has been dying while the musicians play the same tune over and over again. When she dies the Child Princess Mitgu will become Jeddock in the old lady's stead. If, that is, the Child Princess ever lives to come to the throne. For there is the Wise One to consider, and the various captains, all of whom want the power of Jedd." Mok took an enormous drink, put a fat finger alongside his nose and looked wise.

They had been drinking for hours at the table. Blade's head was buzzing and at times he felt ill, but he was still holding up well enough. Mok seemed to have, in addition to an enormous belly, a hollow leg. He was drunk, the fat man, but not drunk enough to inhibit his speech. He talked and talked and talked. Blade listened and learned and tried to make such plans as he could, considering the fact that the liquor was roaring in his belly like a storm at sea.

Now and again Ooma would peer into the room and make signs to Blade, signs of impatience. Always he dismissed her with a brusque shake of his head. He would not get another chance like this. A drunkard Mok might be, but he knew what was going on in Jedd, the country and, more important, what was at the moment transpiring in Jeddia, the city. To Blade it had an old, familiar ring—intrigue and plot and counterplot. Power and death. A situation into which he might move, and exploit it

133

without too much peril to himself, if only he could find the right wedge and the proper moment to use it. And the more he listened to the drunken fat man, the more Blade realized that the time was here and now. Before the old Jeddock, the Empress, actually died.

Blade took a drink, blinked and coughed, and said, "Tell me, Mok, of him you call the Wise One." The man was, he supposed, some sort of prime minister or vizier, and the title more than likely self-bestowed. Blade felt that he could deal with the type—there were plenty of them back in Home Dimension.

Mok burped and rubbed his four chins. "A cunning one, he is. As skinny as I am fat and with not a hair on his great head. He is more brain than body and it is said that he has magic. Perhaps. Certain it is that he has been chief minister to the Jeddock for more years than I can remember, has had her ear and advised her in all things, has had all the power—and he will not surrender it short of death. So it is certain that if he cannot have the care of the Child Princess Mitgu, cannot control her, and Jedd with her, he will see to it that she dies."

Here Mok sighed and took another drink and wiped at a tear that slid down his blubbery cheek. "A pity, my new friend. Truly a pity. She is a lovely child. So beautiful."

Blade glanced through a half-shuttered window. It was dark now, but he reckoned on a moon later on. Even here, high on a hill, the odor of burning corpses came to them and there was a fine sift of ash in the air. Blade decided. Why delay? His own danger could only grow with each passing moment. According to Mok, the Wise One had his own police and soldiery and he was sure to hear of Blade's arrival in Jedd. Perhaps he already knew. Mok had whispered that there were spies everywhere these days. The situation was tense, the rival factions poised and only waiting for the old Empress to die. The sudden arrival of the Yellow Death had only complicated matters, not altered them.

Blade now pretended drunkenness and plied Mok with more and more of the fiery melon juice, interspersed with

134

a host of sly questions. Ooma did not appear again and he saw nothing of the two aunts. By the time Mok gave a last piglike grunt and slid forward to sleep on the table, Blade had all he wanted. More than he needed. He got up and staggered outside, put his finger down his throat and was sick for a long time. Below him, ringing the city on all sides, fires blazed red in the charnel pits.

When he could spew no more and the retching was over, Blade went back into the house. He went up a ladder and found the two aunts asleep in one room, Ooma in another. She was lying on a crude mat in a corner, curled up in the embryo position she favored, and breathing gently. Blade bent over her for a moment, kissed her lightly on the cheek and decided not to waken her. She could have no part in what he meant to do, was in fact best out of it, and the less she knew the better. If things worked out, if he lived and got on with his work in Jedd, he would come for her or send for her. If not—well, she was scarcely more than a child and would soon forget him. He patted her shoulder and left her.

Mok was sprawled head and shoulders on the table, snoring loudly, as Blade left the cottage. He found the path by which they had come and started down the hill. A pale moon was just rising at the far end of the valley. Blade hiked briskly until he was within a hundred yards of one of the charnel pits, then paused in concealment and took stock.

He had only the rough, scratchy clothes he had been given and the stone knife. Not much with which to begin a career in Jedd. This troubled him not at all—he had been in far worse spots in previous dimensions. Weapons would not be a problem, once he came on them. Mok, without knowing he did so, had informed Blade that Jedd was in the Iron Age. For a hundred years now all weapons had been made of the new and miraculous ore that had been discovered in the mountains. Crude iron. Blade chuckled and shook his head. The iron would be brittle and would not hold an edge, but at least the weapons of Jedd were those he understood: swords, lances, pikes, dirks and the

135

like. And armor. Heavy iron armor that weighed a man down.

Blade moved closer to the charnel pit. Fires blazed high and clouds of stinking smoke drifted around him, but by now he had grown accustomed to the smell of roasting flesh and it did not bother him. He moved again, using the smoke as a screen, creeping closer and closer to the pit where the corpseburners were working.

A cart arrived with a new load of corpses. The attendants swore and shouted harsh insults at the driver of the cart. Blade stopped his advance and watched the driver. The man was dressed the same as the corpseburners—yellow breeches and vest and cap. Blade changed his plan and moved away in the smoke to lie in wait beside the cart track leading back to the city walls.

From behind a cluster of boulders he waited patiently, watching the scene in the charnel pit. Inevitably he thought of Home Dimension and of the inferno in which some believed. It was all before his eyes, like a garish woodcut of Doré—the smoldering bodies, the writhing smoke, the moving and cursing figures of the corpseburners playing their parts as demons. Blade observed and reflected and kept the business part of his mind clear and gripped his little stone knife.

The cart started back toward the city. Blade perched atop his boulders and waited. The cart creaked toward him, the solid wooden wheels squealing for lack of grease, drawn by a slow-moving bovine-like creature that to Blade looked like a water buffalo. Horses were unknown in Jedd. Mok, when Blade questioned him about the beasts, had only looked stupid.

The cart went creaking beneath his perch. Blade sprang and, with no compunction at all, cut the driver's throat with the stone knife. The man hardly had time to struggle.

There was a single rein leading to the beast's head. Blade tugged it and the animal stopped and stood patiently. Blade hauled the body into the back of the cart and stripped it. It was the yellow uniform he was after, the breeches and vest and cap. No one in Jedd, Mok had said,

136

would interfere with a corpseburner or even approach him closely if he could help it. The work, and the taint of the plague, made them feared and avoided. A corpseburner could come and go as he pleased. This suited Blade exactly.

He left the naked body in the cart and urged the animal forward, toward the walls of Jeddia, chief and only city of Jedd, where the Empress, or Jeddock, now lay dying somewhere on a pavilion in a lake. Dying to music played by musicians who worked in shifts so that the music never stopped.

The cart creaked onward, the beast plodded and Blade studied the mountains ringing the valley. The peaks glittered in moonlight high above the pall of smoke. Iron. And if there was iron in those mountains—and they but a small part of this dimension—there were certain to be countless other minerals. Perhaps rare ones that could scarcely be found back in Home Dimension. Billions and billions of pounds of treasure just waiting for teleportation. And when that was .one, England would again be the leading power in the world, displacing the United States.

Blade remembered the terrible pains in his head. Damn Lord L and his computer! If only the old man would leave him alone for a time—long enough to get his job done.

But nothing was to be counted on. Blade had to get on with it as best he could and as fast as he could. Establish himself. Take over. Begin his surveys.

That meant risk. To offset the risk he had only his two favorite weapons—bluff and boldness. Always boldness.

He was approaching a gate in the city wall. Soldiers in cumbersome iron breastplates and helmets, wearing baggy, loose breeches and armed with lances and swords, moved back to let him pass through. None spoke or even looked hard at the man in the yellow garb of death. Blade smiled. Fine. Until he was ready for his next step, he would be the man who wasn't there.

137

Chapter 14

It was amazingly easy. Blade sent his cart rumbling through the filthy, narrow streets of the city, pausing now and then to ask directions of men and women who fled even as they answered. He in turn ignored those who carried bodies from their houses and implored him to take them as he passed.

An hour after entering Jeddia, he was concealed in a small copse of trees near a lake. In the center of the lake, mounted on stilts, was a large pavilion. Dim lights glowed through its cloth sides and the strains of music wafted plangently over the water to Blade. The same melody played over and over again by horns and stringed instruments. The old Empress had composed the tune, so Mok had told Blade, and had decreed that it be the national anthem of Jedd, and now she was dying to it. Blade, who could take his music or leave it, admitted that the thing had a certain haunting bittersweetness about it and that, once heard, you would never forget it.

He waited and watched. Barges scuttled constantly from the pavilion to a landing near him. Soldiers—most of them officers, judging from the gilded iron breastplates they wore—and solemn men in long, rich robes and skullcaps of what appeared to be velvet. Ministers of state, advisers, lawyers, merchants and the like. Blade paid them little heed. He was waiting for one man. The Wise One.

Whose real name, Mok had confided, was Nizra.

The moon was falling down the sky when Nizra came from the pavilion to the shore. The music still played on and on, so Blade knew the old Empress still lived. He moved to the edge of the little wood and stared hard as Nizra, the Wise One, stepped from his barge onto the landing. He was accompanied by a sizable retinue, with servants bearing torches, and in the flaring light it was easy enough to see.

Blade saw at once that this Nizra was a macrocephalic. His head was enormous, twice the size of that of an average man, like a giant, pallid flower blooming on a slender stalk. The head drooped continually to one side or the other, as though the weak spine could not bear the weight of it. Blade observed and whistled softly to himself. It was a giant of a braincase and if the brain in any way matched it in size, and in proportional acumen, he had best beware. The Wise One might be just that—and cunning into the bargain.

Now the man was giving orders, dismissing most of his party. Blade peered harder as Nizra stepped full into the glare of a torch. The man wore a flowing robe and a skullcap, as had the others, but the skullcap was a gleaming scarlet. A badge of office, Blade supposed, as was the gleaming chain that encircled the scrawny neck and at which the man continually fumbled with spidery fingers.

Nizra, with four soldiers in attendance, walked a short way around the lake, following a well-worn path, and disappeared into a tall, narrow house of the usual stone and wood. The soldiers did not enter. Blade watched as they spoke for a moment, then split into twos, one party remaining before the house, the other disappearing in the gloom to the rear. This Nizra was well guarded. So much the better. He would be that much more impressed when Blade appeared like a wraith from the very walls. For Blade was counting heavily on the first confrontation. It would decide his fortunes—and whether he would live or die.

He waited patiently until things quieted down. He had about two hours until dawn. Barge traffic between the landing and the pavilion ceased, though the dim lights still glowed and music came everlastingly over the quiet water. Blade made ready. He watched the two guards in front of the house intently. They were bored and sullen and patrolled back and forth, hardly speaking, each intent on his own thoughts. The only light was a guttering torch in a sconce over the door of the house that enlarged and distorted the shadows of the guards as they passed to and fro. Blade moved in closer.

He had only the stone knife. This killing—for he meant to kill them for his own safety and for the effect of it—must be a matter of skill and timing and luck. The skill involved did not worry him—when he had to be, Blade was a most efficient killer.

Still he waited and at last the guards paused to chat for a moment beneath the torch. Blade had been waiting for that. He ran swiftly across the path and ducked into the shadows of a hedge that lay near the end of the near guard's beat. Blade crouched there, stone knife ready, waiting. It must be noiseless.

The guards resumed their pacing. The man was coming toward Blade now, leather harness creaking, short sword swinging in its scabbard, the faintest of star sheen reflected from polished iron armor. Blade took a deep breath and held it.

The guard passed him. He was humming, very softly, a snatch of the refrain that came from the old Empress' pavilion. Blade let him get three paces past, then took him from behind with one brawny arm about his throat to stifle any cry. With his free hand he brought the stone knife around and sought for the man's throat just above the breastplate. The guard was strong and struggled mightily for his life, but Blade held him as he might a babe and slit the jugular neatly. Blood spurted, drenching the dying man and Blade as well. He did not mind. He wanted the blood on him.

141

Time was important now. The other guard would have reached the end of his run and turned back. Blade held the guard erect until he bled himself out, then lowered him and snatched off the swordbelt and scabbard. The sword was short and wide, double-edged with a thick hilt, and very heavy. Very like an old Roman sword.

Blade hauled the body into the shadows, fastened the swordbelt around his slim waist and started walking toward the torch over the door of the Wise One's house. He went slowly, with a measured tread, matching his pace to that of the other guard now approaching. As he drew near the aura of light cast by the torch, Blade drew the heavy sword from its scabbard. He let it dangle by his side, concealing it as much as possible with his leg. The other guard must experience a split second of shock and surprise and terror, and Blade was counting on that.

Both men strode into the flickering circle of light. The guard said, "I have been thinking, Topah. How did you say it was that—"

He stopped, staring, his mouth gaping in surprise at the thing that approached him. This was not Topah! This was not a Jedd! This was not anything in the world he had ever seen before—this yellow-clad and blood-drenched corpse-burner with blazing eyes, this towering and muscular *thing* that was lunging at him now. Topah? Where was Topah?

"Topah—"

It came out as a mere squeak of death. Blade used all his massive strength and put the iron sword into the guard just below the breastplate and above the groin. As he thrust, he twisted the blade in a classic disemboweling cut. At the same time he used a backhand chop to smash the man's throat and voice box. It was over.

Blade put his foot on the corpse and tugged out the sword. He left it bloody. He dragged the body out of range of the torch and then turned and went into the house of Nizra, the Wise One.

He found himself in a short hallway. A taper burned

142

starkly on a barrel-like table. Blade took blood from the sword and daubed it on his face, drawing a crude pattern around his eyes. As a part of his long-ago training as a secret agent, he had studied the ways of American Indians and the ways in which facial paint could be used to induce terror. He could have used a mirror.

At the end of the hall, a steep flight of stairs led upward. Blade leaped up them like a great cat, the bloody sword held at the ready before him. There might be more guards in the house. He hoped not. Dawn would be on him soon and time was at a premium. He wanted to get on with the business at hand.

There were no guards. Another taper gleamed in the upper hall. There was a single door, half open, and through it Blade saw the Wise One asleep in a great bed with a canopy over it. This, if it could be called a luxury, was the only one. The room was barren, stark, with nothing but a chair and a table—on which were piles of books and papers—and a large clay pot near the bed.

Blade went softly into the room, carrying the taper, and closed the door behind him. There was a bolt and he slid it to. He walked to the bed and poked at the enshrouded figure with his swordpoint.

"Wake up," said Blade. "Wake up, Nizra. Wise One. Wake up!"

The head, like a huge bald melon, emerged from the covers. Small dark eyes, like dank moths, fluttered at Blade. The taut white skin, stretched over the massive skull and marred not even by a hair root, mirrored the taper like an ivory ball.

Blade, towering by the bedside like a demon, glowering with his bloody face and clothes and the threatening sword, forever gave Nizra credit for his first words.

The dark eyes blinked. The thin mouth, tiny in the big head, said, "You are a fool. I am not dead yet, corpseburner. Get back to your proper work and leave me to my rest." The voice was another surprise. A rich and robust baritone with the promise of basso.

Blade covered his own surprise with a laugh. "I am not a corpseburner and you know it, Nizra. But that is all you know. Are you awake now? Do you hear and understand me? There is little time for us to reach an understanding."

The black eyes were studying him. Trying to understand, to cope, to sort matters out and decide if this was a dream or reality. And if real, how near was death? Because no man, no matter how dull and sleepy, could stare at the terrible figure Blade made and not know that he was very close to dying. The great bald head nodded and the little dark eyes blinked and the Wise One conceded this.

The marvelous deep voice slid down a note. "True. You are no corpseburner. Who are you then, and what do you want with me? And how came you into this house? My guards—"

Blade held up the blood-gummed sword. "Your guards, the two before the house, are dead. This sword and this blood prove that. I killed them easily and with a purpose— to convince you, Nizra, that I am what I will presently tell you I am. And to show you that I will kill you also, as quickly and as easily as I killed your guards, if you do not cooperate with me absolutely and without question. From this moment on, Nizra, I will order and you will obey. You understand?"

Blade took a step toward the bed and raised the sword a bit. He watched the spidery hands lying on the coverlet. Near the bedpost was a bell pull. The long fingers twitched once or twice, but the hand made no move toward the pull.

"I understand," said Nizra. "What do you want of me?"

There was no fear in the deep voice. The black eyes—for the first time Blade noted that they had no lashes—stared back at Blade. He knew then that he had very nearly met his match. For now he had the upper hand, by brute force, but one mistake could change that. For a moment Blade actually felt disappointment and a sense of pique—this Wise One, this Nizra, was either not afraid at all or he was a master of hiding fear. What he was displaying was curiosity. Plain and simple curiosity. Blade could not help wondering whether he, if awakened in the dead of night under similar circumstances, would have been able to summon such aplomb.

The man in the bed seemed to understand all this. He folded his skinny fingers across his chest and repeated, "What is it you want of me?"

Blade thrust his sword into the scabbard with a ring of iron. He kicked the single chair toward the bed and sat down. He crossed his own brawny arms and matched the dark eyes stare for stare. Blade knew that the time for violence, or the threat of it, was for the moment past. Now was a time for guile and cunning and the matching of wits. For self-interest. For compromise. He had won the first round, but the wedge was barely in the door.

Blade leaned toward the bed. "You will listen. You will not ask questions or interrupt. I will explain as best I can, but I tell you now that you will not understand. Or you will understand very little. It is in the nature of things."

He paused. Nizra nodded slightly and kept silent.

"I am not a Jedd," said Blade. "As you must know. I am not even of your world. Of your universe. I cannot even be properly called a stranger, because that would signify some slight connection with your world. I do not even claim that. I come from out in time and space, from a place you never dreamed of, or ever will, and it would be useless for you to speculate on that—"

The little opaque eyes moved and glittered. Nizra was already speculating. Blade could almost hear the huge brain, beneath its bony carapace, clicking and whirring as the gears meshed and raced. It occurred to him that this Wise One was not so much a man as a thinking machine. It would be his bad luck, he thought sourly, to encounter a genius in Jedd. To make matters more difficult.

But he continued: "I am not a god nor a devil, if you understand those words. I have been sent to your world on a mission, to do certain work, and when I have completed

145

that work I will leave and return to my own world. I would like to complete my work in peace and without more killing. I would like to be a friend and not an enemy. If you will understand this, Nizra, and believe it and work with me and not against me I can finish my task and be gone that much sooner. Now speak—of all that I have said, how much have you understood?"

The massive head lolled on its delicate stalk of spine. The eyes narrowed at Blade. A hand came slowly up to stroke the shining bald dome.

"I understand your words. They are plain enough. If there is a concealed meaning in them I will in time understand that also. If you speak truth or not I do not yet know—but I will know. At this moment I only accept. I do not believe or disbelieve. Let us leave it that way then. I have no wish to be your enemy unless it is to my gain to be so. It may be that you do speak truth, and I would be a fool indeed not to accept that and learn from you. I am not a fool. And I am not afraid of you. Not now. If you were going to kill me you would have done it at once."

Blade raised the bloody sword. "There is still time."

The little mouth smiled. "No. Not now. Because it is plain that you have come to make a bargain of some sort. So get to it. We will leave all explanation and questions for later. What do you want of me? And how are you called?"

"My name is Richard Blade. It will mean nothing to you."

Nizra blinked. "A man must be called something. Richard Blade? Two names? We in Jedd have but one. Did you come alone into our world?"

Blade kept his face impassive. "I came alone. I will leave alone." Ooma must be protected at all costs. He would not have her questioned, probably under torture. Nor the aunts, for that matter. Not even the fat drunkard, Mok, must be placed in danger. They had nothing to do with all this.

Nizra said once more, "What do you want of me, Richard Blade? It will be dawn soon with people astir and

146

if we are to be friends and work together there are preparations and explanations to make ready. So what do you expect of me—and what do you offer me in return?"

Blade answered a question with a question. "How long will the old Empress, the Jeddock, stay alive?"

Nizra blinked three times. The scant brows over the lashless eyes raised in slight surprise, but he only said, "I am called the Wise One by the Jedds, and it is true that I am wise in many things, but I cannot answer that question."

"Guess, then. An estimate."

The tiny mouth pursed, then: "A minute—an hour—a day—a month or a year. That is my guess."

Blade glared, but gave it up. He tried another tack. "Is she senile? What is her mental condition?"

Nizra smiled faintly and interlaced his long, white fingers. "Her mind is filled with mists of the past. She is in a stupor and understands very little of what is said to her. But one thing—if the music halts but for an instant she knows it and complains."

Blade nodded and was silent for a moment, thinking hard. Nizra took advantage of the silence. "How got you past the Api, Blade? I speak of the main post at the valley entrance. I know how you killed Porrex and got past the frontier station, for I received signals, but then you vanished and now here you are. How did you avoid the main body of the Api?"

No mention of the girl. Just as well. Blade said, "I came around, over the mountains."

For the first time, Nizra showed clear disbelief. "That is impossible, Blade. No one can cross those mountains. Nobody ever has in all the history of Jedd."

"I did," Blade said curtly. "I am here, am I not? Threatening your life and giving you orders. But enough of that— Would you say that the old Empress, in her dying state, is highly susceptible to suggestion?"

The great head lolled and the little mouth twitched in understanding. "Yes," Nizra answered. "I would say that she is. At least I hope so. I have been suggesting many things to her these past few days and she has seemed amenable." Dryly he added, "She signs any document I put before her."

Blade gave him a knowing grin. "That will be many documents, I wager. All designed to perpetuate and consolidate your power when she is dead, Nizra? All designed to give you control over the Child Princess, Mitgu?"

The dark eyes met his without flinching. "It would seem," said the Wise One, "that we are men who think alike in certain things. Perhaps we can be friends after all, Blade. Or at least not enemies. Now suppose you tell me—what is it that you wish me to whisper into the old Jeddock's ear about you? And what document must be signed pertaining to you?"

Blade leaned closer to the bed.

"You read me well, Nizra, to a point. You will have a private audience with the Empress and you will tell her that, on this very night, you had a vision—"

The huge head rolled on its frail backbone and the mouth smiled in dry derision. "That will be no lie, Blade. I did. I *am* having a vision. A most grotesque and horrible vision—and visitant."

Blade made an impatient motion. "Listen. Listen well. You will tell your Jeddock that in this vision I came to you, in my very person, as I now stand here, and proclaimed myself as the avatar come to save Jedd. As the savior of your people. There is such a promise, I think, in the Books of Birkbegn? Mention is made of someone who will arrive one day to lead the Jedds to a better way of life?" He leaned to stare hard at the man in the bed.

This time the little eyes avoided him, but not before Blade had seen the surprise and the beginnings of respect and even fear in them. Blade, of course, was only remembering what he had extracted from Ooma and Mok.

"You are most well informed about the Jedds, Blade."

He nodded shortly. "I am. It would be well to remember that, Nizra. But answer my questions. Am I right?"

"Yes. To a point. There is some vague reference in the

148

Books to the coming of a—of such a personage as you mention."

Blade leaned back and crossed his thick legs. His thigh muscles ached and quivered and he began to realize how tired he was. He must sleep soon. When it was safe to do so.

He grinned at Nizra. "I see. You, my friend, are not a true believer in the Books?"

For the first time, the tiny mouth opened in a genuine laugh and he saw that Nizra was toothless. The shrunken gums snapped at Blade. "I have told you," said Nizra sourly, "that I am not a fool. I see what is in your mind and I will do it. I foresee no difficulty there. I will do it because, if you keep your word to me, it will be to my advantage to do so. I will gain by it. When you return to your own world—if indeed you spoke the truth about *that*—I will have gained even more. I am a practical man, Blade, and not so much interested in methods as in results. We have a bargain, Blade."

Blade smiled at him. "A good one for you, Nizra, as well as for me. If I am accepted as the avatar promised by the Books, and I am on your side, you will have a powerful ally against the captains who plot against you and who plan a palace revolution as soon as the old woman is dead. Not so?"

Once again respect glinted in the dark eyes. Respect and a degree of puzzlement.

The great head swayed in a nod. "I could almost think, Blade, that you *are* the avatar spoken of in the Books of Birkbegn."

Blade laughed. "Do not begin our partnership with more lies than you must, Nizra. You do not believe a word of it."

Nizra did not answer. He was getting out of bed. Blade retreated a few steps, sword ready, and watched. It was in its own way fascinating, this little scene within a scene, this mere act of watching Nizra disrobe and dress again. For the man was no more than a skeleton, a walking

149

corpse whose bones showed clearly through the stringy, discolored flesh. Nizra was about five feet tall and Blade doubted that he weighed a hundred pounds. It was as though all the substance of the body had gone to the great head and the brain it encased.

Nizra wore a tent-like gown of a cloth that Blade thought of as tussah, a crude silk. This he took off before Blade without hesitation and with no shame. Then he donned a single undergarment of the same material. Over this he donned the same rich robe he had worn when Blade first saw him. Then the scarlet skullcap to partially hide the bald head. Lastly he took from beneath his pillow the chain of office.

"A moment," said Blade bluntly. He took the chain from Nizra and examined it. It was very heavy, of iron polished to a high sheen, and formed of many small and exquisitely forged links. Blade dangled it in his hand, weighing it, watching Nizra closely. There was anxiety in the dark eyes and the spidery hands reached impatiently for the chain.

"It is nearly dawn," said Nizra. "I must see the bodies of my guards, for if you are a liar I must know it now, and if you are not a liar they must be disposed of and a tale told." Again he reached anxiously for the chain.

Blade handed it back to him. Inwardly he was content. He had judged Nizra correctly. Power, and only absolute power, was all the meat and drink this man craved. Lord Leighton had been right. This Dimension X did, in many ways, closely parallel Home Dimension.

Nizra slipped the chain over his massive head and settled it into place. He looked at Blade with a speculative eye and with an openness that belied the cunning that Blade knew lurked in the man.

"I have been thinking," said Nizra. "There is nothing of it written in the Books of Birkbegn, and I have read them well and know them by heart, but it would be as well if the Child Princess Mitgu had a husband. A certain special type of husband, naturally. Would you be averse, Blade, to marriage with a child of ten? Who, like most Jedd

150

females at that age, is very nearly a woman?"

Blade was completely surprised and taken aback. Nothing like this had remotely entered his planning. He took refuge in brusqueness.

"You look too far into the future," he said harshly. "There is no sense in discussing such matters now."

The vast skull swayed toward him. "I agree, Blade. But think on it. Think well on it."

The dark eyes glittered at Blade.

Chapter 15

During the next few hours Blade saw much to admire in Nizra. The old man was competent and cool and his brain was fertile. And the Wise One commanded unquestioning obedience from his servants and soldiers. Blade was washed and trimmed and given undergarments and a robe as rich as those of Nizra himself. He was given another sword, a better-made one with a hilt adorned with raw, uncut jewels which Blade could have sworn were rubies and diamonds. When questioned about the gems, Nizra said, with indifference, that they came from mines in the surrounding mountains. They were gewgaws, of no real value and used only for show. Such was the Jedd thinking. Blade made a resolve to see those mines as soon as possible.

During the past few months, back in Home Dimension, he had undergone a rigorous and much-telescoped course in geology. Lord L had insisted on it, J had concurred, and Blade, who could do anything when he was interested and set his mind to it, was by now a good amateur geologist, something of a mining engineer. And besides being able to recognize most ores, he was somewhat qualified to judge oil-bearing terrain when and if he came upon it. Now, as he stood peering out a narrow window at the filthy, twisting streets of Jeddia and the mountains beyond, he thought that Project DX might at last begin to pay its way. To return some of the millions of pounds that had been invested in it. All it needed was for the hardworking boffins in Scotland to perfect the science of teleportation.

All that must wait. Survival, prestige, power and status were the important things at the moment. He could accomplish nothing without the latter three, and although survival was as important to Blade as to any man, it would mean little if he could not do his job. He wanted desperately, this time, to take good news back to Lord L and J—and the Prime Minister. News of tangible assets that could be exploited by England.

He watched a death cart creak slowly through the streets not far from him. The yellow-garbed corpseburner paused at nearly every house and waited while a body was brought out and flung into the cart atop the others already sprawled there. Nizra had said that the Yellow Death, this time, was the worst in the memory of the Jedds, and it showed no sign of abating. Blade filed the fact away. It might be a lever he could use one day.

He watched the slow progress of the cart toward the city gates and the dirty smudge of fires from the charnel pits. His lips twitched in a wry smile. Nizra had gotten rid of the guards' bodies in a simple and highly efficient manner—by calling a death cart and having them flung into it and hidden by other bodies. No questions had been asked.

Blade thought of Ooma and, for a moment, experienced a tenderness and a sudden rush of sexual desire. He pushed both out of his mind. Ooma was safe with her aunts and the fat Mok, and so she must remain for now. When the time was right, if it ever was, he would send for her. Or at least go to see her. He did not think that she would come seeking him. Fear of the plague would keep her out of the city. Not that the Yellow Death did not stalk the countryside as well. It did, but the chances of catching it were less in open country than in the crowded and dirty city.

Blade continued to stare out the window. The cart had reached the gates now and was passing out of his view. Blade tugged at his ear and frowned. Rats were unknown in Jedd. He had not seen one and neither Ooma nor Mok had known what a rat was. And insofar as he knew there were no fleas in Jedd. He watched as a window opened down the street and a woman poured the contents of a clay pot down into the street. She drenched a passerby, and there was a great contention.

Blade stepped away from the window and closed it. There was the answer. Human filth. Especially in the city. The Jedds wallowed in it and thought it nothing. Great reeking masses of human excreta clogged the streets and, over the stench of the corpse fires, the city smelled like one vast urinal. Through the closed window, from afar, came the sound of manic laughter as another unfortunate went into the final throes. Blade shrugged, but his spine was cold. It was not a way for a man like himself to die. What was delaying the Wise One?

Nizra, once the bodies were disposed of and his plans made, had been in a tearing hurry to take a barge and get to the pavilion in the lake. He had minced no words with Blade.

"Time works against us. If the Jeddock dies before I can arrange matters, that she recognize you as the avatar spoken of in the Books, I cannot promise the future. All the captains of the palace wish power and each plots against the others. They are in unity only against me. Thus far I have managed to keep them divided and weak, but when the old lady dies it will be another story. Then will come the showdown. We need each other, Blade."

So Blade waited, pacing the little room impatiently. He had promised Nizra that he would not venture out and indeed had no wish to do so. Still he was beset by anxiety—the terrible pain might return at any moment and Lord L snatch him back before his task was done. Or he might catch the Yellow Death and die laughing in torment. Or Nizra might suffer a change of mind and betray him, have him slain out of hand. With all these doubts to plague him, it was little wonder that Blade was in a foul mood when at last Nizra came into the room. By the slant of sun through the window, it was well past midday.

"You were long enough," Blade said roughly. "How does it prosper?"

Nizra fingered his chain of office and nodded, his huge

head bobbing like a balloon on a string. "Well enough. I told my story of the vision and she believed. Or seemed to. She is always in and out of coma and it is hard to know how much she hears and understands. And she is very close to death. Are you ready? There is not a moment to lose. I had private speech with her, but the captains are alert and prowling like lice on a corpse. If the Empress dies before we can get her blessing and recognition, Blade, we are likely to find ourselves in a chancy spot."

Blade, as he left the house with Nizra and an escort, thought that he had cast his die and must now abide it, but that he might have chosen a better ally. One of the disgruntled captains, for instance—the one most likely to win out. But there had been no time, nor sufficient knowledge for that, and now he and Nizra were bound together for better or worse. For the time being.

They were barged out to the pavilion with great panoply. The music was, as always, sad and sweet and bitter with death, with now and then a lively passage in memory of youth and life. Blade, himself the target of many curious stares, was aware that men hated Nizra. It was evident in the sullen looks, the mutterings, the barely-concealed defiance. Again Blade felt unease. He was plunging farther and farther into a maze that might have no exit. And, being sponsored by the Wise One, he might very well inherit a whirlwind that he had not sown.

They docked at the pavilion and Nizra, taking second place, bowed Blade out of the barge with great obsequiousness. The play had begun.

The pavilion, a large floating platform anchored to the lake bottom, was covered with a high-ridged tent of bleached cloth. There were many small compartments and one spacious chamber where the old Empress lay like a mummy in an enormous bed. The musicians were invisible behind a cloth screen at one end of the chamber.

As they approached the death chamber, Nizra nudged Blade and indicated a little group of men clustered around the entrance. "The captains," he whispered. "Like corpsebirds awaiting a meal. Five of them. Observe them

156

well, Blade, without seeming to, for they are my enemies and also yours the moment you are pronounced avatar."

Blade did not need to be told. There could be no mistaking the enmity of the five men who waited outside the double-draped entrance to the royal chamber. Blade, long skilled in such matters, read the situation at a glance. They were like five pages in a familiar book: hate, envy, greed, pride, arrogance, self-righteousness—and doubt. Doubt! Doubt about Blade himself, as to who and what he really was. In that doubt, Blade knew, lay his temporary respite and hope. Keep them guessing.

Nizra whispered again. "I must make you known to them, and now is as good a time as any. Play your part and do not appear surprised by anything I say. This is a time for boldness."

Blade was a superb actor when he had to be and he needed to be one now. It was simple enough in essence. He *was* a superior being from a superior world and so he had only to play himself. He stiffened his back, raised his chin and stared with cold indifference as each captain was introduced in turn.

Nizra, with a mixture of humility and authority, fluttered his thin fingers from man to man: "Bucelus, Crofta, Holferne, Chardu—and Gath."

Each captain inclined his head as his name was spoken. None but Gath offered his hand. The latter, when his turn came, stepped close to Blade and proffered his hand along with a steely glance from a pair of steady blue eyes. Blade took the hand and found that he had walked into a trap. This Gath was of slim build, though sturdy and wide-shouldered, and had enormous strength in his hands. His intent was apparent at once. His hand closed on that of Blade like a merciless steel vise and began to squeeze. His clear purpose was to make Blade cry out or even to sink to his knees and cry quits. The four other captains watched and Blade knew it had been prearranged. They were already testing the avatar who, so strangely and at such an opportune moment for Nizra, had fulfilled the promise of the Books of Birkbegn.

Blade, his face impassive, did not betray his first pain, though he felt the bones of his right hand being crushed to powder. He smiled at Gath and returned the pressure. Only for a moment did he doubt, then as the seconds passed he knew that he was the stronger. The great muscles of his forearm knotted and coiled as he exerted more and more of his strength. Gath, who had an open and friendly face above a flowing mustache and whose blue eyes lacked the hate and fear of the other captains, began to change expression. At first, surprise was predominant and Blade guessed that Gath had never been beaten at this game before. He squeezed harder and all heard the bones of Gath's hand grind together.

Gath's mouth was open now and beads of sweat started on his high forehead. Blade kept up an unrelenting pressure. Gath went suddenly to his knees with a little cry of pain. "Enough—enough! You are stronger. I, Gath of Jedd, admit it. Give me back my hand."

Blade released him with a smile. "It was a good contest, Gath. I enjoyed it. You have great strength. When there is time we will try again."

Gath was silent, ruefully contemplating his crushed hand, but one of the captains muttered, "He has strength, then. That does not prove him to be the avatar."

Another captain said, "With that I agree. Nizra's visions are most convenient to his cause."

Nizra, acting as if he had not heard, bustled Blade past them and into the great chamber. It was in semigloom and filled with the music. In a far corner, tiny on the huge bed, lay the unmoving figure of the old Empress. Nizra plucked at Blade's sleeve and whispered.

"Go to her now. I have done all I can. You saw the temper of those five and you know how much is at issue. If I am to serve you, Blade, and you me, we must have the blessing of the old woman. How you get it is your concern. Go."

Blade walked slowly across the wooden floor of the chamber. The hidden music swirled on and on. Blade came to the side of the bed and stood looking down at

158

the old woman who lay there. The face was a wrinkled skull—she might have been dead for weeks—and the eyes were closed. She was clothed in a single shroud-like garment and covered with a light coverlet so adjusted to the frail body that he could detect the bone structure. This old woman was, in truth, nothing but bones covered with a scant layer of brown parchment. Blade stood staring down at her, his arms crossed on his broad chest, and marveled that life could still flicker in so worn a vessel.

For a long time she did not stir. Her eyes remained closed, though he had a distinct impression that she knew he was there. He waited and, after a time, began to wonder. Perhaps she *was* dead.

The eyes opened and stared up at him. Clear, dark, old eyes in a wizened monkey face. Blade felt a shock at the intelligence in her eyes as they examined him from head to toe, in no hurry, roving back and forth over his big frame. Weighing and assaying him. At last the shriveled lips moved.

"You are he called Blade? He who came to Nizra in a vision? You are the avatar so long promised to my people by the Books?"

Blade nodded gravely. "I am he."

There was a long silence. The clear eyes studied him again. At last the desiccated mouth twitched in what might have been a smile, a signal of inner laughter at a final jest.

In her surprisingly audible whisper she said, "Who is present? Do we speak alone?"

Blade glanced back at the entrance. Nizra waited there in the shadows, his hands buried in the sleeves of his robe, peering anxiously toward the bed.

Blade stepped nearer the pillow. "Nizra is in the chamber, but he cannot hear us. What would you say to me, Empress?"

When she spoke again the words came blurred and with what he knew must be a great effort of will.

"You are a liar," said the old woman. "Nizra had no vision and you are no avatar. I know he is promised in the Books of Birkbegn, but those are all lies and the avatar

159

will never come. But none of this matters. You are here and you are no Jedd. I see in you intelligence and great strength. So perhaps the Books do not lie so greatly after all, but keep their promise in another way. I am a great fool, Blade, as all Jedds are, but in some ways I am not a fool at all. I also have had dreams and private visions, many of them in my long life, and I told no one of them. Now you come and I will trust you. Whoever you are, from wherever you come, I now deliver my people into your hands. There is about you the look of a god, Blade, and yet I know you are no god. But perhaps you will serve. You will undertake this task? It is not an easy one."

The old face crinkled again in what must have been laughter. "I should know. I have lived a long time and have never known any peace of mind. I have been forced to use such as Nizra because there was none better. How many Nizras have I tolerated and used because I must—"

She lapsed into silence. Her eyes closed and she breathed heavily and Blade knelt by the bed. Had she gone?

The ancient eyes flickered open. "Do not be afraid. I will live long enough to do what I must. So hear me—never trust Nizra. He is cunning and treacherous."

Blade nodded. "This I already know, Empress."

The living skull moved on the pillow. She was bald but for a few weak hairs that sprang like gray wires from the bone.

"You shall marry the Princess Mitgu, Blade, and lead my people from this valley. We Jedds have been here too long and so my people are born and die in misery. So this is my wish, Blade—when I am dead, you will rule, with Nizra to aid you, for that cannot be helped, and you will burn Jeddia and everything in it. Then you will take my people to the north, to the land of the Kropes and the Shining Gate. The destiny of the Jedds, whatever it is to be, lies there beyond the Gate. Go north, Blade. Go upward. It is forbidden to go back. You hear? You understand? You promise me this?"

Blade, mystified and far beyond his depth, could only

160

nod and say: "I promise you this, Empress. I will do my best for your people. For the Jedds."

The Empress tried to lift a hand, but the effort was too much. She whispered to him. "Then summon Nizra and all my captains. Make haste."

They assembled at the bedside, the five captains on one side of the dying old woman, Blade and Nizra on the other. Nizra, now that things were going his way, was clever enough to remain silent and a step or two behind Blade. The captains were sullen and hard-faced, though respectful enough, and Crofta and Holferne had tears in their eyes. Only Gath deigned to glance at Blade. His blue eyes were speculative and, Blade thought, not unfriendly. He marked Gath as a possible ally in the future.

Somehow the old woman found strength to raise her voice. It filled the gloomy chamber, firm and without a quaver as she gave them all her final instructions. Richard Blade was the avatar, come to save the Jedd people. He had made certain promises to the Empress, and Nizra and the captains were to aid him in keeping those promises. Blade was their leader now and must be obeyed in all things. He had to marry the Child Princess Mitgu as soon after her death as was possible. These were her dying wishes and commands.

The old voice faltered at last. There was a moment of absolute silence save for the music. Blade stared across the bed at the captains and met only hatred and disbelief and enmity, except for the blue gaze of Gath. Behind him Nizra moved uneasily and his robe made a rustling sound. The music ceased abruptly. Somehow the musicians knew.

Nizra cleared his throat. Blade half turned, fixed the Wise One with a hard stare and raised a hand. This was his moment for taking charge.

Blade bent over the Empress as the others watched in silence. The eyes stared up at him. He closed them and pulled the coverlet over the face. Then he faced them all and gave commands, his voice calm and level and laden with poise and authority. His voice and his exterior carriage gave the sure impression that the orders of the dead

161

Jeddock, and his own, would be carried out without any slightest question. It was one of the magnificent bluffs at which Blade was so adept.

He put extra depth into his voice and let the words roll out, orotund and sonorous, as befitted the new role he now played. Avatar! He who had been promised to the Jedds by the Books of Birkbegn.

"You," he said to Crofta, "will make the funeral arrangements. Follow your customs in all things, but it must be done this day. If I am to keep my promises I have no time to waste. Go."

Crofta, a swarthy fellow, stood in indecision for a moment, his helmet under his arm and one hand on his sword-hilt. He glanced uneasily at his fellow captains. They evaded his glance and watched Blade. Blade smiled inwardly and waited. None of them wanted to be first in direct opposition.

Crofta suddenly clicked his heels, bowed slightly and yielded Blade his first small victory and a title as well. "Yes, Sire Blade," said the captain. "As you command. At once." He hurried from the chamber.

Blade heard the faintest of chuckles behind him. Nizra. He ignored the man and pointed a finger at Bucelus.

"I do not know your order of command, and it does not concern me now. As of this moment you, Bucelus, are in high command of all the military. You have the entire authority and the responsibility. You will at once, on leaving this place, gather all your troops outside the city, on the plain to the north of Jeddia. All soldiers must be brought together and kept together until I order otherwise."

Bucelus, a giant of a man and amazingly ugly, came near to scowling. "To the north, Sire? That is not wise. The Kropes watch always from the Shining Gate and they do not like soldiery in any degree north of the city. But perhaps you do not understand about the Kropes? I—"

Blade gave the man a cold stare. Kropes and the Shining Gate? He must know about these at once. But he said,

"Do as I bid you, man. Leave the Kropes and the Shining Gate to me."

Bucelus left the chamber, muttering to himself.

Blade turned next to Holferne, a skinny little man nearly as bald as Nizra. "You, Holferne, will take as many men as you need and begin preparations for a march. Not for the army alone, but for all Jedds, everywhere in the city and the valley. This you will keep secret until I give the word, but I intend to take the entire population on trek. You will keep that in mind and begin assembling transport and food and water and anything else that is needful. I leave the details to you, but do it quickly and without fanfare. I will expect reports from time to time. Go now."

Holferne glanced once at Chardu, the one remaining captain other than Gath, then bowed and clapped on his helmet and left without a word. Blade glanced at the Wise One. Nizra was not chuckling now. His great head was leaning to one side as he studied Blade with a puzzled expression on his face.

Blade looked at Chardu. "To you I will entrust a most sensitive task. You will tell no one why you do this or on whose orders you do it. You will, in great secrecy, make ready to burn the city to the ground."

Nizra gasped aloud. "Burn Jeddia?"

Blade did not look at him. "It was my promise to the Empress. The city is a dungheap, rotten to the core, and breeds plague after plague. If you Jedds remain here you will in time all die the Yellow Death. You must know this, for each outbreak of plague is worse than the last. So make your preparations, Chardu. Assemble your firestuffs and your men so that when I tell you to begin, the city will burn in minutes. All this in secrecy for now. I have no wish to see rioting. Go and begin."

Now only Gath was left of the captains. Blade smiled at him. Nizra plucked at Blade's sleeve but was ignored. Blade was playing for high stakes now and letting his intuition guide him. The next few moments would tell if that intuition lied.

163

Blade walked around the bed and approached the captain. Gath eyed him doubtfully. Blade held out his hand. "Another test of strength, my friend?"

Gath made to hold out his hand, then drew it back. His blue eyes narrowed, then widened and a hint of smile touched his well-formed mouth under the flowing mustache. "I think I will not, Sire. My hand still aches from our last try. I admit you stronger."

J often said that when Richard Blade really tried he could charm the birds out of the trees and make fast friends of the serpent and sparrow. J's allusion had been, in the main, to Blade's prowess with women. But it could apply to men as well. And Blade was really trying now. He needed Gath and now he staked everything on his knowledge of men and his reading of character.

So he clapped Gath heartily on the shoulder and stared deep into the man's eyes. Gath gave him back stare for stare, his eyes unblinking and cool, yet with a latent promise of friendship.

Blade crossed his arms on his chest. Both men ignored Nizra, who was at the bedside staring down at the dead body of the Empress, his great head bowed on his scrawny chest.

"You I will not order," said Blade to Gath. "I will ask you to be my first companion, my aide and chief lieutenant in all that I do, to trust and be trusted. I like you, Gath, and I would have you as my friend. What do you say to this?"

Gath did not answer at once. He looked from Blade to the bed and the corpse there, and he stared long at the Wise One seemingly lost in contemplation. Blade sensed the struggle in the captain and said, "You know the situation in Jeddia, Gath. You know the caliber of your fellow captains, you understand what they are and what they want and how they would use power. Against all this I am new come and you know little of me. Yet this decision must be made by you alone. You can walk out now and be none the worse off because of me. I do not want or trust service that is not freely given."

164

Gath met his eyes again. He nodded and pulled his short iron sword from the scabbard. Nizra looked up in alarm at the sound. Blade tensed.

Gath looked at Blade for a long moment, then kissed the hilt of his sword and extended it to Blade. Blade in turn kissed the hilt and handed it back to Gath. Then he extended his hand. Gath took it with a smile and this time there was no trial of strength. Gath took a last glance at his dead Empress.

"I will obey her last wishes," he said gravely. "I still serve her. And I will serve you."

Blade touched his shoulder again. "My thanks, Gath. You will find me loyal to my friends. And now listen well—you will form a bodyguard for me, say fifty of your best men, and, subject to my orders, you and they will not leave me. You will muster and disarm all other contingents in the city and throughout the valley, other than the regular military under the command of Crofta. This must be done at once."

Gath could not restrain a grin as he looked at Nizra. That personage was staring at Blade in dismay, but said nothing.

"Yes," said Blade. "Even the retinue of Nizra will be disbanded. He is my chief adviser now and in my care, and has no need for a private army. This will save him much expense."

Nizra, ignoring them, went to a shadowy corner of the chamber, put his hands in his sleeves and began to pace back and forth. The head lolled from this side to that as he paced, and Blade would have given much to know what went on in the oversize skull.

"So I place my safety in your hands," he told Gath. "And leave it to your conscience. Now—I am to marry the Child Princess Mitgu as soon as possible. This will be immediately after the funeral"—he nodded to the bed—"and just before we begin the trek to the north. You will make all arrangements for this wedding. But first you will arrange an audience for me with the Princess, for I must know her thoughts in this matter. If she does not wish marriage, there shall be none. And I tell you now, Gath, that you may tell others, if need be, that I understand that she is but a child and the marriage will be in name only. So I may keep my promise to the dead Empress. Between ourselves we may speak freely and I tell you plain that I am not the sort of man who wishes to bed a child."

An odd look came over Gath's face. His blue eyes twinkled and his brushy mustache seemed to twitch. He asked, "You have not seen Mitgu, then? Have not met her? She who is known to the Jedds, among the common folk, as the Golden Princess?"

Blade admitted that he had not yet made the acquaintance of the little girl in question. This was not very strange, he added, since events were rushing at such a torrential pace.

Gath bowed and did not wholly succeed in repressing his smile. "You are strange here, Sire, and know little of Jedds. The Golden Princess, our Mitgu, is not such a child as you seem to think. But you must see for yourself. I will arrange it at once. Is there anything else you wish of me now?"

Blade glanced to where Nizra still paced in the shadows. "Only that you summon six good men, whom you trust, and post them about me before I leave this place. And that you pass this on to the other captains—there will be a council of war tonight in the house of Nizra at two hours past sundown. I want all the captains there, including yourself. You will be responsible for the safety of all."

Gath saluted with his sword. "All shall be done."

"Then my hand to you again," said Blade. They shook hands once more and Gath left. Blade and Nizra were alone in the chamber with the corpse of the old woman.

Nizra spoke first. "I feared all this, Blade, but went against the warnings of my mind. I thought to use you and instead I have been used. It will be a lesson to me, if I live to profit by it."

Blade was silent, watching the Wise One continue his pacing.

"What of it, Blade? Am I under arrest, then? Am I to be killed or kept prisoner?"

"None of those," Blade said curtly. "So long as you make me no trouble and do not plot against me. I need you, Nizra, as much as I ever did. I need your wisdom and your vast knowledge of this city and the Jedds. Give me freely, without stint or self-interest, of that wisdom and knowledge, and we will get going. Until my work is done and I must go from here. After that I cannot help you and you and the captains must have it out. Until that time, if you do not play me false, I will be your friend. But understand one thing—I am leader. I alone give orders."

Nizra came into the light of the tapers near the bed. He glanced across the withered corpse at Blade and a faint smile touched his tiny mouth.

"To all this I agree, Blade. Because I believe you when you say that you will go soon. So, as I am no fool— despite having been made to look like one this past hour —I will wait and bide my time. When the time comes I will handle the captains. So much for all that.

"And now—this trek you speak of to the north. To the Shining Gate and the land of the Kropes. It is ill-advised, Blade. Worse, it is an impossible madness. The Kropes have held the Jedds in thrall since time forgotten. To so much as approach the Shining Gate is sure death for all of us."

"I know nothing of this," said Blade. He nodded to the dead woman. "But it was her wish, and she was not as senile as you thought, Nizra. But I will listen and then decide. Tell me of the Kropes, Nizra, and of this Shining Gate."

Nizra made a little bow and for once could not hide the bitterness and hate that boiled in that huge skull. "As you command, avatar."

Blade smiled calmly. "Yes, Nizra. To all purposes I am the avatar. It was you who named me so, remember?"

167

"To my sorrow."

"The Kropes, Nizra! The Shining Gate."

Nizra told him. Blade listened with dismay clotting like lead in his chest. But he shook it off. It was simply another impossible task and he had, since the forays into Dimension X began, gotten quite accustomed to doing the impossible.

Chapter 16

Richard Blade and Gath strode through the narrow streets of Jeddia. Two of Gath's stalwart soldiers were in the van, two behind and a man on each side of them. They made their way around a death cart halted before a large inn. Blade was on his way to his first audience with the Child Princess Mitgu, she whom the folk of Jedd called the Golden Princess.

Blade glanced at the corpseburners carrying out three victims of the plague, a child and two women. He looked at Gath. "You will give orders that no more death carts are needed. All corpses are to be left in the houses, where they will burn with the rest of the city. Find some other employment for the corpseburners—use them as you will."

"Yes, Sire."

A burst of crazy laughter came from a house as they passed. Gath doffed his helmet and wiped his face with a cloth. "At first I doubted, Sire, but now I see that you are right. The sooner this accursed city is burned the better."

They approached a tall wedge-shaped building, of the usual stone and wood, but much finer than even Nizra's house. Here Mitgu lived and here she had summoned Blade to visit her. It had been an order, not a request, and Blade smiled when he heard it. He must not forget that, with the old Empress dead, Mitgu was the new Jeddock. He had begun to look forward to the meeting—never before had he had dealings with an imperious little girl of ten. It would, at least, be a different sort of confrontation.

Gath, on Blade's orders, had posted a strong guard around the home of the little Princess. A junior officer saluted with his sword as they passed and both Blade and Gath returned the salute. They paused at the door and Gath sent the sentry away for a moment.

Blade studied his chief aide. "You are mindful of my orders about Nizra?"

Gath said, "I am, Sire. He is not to be harmed, unless on your explicit orders, and he is never to go unwatched. My spies are busy, Sire, and they are good men. Nizra may do what he will and go where he chooses, but he will always be watched. My men report to me on the hour."

Blade nodded in approval. "Good. But remember that he is not called the Wise One for nothing—and I daresay his spies are as good as yours. Probably he has more of them. When did you see him last?"

Gath grinned. "I left him in his house, Sire, after I had disbanded his guard of honor and taken their weapons. To tell truth he did not look too unhappy, and there was a great coming and going of men. Spies, no doubt. Would you have me stop this traffic? It would be easy enough to do."

After a moment of hesitation, Blade said, "No. I want to give him rein, see what he will do. So long as I *know* what he is doing I can see no great harm. So carry on as before, Gath. Do not impede him in any manner unless he threatens me or the Child Princess. This is understood?"

"It is, Sire."

"And now," said Blade, "I must go and meet your little Princess." He twitched his swordbelt around and straightened his helmet. He had changed his robe for a soldier's tunic over which he wore a highly burnished breastplate. Short trousers of fine cloth and high-laced sandals completed his dress.

Gath was staring. Blade laughed and said, "I am a little nervous, to tell you true. How does one handle a ten-year-old? But I will cope. How do I look, Gath?"

Gath saluted with his sword. "Just as I would have you look, Sire. Like my leader." He saluted again and stepped

170

back. "I wish you fortune with the Child Princess, Sire, but only remember this—words sometimes lie, and among us Jedds a ten-year-old is not exactly a child. Not yet a woman, perhaps, but not a child."

Blade thought of Ooma and wondered. He had put her age at fourteen or less, and still marveled at her experience and skill in lovemaking. Was Ooma even fourteen? His doubts came back.

But a child, a girl, of ten? Surely she could present no problems. All he had to do was humor her and win her confidence, show her that he was honest and meant her only good. Yet he was faintly uneasy as he went into the house and mounted a stair to an upper chamber where he was awaited.

He approached an ornate door. A middle-aged woman, dressed all in black and wearing an iron chain much similar to that of Nizra, bowed to him and opened the door.

"The Princess Mitgu awaits you, Sire."

Blade halted and looked at the woman. "I would be alone with her. This is understood?"

"It is understood, Sire. You will not be interrupted."

Blade stepped into the chamber. It was spacious and very dark except for two tapers gleaming at either end of a large cushioned seat. Rugs and pillows were scattered all about and there was a taint of incense in the room. Blade halted and gazed around. Where was this Child Princess, then?

A close-cropped head of golden hair appeared from behind the divan-like seat. The tapers sparked and reflected themselves in that smooth poll and a pair of wide-set and narrowed eyes studied Blade. For a moment he was shaken, thinking himself the butt of some outrageous joke. This was a boy!

The voice, high and clear and lilting, was that of a girl. "I wanted to see you first," it said. "That is why I hid and spied when you entered. All of Jedd whispers of you, Sire."

Blade, one hand on his swordhilt, bowed low and was

171

silent. He did not really believe his eyes, Blade who had been in so many dimensions and had seen sights that few men in his own world could believe.

She had come around the divan now and was confronting him and matching him in silence while each studied the other. Her poise and bearing left no doubt that she was a Princess born. Her flesh—and she displayed a great deal of it—glowed with a coppery-yellow translucence that seemed to give color to the tapers. Blade had the fleeting impression that he could see her fine bone structure trimmed beneath the satiny flesh. This illusion soon passed and his throat dried and his hands were moist in the palms and he, of all men, felt and admitted a fine trembling in his knees. This was youthful beauty incarnate. He had never seen its like before and knew that he would never see it again. And also knew, that if he married this child, he would be powerless to restrain himself from consummating the marriage. Already his groin tingled and for just a moment Blade felt shame.

"Yes," said the Princess Mitgu. "I *will* call you Sire. I was not sure I would, but now I see that I must. You look like a Sire. And I think I will marry you. I was not sure of that either, but now I will. You are the handsomest man I have ever seen and not at all like the Jedds. That is a pity in a way, because all the captains will be jealous and make much trouble for you. But that cannot be helped, I think."

Blade felt like a fool and supposed that he looked a bit like one. Had his mouth been hanging open?

He bowed again and said, "I have much to learn, Princess. I did not know that you had been courted by any of the captains." It was true. Nizra had said nothing of this, nor had Gath mentioned it. He wondered if it meant new complications, new jealousies? His plate was full enough as it was.

Mitgu cocked a tiny finger at him. "Come further into the light, Sire. Sit with me and we will talk and make ourselves known to each other. A girl should know something of the man she is to marry. And I would have you tell me of great-grandmother. How did she die?"

"She died well," he told her. "Well and in peace. And it was her wish that we marry, Princess, not mine. I promised her, else I would not be here now."

Her face, with its small, perfect features, reminded him of a copper rose. The corners of her red mouth turned down. "I loved her, even though she was often stern with me. I would have been at her bedside, but it is against Jedd law for the young to watch the old die. A stupid law, I think, as so many things in Jedd and Jeddia are stupid. But now that you are here, and to be my husband, all that will change. Come, I said. Sit with me."

Sweat trickled down the back of Blade's stalwart neck. She came to him and took his big hand in her tiny one and led him to the divan. She wore very little, just a vestige of white bra over her small, virginal breasts and the miniest mini-skirt Blade had ever seen. The skirt barely sufficed to cover her and Blade would not let himself look at the slim golden legs beneath the skirt. They were long, perfection in form, and in exactly the right proportion to the compact little torso above them. He could almost have spanned her waist with one hand. But it was the odor of her that most intrigued Blade. And made him extremely nervous.

If it was perfume he had never known any like it. Indeed he did not think it was perfume—it was the clean and uncloyed scent of a well-scrubbed child, a girlchild just hovering on the brink of womanhood. Her tender flesh glowed at him, emanating a warmth and a fragrance and, yes, a golden color that made his face redden and his own flesh sticky with sweat. Richard Blade was finding out things about himself—things that he did not really want to know. Was he really this much a lecher? For honesty bade him admit that he was sexually excited, but this fragile and lovely child had aroused him almost beyond bearing. Yet bear it he must. At least until after the marriage. Beyond that he did not dare to think.

Mitgu pulled him down beside her on the divan. She took one of his hands in both of hers and laid it on her bare leg. Electricity seared through the big man and he made a final effort. He sat bolt upright, took his hand back and put on a most solemn visage.

"We will speak of marriage later, Princess. Plenty of time for that. I came to inform you about my plans and to know if they meet with your approval."

A formality, but one he deemed necessary. This girl was now the nominal ruler of the Jedds and, though he meant to go through with his plans in any case, it would be easier with her cooperation. He told her of his plan to burn the city and trek to the north.

She was watching him closely. Her eyes, sloe dark and in startling contrast to the golden head with its boyishly cut hair, were tip-tilted at the outer corners and when she smiled with her mouth her eyes smiled too. They smiled now at his attempt to be formal. She squeezed his arm and laughed at him, gold and silver notes that tinkled through the great gloomy chamber.

"You are afraid of me," she crowed. She clapped her hands in glee. "You are like all the captains, except that you do not go down on bended knee. But you are like them all the same—you think I am a little girl who must be given sweets and humored." She moved away from Blade and twisted lithely on the divan to face him. Blade was permitted to gaze for an instant between those girlish golden thighs, to explore a silken, coppery cavern where lurked a fuzzy golden shadow. Mitgu wore nothing at all beneath the brief skirt. His heart thudding, his breathing strained, Blade tore his glance away from that virginal target. He felt dizzy and his head spun. Sweat drenched him. He did not understand this—never had he suffered such an onslaught of unbridled animal lust. And for a child of ten! He stood up, conscious only that he must get out of this place before he lost control.

Mitgu clapped her hands again, unmindful of his torment, and laughed at the big man towering over her.

Suddenly she sobered, frowned and extended her hand to him again. "I am sorry, Sire. And I did not speak true—you are not at all like the others. But I would have you know that I am not a child, not a little girl. I am a woman."

174

Blade, having got well away from the divan and the temptations there, paced a few steps back and forth and then faced her again.

"Are you, then? A woman?" Blade had won his battle now and felt calmer. His look, still in self-defense, had a hint of coldness and mockery in it.

"If this is so," he continued, "and you are indeed a woman and no child, then you will understand that I am a man and you will know what is in my mind."

The sloe eyes narrowed at him for a moment and she laughed again. With one supple movement she twitched off the tiny bra and flung it aside. She gazed down at her breasts, then up at Blade.

"See, then. Are these the breasts of a little girl, a child?"

To Blade, of Home Division, they were indeed the breasts of a child, of a tender and unsullied girl verging on womanhood, and therein lay his greater agony. Her breasts were small and plump and perfect rounds of flesh unspoiled by fondling. Coppery mounds as soft as the flesh of inner thigh. Moving now to her breathing, trembling with life of their own, tipped with pink buttons of erectile tissue now responding to her inner excitement.

Mitgu put her little hands under her breasts and cupped them and lifted as if to offer them to Blade. She caught her breath and with a half sigh, half gasp, repeated, "Are these the breasts of a child?"

Blade stood tall, his shadow etched by the tapers and falling across that golden little body. As he could cover her, then and there, if he wished it.

Mitgu trailed her fingertips across her nipples, then extended her arms to Blade. "Would you kiss me, Sire? And so find out how much child I am?"

He had taken a step toward her when the door was flung open and the lady-in-waiting entered. Mitgu squealed and disappeared behind the divan. Blade, feeling like a man who has seen the axe begin to fall and then been reprieved, yet turned on the woman with a scowl. An order was an order!

"I was not to be disturbed—"

The woman bowed low and her voice quavered as she nervously fingered her chain of office. "I know, Sire, but there is one who insists. He would not be turned away. He is a cornet, sent by Gath himself, and he has news of the greatest import. He threatened to kick in the door and enter unless I—"

"Enough," Blade said gruffly. He brushed past her without a backward glance. But he thought he heard a subdued giggle from behind the divan and his face grew hot. That had been a near thing. But one thing he knew—in future, if he had a future in Jedd, he would treat Mitgu as a woman. She was right. She was no child.

The young Jedd waiting for him in an anteroom was one of Gath's sublieutenants. Blade recognized him vaguely and spotted the polished iron cornet around the man's throat. The little iron half-moon was engraved with a large G. This was one of Gath's men, right enough.

As Blade strode toward him, the young officer saluted with his short sword, then touched the blade to his chest armor over his heart. "I am Sesi, Sire Blade, sent to you by the Captain Gath on an affair of the utmost importance. The Captain is busy elsewhere and could not attend you in person."

Blade crossed his arms on his chest and nodded. Smiled encouragement. "Then out with it, Sesi. What is this great news?"

The cornet, a stripling with a few chin whiskers and very light gray eyes, met Blade's glance for a moment and then looked away. He stared hard at the floor in concentration. Here, Blade thought, was no great intellect. This Sesi would never be a captain.

"I am to give you this message word for word," the young officer said. "It comes from the Captain Gath as given to him by another. But first I am to tell you that the message was delivered by a fat man."

Mok. Mok the drunkard! Blade stepped close to the cornet and scowled at him. "The message, then? Get on with it, man."

Sesi would not be hurried. Evading Blade's eye, staring at the floor and the walls, he labored through it.

"Gath bade me speak thus—a fat man came to the house of Nizra, the Wise One, looking for Sire Blade. I, Gath, halted him and took his message instead. The fat man said: 'The girl Ooma, of whom Blade knows, is in danger and has great need of him. Ooma begs that Blade come at once to her.' "

Ooma! Blade's heart pained and remorse struck at him. He had been so busy, so caught up in a frenzy of events, that he had spared the girl little thought.

He seized the young officer by the shoulder. "You saw this fat man?"

Sesi shook his head. "I did not, Sire. I was given the message by Captain Gath. *He* saw the fat man."

But Blade had turned away. "No matter. You will come with me. I have a bodyguard of six below stairs. You will take command of them and follow me without question."

He went vaulting down the stairs, three at a time Ooma in trouble, in danger. Again he cursed himself for his thoughtlessness. He owed the girl much, had a tenderness for her and yet had been so neglectful.

Blade set a blistering pace out of the city. Through the gates to the south where no guards challenged them and no death carts rumbled. His orders were being obeyed.

The young sublieutenant and the six soldiers panted along behind the big man as he increased his pace. There was no semblance of a formation and they were all trotting to keep up with Blade's long strides. He had noted it before—most Jedd men were short of leg.

They skirted the charnel pit and the rocks behind which Blade had lain in wait for the corpseburner and his cart. He spared them hardly a glance as he started up the hill to the house of Mok and the aunts. The soldiers and Sesi came after him as best they could, sweating and cursing and stained with dust and smoke from the smoldering pit.

Blade could see the house now. There was no sign of life. The humble little cottage brooded, desolate and alone, on its hilltop. The path here wound through a copse of melon trees and Blade halted just at the edge of the grove. His followers slumped to the ground, panting.

Blade studied the cottage. The door stood half open and his heart contracted painfully as he saw the mark—a splash of yellow paint. The plague mark. Ooma?

The young cornet and the six men saw the mark also. There was a frightened burble and Sesi came to stand beside him. "There is plague in that house, Sire. The men will not go nearer."

Blade shot him a sideways glance. "I have not asked them. And you?"

Sesi would not meet his eye, but mumbled, "Nor I, Sire. My duties do not require that—"

He was cut short by a peal of maniacal laughter from the cottage. The young officer shuddered and stepped back a pace or two. Blade stared up at the cottage. That had been a man's laughter. Laughter?

Peal after peal now, of a man mad with fear and pain, the eerie laughter of a man who sees Death looming out of the black mists. Mok. It could only be Mok.

Blade snapped an order over his shoulder as he sprang up the path. "Remain here, Sesi. Form up your men and keep discipline. Wait for me." He broke into a run.

The yellow plague mark was like a running sore. Blade kicked the door open and entered. Mok lay on the floor near the table where he had passed out that night. He was on his back, his face saffron and twisted with pain, his mountainous stomach thrust up. He was laughing, the gaping mouth disclosing the ruins of blackened teeth. Laughing and laughing.

Blade, ignoring Mok, vaulted up the stairs, calling out as he went. "Ooma? Ooma—Ooma?"

Echoes mocked him. No voice answered. He peered into the room where he had left her sleeping. Empty. He ran down the corridor and glanced into the only other room. Both the aunts lay in their beds. One look at their yellowed faces was enough. Dead of plague. But where was Ooma? She had sent a message and surely she would wait here for him.

He ran down the stairs and approached Mok. The man still lived, though for the moment he had stopped that terrible laughing. Blade knelt beside him. "Mok! Mok—do you know me? It is Blade."

The little eyes, lost in folds of jaundiced fat, slowly opened and Blade could discern a last intelligence in them. The mouth opened and words tried to slip past the swollen black tongue and were blocked. Blade bent closer, trying to understand, to make sense of the jumble and slur, of the agonized attempt to speak. Nothing.

He glanced at the table. There was a clay vessel of the powerful fermented melon juice. Blade seized it and dashed half the contents into Mok's face, then he pried open the mouth and poured the rest down the fat throat. It was a faint hope, but the stuff might jolt Mok into a few last moments of lucidity.

The fat man choked and retched and spat. Blade knelt and put his ear close to the frothing mouth. "Mok—Mok! It is Blade. Ooma sent for me. Where is she, Mok? Where is Ooma?"

The fiery liquor did its work. Mok's eyes cleared for a moment and he looked up at Blade with comprehension. His first words nearly tore Blade's heart from his chest.

"Api," burbled Mok. "Api came. They—they took Ooma and used her, all the Api soldiers, and then bound her and threw her alive into the charnel pit. She would—would not tell them of you, Blade. They would have spared her, the Api, but she would not tell them of you. A-alive—in the pit—"

Mok closed his eyes and let out a deep groan. Blade struck him hard across the face while his guts twisted with horror and remorse. Api? They were immune to plague. And who controlled the Api? Who but Nizra. The Wise One. Blade struck Mok again and damned himself bitterly for being the fool of all time.

Mok was speaking again. "Trap, Blade. T-trap. Ooma did not send for you. She was content to wait until you came. B-but Api came first. Took her. G-gave us all plague with knife. You see—"

It was his last moment of lucidity before death. He raised a fat arm and Blade saw the cruel knife gash. They had inoculated Mok and the aunts with plague. Simple enough. Let a dagger fester in a corpse for a time, then plunge it into living flesh and plague would follow almost instantly. But this time it had not struck fast enough. Mok had lived long enough to talk.

There came a scream from the copse where he had left his bodyguard. Then a clash of arms and more screams and cries and the curses of men locked in battle. It *was* a trap. The Api had been waiting.

Mok's arm dropped to the floor. The fingers curled, stiffened, then relaxed. Mok was dead.

Blade drew his sword and ran to the door and peered out. Three of his men were already down and the remaining three were retreating up the path toward the cottage and giving a good account of themselves. They were being hard pressed by half a dozen Api warriors, as hairy and long-snouted as Blade remembered them.

Blade stepped outside the door and raised his sword and bellowed, "To me, guardsmen. To me! Break off and form around me here."

His stentorian roar for a moment broke off the hot little battle. The Api paused in their attack and stared at Blade, their pale eyes feral beneath the horned helmets, the pointed baboon muzzles dripping with sweat and slobber. The goons rested for a moment, leaning on their long wooden swords edged with flint; and Blade's remaining three men broke off and ran to join him.

One of the soldiers was bleeding badly from a shoulder wound. Blade ripped away part of his tunic and bound it up as the man gasped out his story.

"They were concealed in the melon trees, Sire. We were betrayed by Sesi, who led us here. And now we die, for there are many of them all around the house."

It was true. Blade could hear the high-pitched, effeminate calls of still more Api as they emerged from the trees at the foot of the hill behind the cottage and began to ascend. But he patted the wounded man on his unhurt shoulder and smiled at them all. "We are not dead yet, guardsmen. Only obey me—obey me absolutely and keep your courage and we may come out alive yet. They are only Api after all and we will out-think them."

Yet as he gazed down the hill to where the Api leaders and the traitor Sesi were conferring, Blade did not feel so confident. It was going to be a near thing. Yet such was his rage and despair at the moment that he welcomed it. Let them come on. They would find a Blade as cruel and brutish as themselves. His eyes narrowed as he sought out the young sublieutenant Sesi. How skillfully, how carefully, the cornet had carried out his master's orders. Blade cursed himself again and again. He had made what might be a fatal mistake—he had underestimated the Wise One. What was worse, Blade had ignored the clear indications that this might happen. Nizra had told him of signals from the Api, and Nizra had carefully avoided mentioning the girl Ooma. Blade, busy and full of his own conceit, had let it pass unnoticed. How Nizra must have chuckled, how that ghastly head must have lolled. For by torturing Ooma he could learn the truth about Blade, at least to a point, and thus seek to discredit him as the avatar. Fool, Blade called himself. Fool—fool—*fool!*

At the foot of the hill the conference broke up. Sesi turned away and sat down beneath a melon tree. Blade smiled grimly. The cornet had done his part and would not fight.

The Api leader, a goon not so large as the slain Porrex, but who looked to be shrewder, began to squeal out his orders. Blade followed suit.

"Into the house," he ordered. "There are four windows and the door to guard. I will take this door and the near window—each of you will take one of the remaining windows. They are large and clumsy, these Api, and not made for climbing through narrow windows. Now—keep your spirits up and fight for your lives."

One of the men gazed at the yellow mark on the door and cringed away, crying out, "But there is plague in this house, Sire. We will—"

181

Blade gave him a brutal shove in through the door. "There is a greater plague out here, fool. In! Must I think for all of you?"

The Api were slow in approaching and Blade understood why. He reckoned some two score of the goons, against four. Impossible odds. Once inside the cottage he cast about for some manner of evening them a bit. He stared at the corpse of Mok and had an idea. There was still time, for the overconfident goons were shouting and jesting among themselves as they moved in to slay the four men.

Blade pointed to the vast body of Mok. "Wedge him into one of the windows. Quickly. All that blubber will barricade it as well as an iron shutter."

And so poor Mok, and his bloated body, did some service as he was thrust head first through a rear window and wedged tightly there by men who groaned and sweated as they lifted the great bulk.

Blade glanced through the remaining rear windows and saw a line of Api coming up the back slope. They were fifty yards distant, some twenty of them, and squealing with battle glee as they swung their long, pointed swords over their heads.

Only two of his men had lances. The remaining guard, he who had been wounded, had only his short iron sword, as had Blade. Blade posted the men with lances at two of the remaining three windows, one facing to the rear, the other forward, and he himself took the door and the window nearest it. He posted the wounded man in the center of the room as a reserve and indicated the body of Mok where it served as a stopper.

"Keep an eye on him," Blade commanded. "If they dislodge the body, or cut it up or pull it out, then you must guard the window. Otherwise you will be alert for a call to aid any of us that needs it."

He advised the men with lances: "Make your thrusts short and fast. In and out, quickly. Do not let them seize the lances or break them off. If any of them succeed in getting halfway through a window do not kill them until

182

they are well wedged in and blocking the way to others. You understand why I say this?"

One of the guards, younger than the others, laughed and pounded his companion on the back. "We understand, Sire. Do not fear but that we will do our duty. If we must die here we will make it a dear victory for the Api."

Blade smiled. "Good man. I do not ask for more. Now take your posts and make ready, for the fight is here."

As he stalked to the door he heard the other lanceman mutter, "I have *heard* that he is the avatar—now I begin to believe it. I do not think fear has yet been coined for him, and I am a Jedd who does not believe in much."

Blade grinned. He stood in the open door, hands akimbo, and watched the Api storming toward them. They had been bunched into two files, each of ten men, and Blade made a sound of derision. This was not the way to do it, not at all, but who was he to tell them?

They were twenty-five yards distant. Fifteen yards. Ten yards. Five yards.

Blade leaped from the door with a bull-like roar, a shout that sounded up and down the smoky valley like a horn calling men to battle. A fine tremor beset his nerves and bloody mists moved in his brain. He knew the signs, knew that the battle madness was upon him, and he welcomed it.

His great hoarse voice sounded over the clash and the screaming. "Come, Api! Come to me. Come to Blade. Come to my sword, my thirsty sword that lusts for Api blood! Come and die, Api."

For a split second, the shock of his voice halted them in confusion. The forward files milled in confusion. Blade leaped at the nearest goon and swung his sword in a glinting arc, slashing off a hairy arm. He lunged and put his iron into a massive chest, through armor and bone, and kicked swiftly with his foot to disengage. Then, before they could recover and move in on him, he was back in the doorway, brandishing the bloody sword and screaming defiance.

For a moment the Api seemed on the verge of breaking

and running. So terrible a foe as this was new to them, though by now they had all heard the tale of how Blade had blinded Porrex. But this was different. Now it was *they* who must face this mad creature, this warrior whom their quasimasters, the Jedds—and all Api despised Jedds —whom the Jedds called avatar and obeyed as some sort of god.

Blade had a moment of surcease. He made a brief glance of inspection. Mok's corpse was holding up well and both lancemen had bloodied points. There were no Api snouts at the rear windows. Blade nodded and turned back to his own affairs.

The Api officers, a senior and a junior, were flailing at their troops with the flats of their swords, trying to drive them on. Near the door was an Api corpse, and the beast that had lost its arm was lying nearby watching itself bleed to death.

Over the squealing and screaming and cursing, Blade heard the Api commanding officer shouting threats and promises.

"Forward! On! Are Api warriors to be halted by four men? You had the woman, all of you, and now payment is due. On! And think—you all heard the promises made in the name of the Wise One. Power in Jedd and women—women for all. Think—power and women and food and easy duty for the rest of your lives. Now forward and kill them!"

Even besotted as he was by battle lust, Blade heard and understood. This was Nizra's great ploy. How carefully he must have planned it all in advance. First to discredit Blade as avatar by information tortured from Ooma; this failing, to trap and kill Blade and then loose the fierce Api on the Jedds. Blade cursed himself again, grimly. It was by his orders that Crofta had pulled out all the Jedd troops and taken them to the north of the city, thus leaving the southern approaches wide open to the Api.

No more time for thought. The Api had been whipped into line again and charged forward. Blade slipped out of the door and killed one of the goons, suffering a slight gash in his thigh, then as fast as a heartbeat he was back and defending the door. The Api were hindered by their very numbers. The door was narrow and Blade could only thrust, not swing, his sword, but he did fearful execution. The short iron sword was a live thing in his hand, slashing and hacking, in and out with serpent speed. A long wooden sword slammed down across his helmet and broke in two. Blade killed the Api who had wielded it, had trouble extricating the weapon from the goon's leather harness, daggered another Api who charged him from the flank, and finally got his sword free and darted back into the doorway. Just in time.

One of the smaller Api was trying to get through the near window and take Blade from behind. He had his head and shoulders through and was being shoved by two of his comrades. The Api could not use his weapons, but snarled and lunged at Blade's throat with his fangs as the man brought his sword around and up and down in a terrible stroke. The goon's head fell into the room and bounded across the floor. His headless trunk twitched and writhed and remained stuck in the window.

Now two of the goons were trying to get through the door at the same time. Blade found foot room and thrust them both through, hacked their awkward swords from the hairy paws and cut their throats with backhand strokes. Blood sprayed him. He let the bodies settle in the doorway as a barrier.

The junior Api officer snarled and thrust at Blade. Blade barely turned the point in time, let his short sword slide up the other weapon and slashed the young officer across the eyes. The Api fell back with a high scream. At this sight, the remaining Api in front of the house began to fall back to rally around their remaining officer. Blade, his head roaring with blood frenzy, drenched with sweat and the blood of Api mixed with his own, had a moment of respite.

It was just as well. The Api attacked the rear of the

house with no liaison with those in front and did not know the battle was going against them. They were attacking with zeal, in waves of ten, and just as Blade turned he saw the corpse of Mok, hacked to bits, being pulled out of the window. He shouted at the guardsman in reserve, the wounded man, who had already seen the danger and was running to the window. As he reached it a spear was hurled squarely through the window and took the guard in the chest, piercing his armor and standing a foot out behind his backbone. The man fell to the floor with a dreadful scream and began to thrash about.

There was no time for mercy or compunction. Blade needed the spear. And the man was as good as dead. Blade turned him over, seized the shaft just below the point, and drew it on through the dying man's body. The shaft was slimy with blood and gut tissue and he wiped it on his tunic. An Api face appeared at the window and Blade thrust hard with the spear into the beast's braincase. The Api fell back with a shrill death cry.

Blade spun around. The door was still empty of the enemy. They were disorganized on this side. The headless goon blocked the near window. The guardsman at the other front window was resting, reeking with blood, and gave Blade a dull and uncomprehending look of battle fatigue. Blade went to the remaining rear window, walking sideways to keep an eye on the door. Judging from the Api sounds out there, they were some thirty yards down the slope. He was sure they would attack again. The remaining officer would harangue and beat them into it.

The guard at the other rear window was engaged in a tug-of-war. One of the Api had thrust a spear through the window and the guard had seized the shaft and was now trying to wrench it from the holder and bring it inside. But the brute Api was the stronger and was winning.

"Hold on," Blade shouted. He leaped forward and severed the shaft with a downward stroke of his sword. His man now had two-thirds of a spear and the working end. Blade grinned through the mask of blood caking on

186

his face. He slapped the Jedd on the shoulder and shouted, "You do well. Half a spear is better than none, and you have the point. But be not selfish—share it with them when they come again."

The man managed a feeble smile and nodded. Blade turned back to the door to await the new onslaught. With misgivings. They were only three now and the Api must have near thirty left. This time, if the enemy pressed hard enough, they must win by sheer weight of numbers. Blade thought this, speculated for a moment, then forgot it. It was not in his nature to wish that Lord Leighton might find him with the computer at that perilous moment.

The frontal attack did not come. The Api to the rear fell back down the slope. Blade peered and frowned. What now? This he did not like. He would almost as lief have them come on in strength, for he had a plan forming. If he could sally out and kill the remaining Api officer he and his two Jedds might yet win the day. But now there was only silence.

Blade waited, his uneasiness growing with each moment. He knew what he would have done in the Api commander's place and now he was afraid that the goon leader would think of it. The two guards left their posts and joined them. Both were wounded, weary to the bone and frightened, and he knew they could not fight much longer.

One of them, peering past Blade to where the Api were conferring with the traitor Sesi, shook his head tiredly and said, "I like this not, Sire. The Api are no thinkers, but Sesi is a Jedd and has some brains. See how he gives orders to the Api captain!"

Blade kept a confident smile on his gory features, but his heart sank. Sesi was pointing down the hill toward the smoking charnel pit and arguing with the Api chief. Blade nodded to himself. Yes. Sesi had thought of it. He watched as two of the Api goons broke away from the main body and went running down the hill.

Blade and his two Jedd guardsmen waited. They were

near to perishing of thirst, but there was no water in the house. Blade tried to keep up the spirits of the other two as best he could.

He watched the group of Api on the front slope. They were gathering dry faggots and, using vines for cord, were binding them into compact bundles. Blade said nothing. He knew that the Api behind the house would be doing the same.

The two Api came back up the hill carrying torches, flaming red and yellow and giving off streamers of black smoke. Fire from the charnel pit.

One of the guards looked at Blade in fear. "They are going to burn the cottage, Sire. Drive us out into the open."

Blade could only nod. "Yes. I was afraid they would think of it."

The other Jedd dropped his sword and began to weep. "I have fought well, Sire, but I cannot face the fire." He went to his knees and rocked back and forth, his features contorted and tears streaming through the blood on his face. Blade fought against turning away in disgust. The man had fought well and every man had his breaking point.

The weeping man clutched at Blade's knees. "Surrender, Sire. Surrender now and it may be they will spare us—at least ask for a parley."

Blade laughed harshly. "No parley. And if you think they will spare us you are as big a fool as I for walking into this trap. No! We must see it through."

It happened so fast that he could not have stopped the man even had he tried. The guard leaped up and ran out the door, his hands flung high, and screaming at the top of his voice: "Mercy—mercy. I surrender to you, Api, and beg for mercy. Sesi—you are a cornet and a Jedd and I beg you to save me. Mercy—mercy—"

All the Api stared at the running man. Blade felt a sickness grow in him. The guard reached the Api group and they parted to let him through. He flung himself to the ground before Sesi. The young sublieutenant made a motion with his right hand and one of the Api raised his long sword and, using both hands and great force, impaled the guard and pinned him to the earth. As he was still thrashing and screaming in his death throes they cut off his head and mounted it on a spear and waved it up the slope at Blade.

The remaining Jedd stared at Blade and said, "He was a fool. I am not. Better to die here with you, Sire, in honor."

Torches were being applied to the faggot bundles now Half a dozen of the Api, each carrying a flaming sheaf of faggots, ran up the slope. There was nothing Blade could do. If they ventured out to fight they would be cut down in minutes. He strode to a rear window in time to see more Api creeping up with flaming bundles. Blade cursed and chewed on his parched nether lips. Not much of a choice Go out and fight to the death, or stay and burn to death

But it was, at least, an easy enough choice to make

The Api cast their fiercely-burning flambeaus and sped away. Smoke began to seep into the house and tongues of flame were already licking up the walls and devouring the dry wood. Masonry began to crumble as the wood support was eaten away. The Jedd began to cough and swipe at his eyes. He peered at Blade through the dirty gray swirls of smoke.

"Why do we wait, Sire? I do not intend to burn, nor do I think you will so choose. Let us go now and die like men."

Blade did not answer for a moment. He was peering intently out a window, shielding his eyes from the smoke and hoping they did not deceive him. It was cruel to hope and be disappointed—and yet had he not seen the glint of sunlight on metal? Behind the Api, near the charnel pit. was not the sun reflecting itself in *highly* furbished iron?

He said nothing of this to the Jedd, but put an arm about his shoulders and asked, "How are you called? Your birth name?"

The Jedd stared back with bloodshot eyes "I am Kaven and I have served Gath since I was hardly more than a weanling. And my father served Gath's father."

Blade squeezed his shoulder. "Now, Kaven, make ready. For you are right. We will not stay to burn." He said nothing of what he had seen. No point to raising hopes on what might be only an illusion. Blade shrugged his massive shoulders and picked up the lance he had captured. What was to be—would be.

The floor was red-hot now. Walls were aflame and ready to crumple. The smoke would kill them quickly if they stayed. Blade led the way to the door.

A high shrill of triumph came from the Api as they were seen. A score of the creatures, led by the officer, charged up the hill at them.

Blade found a level spot and spat out a final command. "Back to back, Kaven. Fight as long as you can."

The man did not answer and in the next moment the horde of slavering Api was upon them.

Blade shortened his grip on the spear and fought with it in his left hand while his right wielded the iron sword with terrible execution. His rage flamed hotter than the blazing cottage. He was in and out, thrusting and backing and cutting, standing astride the Api corpses as they piled up. Kaven too was doing his share of killing. Their backs joined, their sweat and blood mingling, they fought for life.

Blade lost his spear. An Api died with it through his guts and, in falling, tore it from Blade's hand. Blade bellowed in rage and swung his sword with two hands. He heard Kaven scream as he took a wound. Blade chanced a look and saw the Jedd on one knee, still fighting with his lance, his sword arm spurting blood and useless at his side.

The Api leader, forgetting his weapons, leaped in to grapple with Blade, seeking to tear out his throat with the long baboon fangs. Blade drew back in time, shortened his thrust and put it into the leader's chest up to the hilt. The beast screamed a final defiance and tried to close in, his fangs cutting and slashing at Blade's flesh. Blade lost his sword. It would not disengage. He smashed at the long-snouted face with his right fist, a terrible blow that sent

190

the Api spinning away with Blade's sword still embedded in his chest. Blade stood alone, feet outspread, his big hands curved into talons, a gigantic bloody figure now fighting with only his bare hands.

A horn blew in the melon trees. It was a short blast, raucous and brassy and lacking any tone, but the sweetest music Blade had ever heard. Gath's men charged up the hill, an entire troop, some two hundred Jedd warriors. It was over.

Even now he could not spare himself or rest. His plans must go forward. He took a moment to catch his breath, then standing astride a high pile of Api corpses, he cupped his hands and bellowed harshly over the clangor of battle.

"Gath—hear me. Take the Api alive, if you can. Alive, I say! I have use for them. And do not kill Sesi! That is an order, Gath. Do not kill the cornet! I also have use for him. Do you heed me, Gath?"

The captain Gath, his armor slightly bloodied, fought his way through the thinning Api ranks to where Blade stood. He saluted with his sword and panted, "I hear you, Sire. I obey."

He turned and shouted orders to his officers, who in turn passed them on to their men. The Api began to throw down their weapons and surrender and were herded into groups.

Blade turned to find Kaven trying to get to his feet. He was clutching his right arm and trying to stanch the blood. He gave Blade a grin of joy and utter weariness. "It is good to live, Sire. And the better so because it is such a surprise. Unless I dream and we *are* dead."

Blade set about bandaging the man's hurt. It was deep and long, the slash, but in time would heal and leave an honorable scar. "You do not dream," Blade told him. "Nor is this a dream—you are now a captain. You will serve me as second in command only to Gath."

Kaven shook his head in wonder. "Another miracle, Sire. I live—and I am a captain. Are you sure I do not dream?"

Blade laughed and turned away to meet Gath. The captain was angry and spared Blade nothing. His blue eyes shot cold sparks as he said, "I had not thought to serve a fool, Sire, when I gave you my sword and heart. But it seems I do, for only a fool would have fallen into this trap. Only a fool would have been lured to this place with but six men to protect him. Why, Sire? In the name of all that is sacred to the Jedds, and that is not much, tell me why!"

Even bloody, nearly naked, hurt and near collapse, Blade could use his charm. A sheepish charm now, because he knew he deserved the rebuke and did not fault Gath for giving it.

His white teeth flashed as he smiled and said, "Because I *am* a fool, Gath. I admit it. But it was your trusted man who led me here." And Blade pointed to where Sesi stood, bound and guarded by a few of Gath's men.

Gath flushed and looked downcast in his turn. "I am sorry for that, Sire. But how was I to know that he had sold himself to Nizra? In every brook there is one fish that stinks. But Sesi will pay—how he will pay."

The fight was over. The Api, disarmed and sullen, were being rounded up and heavily guarded. Blade, watching this for a moment, gave brief orders concerning them and Gath passed it on. Then Gath was informed of Kaven's new rank and the newest captain was led off to receive medical attention. Blade and Gath walked a little apart from the soldiers.

Blade looked at Gath. "There will be no torture. I speak of Sesi now. I will question him myself, when I am ready, and I will learn all I need of Nizra's plotting. When I have done this, you will kill Sesi. Quickly and cleanly. You will cut off his head."

"But, Sire! This is not the way to handle it. Sesi's treachery was great, as much to me as to you, for it was I who sponsored him from the ranks as cornet. He must take a long time dying, be tortured as no Jedd was ever tortured before. It will serve as an example and—"

Blade gave Gath a cold look, then reached to touch his shoulder. "Do it my way, Captain Gath. I know what I do.

192

No torture. This is understood?"

And Gath, still grumbling, said that it was understood. He also said, half under his breath, that he did not now, nor ever would, understand the Sire Blade.

Blade grinned and said, "Then you will not understand this, either. I want Nizra taken unharmed. Where is the Wise One now?"

Gath, still sulking a bit, would not look at him. He watched the last of the Api being led away.

"Nizra is in his house, Sire. I doubled the guard and gave orders that he was not to leave. I know that in this I contravened your orders, but I was worried and fearful and I did what I thought best."

"You did well," Blade admitted. "I am glad that we are not both fools and that you have Nizra safe. I still have use for him. For one thing, he controls the Api, all that are still free. I would have them all rounded up and disarmed. You will have Crofta's men build a cage for them, as large as is needed, and assemble them on the northern plains."

Gath shook his head doubtfully. "They will serve only Nizra, those stupid beasts. When they learn that he is out of power they will desert and scatter into the forests to the south. You will not catch many of the Api."

"Nevertheless we will try. Now, Gath, one last question before I leave you, because I have a task that I must do alone. How came you to know of my danger? What brought you to me?"

Gath gave him a sly look. "Chance, in part. I spoke to the lady-in-waiting of Mitgu and she told me of Sesi and his message. The lady must have been listening at the door. And then I knew all Jedd troops had been ordered out of this region, and where there are no troops the Api like to pillage and rape. So I knew it was not safe for you to wander here with so small a guard." Gath stopped and shrugged his shoulders. "And I had a feeling in my stomach that all was not well."

He would not meet Blade's eyes. Blade touched his shoulder and said, "And the rest of it, Captain? Tell me."

193

Gath looked directly at him and the skin about his blue eyes crinkled. "I have my own spies, Sire. And they have brought me reports about Sesi. For long now I have thought he was Nizra's man, but I had no proof and so gave him leave to hang himself. So, on hearing all I heard, I myself went to call upon Nizra."

Blade felt sudden shock. He frowned. "You did not kill him?"

Gath tried to look innocent, failed at it and broke into laughter. "Not I. He is well and secure a prisoner. The thing is—he may have a few cuts and bruises. Nothing that will not heal in time."

"That is good. I thank you, Gath. You saved me this day and it will not be forgotten. But there is one thing—"

Gath, on the point of turning away to attend to business, halted and looked back. "And that is, Sire?"

Blade grinned. "Next time do not leave it so long. I thought you would never get here."

Blade made his way down the hill alone, oblivious of the stares of Gath's men and the defiant snarls of the Api prisoners. He went to the smoking charnel pit and looked into it, near to gagging on the sulfurous fumes and sick at his stomach. Row and criss-crossed row they stretched away, the lines of fire-blackened bodies. Blade leaped into the pit and began to search along the paths left by the corpseburners.

It was half an hour before he found the ravaged little body of Ooma with the marks of savage torture everywhere on that once smooth and tender flesh. She had not been burnt and for this much he was grateful. He picked up the frail body and carried it out of the pit and, avoiding the hill, skirted around it and walked until he came to a melon tree growing out of the ruined pavement of a long-forgotten temple.

Blade put her body down and stood gazing at it for a moment. One of her crude wooden combs was still caught in the dark tangle of hair. His face flamed, he choked, and was not ashamed of the hot tears crowding behind his eyes. For a moment he was blinded by the moisture, and the old temple, the courtyard and the single melon tree, disappeared in a scalding haze. Blade gulped, cursed himself softly and began to work.

He knelt and tore out the ancient stones with his hands. He scooped a grave in the soft earth below and placed Ooma it it. He arranged the small, twisted limbs as best he could and covered her face with a bit of his tunic. Then, for a minute or so, he stood looking down at her.

At last he took a double handful of the earth and let it spray through his fingers onto her body. He did not speak aloud, but in his mind he said, "Goodbye, Ooma."

He filled in the grave, replaced the stones atop it, and left it unmarked. He would never come this way again.

Then Richard Blade trod wearily back up the hill to where Gath and his men were waiting to march.

Chapter 17

Two weeks passed. A week of preparation and a week on the march. Blade, encapsuled in work, sleeping but two or three hours a day, was so snared by the flow of time that he forgot it. Jeddia was burned and he married the Child Princess Mitgu who, on their wedding night, proved no child after all. As dawn broke, Blade was near exhaustion and salved his conscience by admitting that a Jedd girl of ten was like a woman of thirty in Home Dimension. Mitgu had been a virgin, had bled copiously, but if she felt pain it in no way dimmed her ardor. And when she left him alone at last and he tried to sleep he was stricken with new head pains as the computer probed for him. The pains were fierce but short-lived. Lord L had missed him again.

This bright morning Blade, accompanied by Captains Gath and Kaven, had gone far ahead of the long column of trekking Jedds. They were nearing the valley mouth to the north, where the ascending terrain funneled through a narrow gut and spread out in a broad and spreading plain. And there the way was barred by the Shining Gate.

Now, high on a crag, the three men stood and gazed, near blinded by the dazzling reflection of the sun on metal. Both Gath and Kaven were astounded and afraid at the sight. Blade was only astounded. He recognized at once that the gate, dam, wall or rampart—call it what you would—was of stainless steel. Half a mile across and some two hundred feet high, it blocked the valley mouth. There was no sign of life on or near it. Desolate, towering, brooding, it shimmered in the heat and mirrored the valley in itself.

Some of the desolation touched Blade and by the alchemy of time and place was turned to loneliness. It was his first leisure in weeks and now it turned sour—he sensed the beginning of an end. What the end would be he could not guess. He recognized the pattern as before, the ever upward terrain, the sense of forward progress, of wandering through the evolutionary process with eons compressed into days and weeks.

None of this could he share with his companions. No more than he could explain to them that the dam, or wall, or gate was of steel and so the Kropes who had built it must be an industrial people. There must lie, beyond that shining barrier, a highly sophisticated civilization.

Gath said, "And now, Sire Blade, now that we have reached the Shining Gate—what?"

Kaven peered at Blade anxiously, the same question in his eyes. He was awe-stricken and afraid and trying not to show it. His sword arm, still heavily bandaged, was in a sling fashioned by Blade.

Blade did not answer for a moment. His eye was on another crag, a jagged, bent needle of stone that reared far overhead and, he was certain, would overlook the shining barrier. After studying it for a minute he turned to them with a grim smile.

"Do not ask me riddles. You have never seen a Krope?"

Both men said they had not. No Jedd had actually ever seen a Krope. In long years past a few exploring parties had been sent up the valley to the wall. None had ever returned. No word had ever been sent. The Shining Gate spoke in silence. Stay clear.

Blade nodded. "They why ask me? I know as little as you Jedds. But I intend to find out." He pointed to the hook of stone outlined far over them. "From that vantage I can see over the wall."

Both Jedds gazed up, craning their necks, then said in

198

disbelief, "It cannot be done, Sire. No man could climb that."

"I can. I will. But it will take me all day, and in the meantime here are orders. Get back to the column and see they are carried out at once."

When they had gone he made his preparations for the climb. He lay on his belly and studied the terrain for an hour, formulating and discarding various attacks on the crag. For a short period disillusionment set in—this task would make Sir Edmund Hilary, the great mountaineer, himself quail—then Blade chuckled and told himself that he had no choice. Press on. He sensed that his time in this Dimension X was growing short and he still had his job to complete. It was but half done. He had made tools, or had them made, and had explored the mountains as they trekked between the ranges. They were indeed rich in every mineral known to Home Dimension. Blade had tested samples and sealed the knowledge gained away in his memory file for Lord L to unlock and record. And yet there was more to do—he must press on and on, learning all he could, until this mission came to a natural and inevitable end. When that would be he could not know.

The sun was near to setting when at last Blade lay exhausted on the upjutting needle of rock. He had done it and had cheated Death a dozen times in the doing. Now he clung to the smooth gray surface, his fingers and toes digging into crevices, and stared out over the steel wall. With the sun behind him he could see well and clearly.

The vast plain stretched out to infinity. Here and there it was dotted by small houses, also seemingly made of steel, and beyond the houses he saw row on row on row of what looked like huge factory buildings. Yet there were no chimneys, no smoke. And nothing moved. No sound came. It was like an industrial town deserted, a wasteland barren of people, lacking any slightest human touch.

Yet near the shining barrier itself there was movement. Near one end of the wall, closest to Blade, was a large structure built of the same metal as the gate. Through its

199

doors the figures constantly came and went. Blade frowned. If they were men—and they moved and looked like men—they were the strangest he had ever seen. They were made of metal and they glistened in the last rays of sunlight falling over the great wall.

Blade frowned and considered. Then he had it, given the hint by the very faint awkwardness of articulation. These Kropes, if they were Kropes, moved with an arthritic stiffness.

Robots!

Blade studied the figures for a long time, checking and doublechecking, then accepted it as fact. He was up against robots. Mechanical and electronic men.

That meant a central control. Blade took the risk of standing on his crag and, shading his eyes with a hand, sought to find again what he in one fleeting second thought he had seen. Something floating in the clouds far away over the plain.

He *did* see it. Saw it for a microsecond before the low clouds closed in again. The very tip of a tower, the spire of a tall building far away, the upthrust lance of a skyscraper that took his breath away. Then it was gone, wrapped in moist clouds, but not before he had made a rapid triangulation and worked it out in his head. He slipped down to his rock again and did the computation over and did not believe himself. And yet he had seen it.

The tower he had seen must be twice as high, plus a little, as the Empire State Building!

Central control.

He shook off his awe and turned to tactics, to practical things. And was in luck. Within five minutes he had located a possible way around the steel barrier. The Kropes were careless, or their control inefficient, for at the end of the wall nearest Blade, where the wall abutted on the sheer cliffside of the valley, erosion had taken a minute toll. But it was enough. Centuries of rain and wind had so eaten away the living rock that a narrow and shallow trench had been dredged between the end of the wall and the cliff. One resolute man might worm and squeeze his way through. Blade marked it well and began his descent, thankful for the moon that would rise soon. It would take him nearly all night to get down from his perch.

It lacked two hours of dawn when he rejoined the Jedds. The orders he had given Gath and Kaven had been carried out to the letter. The main body of the column had camped far back in the valley, protected by its twisting and turning course, and out of sight of the Shining Gate.

Kaven and Gath, along with Captains Crofta and Holferne, met Blade a mile north of the camp as had been arranged. They were accompanied by a few Jedd soldiers carrying torches. Blade fell into step with the captains.

"Put out all torches before we round the next bend," he told Crofta. "For there we will be in sight of the wall."

When Crofta had left to execute the order, Blade looked at Gath. "All is done as I wished?"

"It has been done, Sire. Not without difficulty. We had to kill several of the Api before the others would obey."

"That is no matter. And Nizra? The Wise One? How is he taking it?"

Kaven laughed. "In silence, Sire. He sits in his iron cage, with that huge melon head of his sunken low, and will say not a word."

Blade smiled. "I can understand that. You have not allowed him to be tormented?"

Gath shook his head. "No, Sire, though it has not been easy. I have had to station a guard around his cage to keep the people from stoning him and poking sharp sticks into his cage."

For a moment Blade made no comment, then he said, "Let us go and have a look, then. It will be dawn soon."

The little party halted at the next bend of the valley. False dawn tossed pearly shadows on the cliffs to their left as they sought concealment among the rocks and boulders littering the valley floor. Blade kept Gath and Kaven with him.

From their vantage they could look straight down the valley to the Shining Wall. Just in front of them was a narrow cut, and beyond it the valley floor ran fairly level to the wall. Crofta's engineers had erected a fence of sharpened iron stakes across the cut and beyond this, between it and the wall itself, were half the Api captives. They milled about in confusion or sat in groups and chittered in their high feminine voices. Nearest the wall, in a small iron cage so constructed as to be carried on poles, sat the Wise One, Nizra. In the faint light Blade could make out, barely, the slumped figure of the former High Minister, the great head sunken forward on the scrawny chest. The Api, for reasons of their own, stayed well away from the cage.

Guinea pigs, Blade thought. They were expendable. He had a moment of pity for the brute Api, who had only followed orders, and no pity at all for Nizra. By his orders Ooma had been raped, tortured and flung into the charnel pit.

The light grew steadily. Soon they would know. Blade, watching Nizra intently, saw the big head come erect as the man gazed around. Nizra knew what was happening and why he was there. He also knew he was being watched. As a first ray of sunlight lanced into the valley and splotched golden on the cliff walls, the Wise One lifted his puny fist and shook it at Blade and the other watchers. He knew. He was defiant to the last.

Full dawn. Broad daylight and nothing happened. Blade frowned and stared at the glistening steel wall that dammed the end of the valley. Could he have been so wrong about the danger? It had been a hundred years or more since the last Jedd exploring party had been this way. Things could have changed and—

It was over before Blade and his party could see what really happened. A huge ball of blinding white light, shaming the sun, rolled out from the steel wall and burst over the Api and the iron cage. It vanished as suddenly as it had appeared. For a moment the morning air was tainted with the harsh acridity of scorched flesh, then even that was gone.

Everything was gone. Nizra, the iron cage, the Api—all

had vanished. Not even bones remained. There was, where they had lived but a second before, just the faintest trace of scorching, of burnt earth, nothing else. Blade nodded to himself and drew farther back into concealment. Some sort of ray. Disintegration ray. Control, somewhere beyond the steel wall—probably in the tower Blade had spotted—was not asleep.

And now Blade knew. Knew what he must do. Alone.

Gath and Kaven, at his side, were stricken with fear and awe. He did not blame them. They were the bravest of the Jedds, but this thing they had just seen was too much for them to cope with. Blade smiled at them and smote Gath on a shoulder.

"It will be all right. I will see to it. Now give the order to turn back. Quietly, and stay out of sight of the wall."

The journey back to the Jedd camp was a somber one. Little was said. Blade, his mind crowded with plans, stalked on ahead and the captains, sensing his mood, left him alone.

He did not go at once to the tent where Mitgu waited. Instead he sent for servants and was barbered and washed and arrayed in fresh clothes. When at last he entered the royal tent, the little Empress—for Mitgu was now Jeddock and Blade her Regent—was anxiously awaiting him. With her first words Blade knew that the servants' grapevine had been at work. He never ceased to marvel at its efficiency. Anything he did, or had done to him, was known immediately among the people. Sometimes before he had even had a chance to weigh and judge the matter.

Mitgu, her naked golden body gleaming beneath a near-transparent coverlet, stretched her arms to him and laughed in relief. "Sire—Sire! You have come to me. I—I feared. I have been told an awful tale of—"

He stood tall beside her pallet, looking down at this miniature beauty, his child-wife, with a half frown and half smile. "Put it out of your mind, Empress. Servants lie, and when they cannot think of a lie they make one up."

She put a small hand on his brawny leg. "Do not call me Empress when we are alone! You promised. I am

Mitgu. Your wife, Sire, who adores you. And do not belittle my servants." She laughed again. "They are stupid and lack imagination to invent the tale I have heard. Is Nizra really dead? Gone and nothing left, not even a corpse?"

Blade nodded. "That is true."

She nodded in satisfaction. "Then it is not all bad, this thing I hear. We are rid of Nizra—he cannot plot against us now."

Blade sat down beside her on the pallet. "That also is true. Now enough—do not concern yourself with these matters. It is my province and I will deal with it. And I did not come here to discuss such affairs."

Mitgu showed her little white teeth behind a scarlet mouth. "Then why did you come, Sire?"

"For this." Blade caught her to him and kissed her. Her slim arms wound around his neck and her lips opened beneath his and her tongue flickered into his mouth. In that moment he thought of Ooma—they were much alike in their loveplay—and he was glad when the urgency of his desire took over and banished the shade of the dead girl.

In a very few moments the tiny Empress also was caught up in the toils of passion. She was, like all Jedd women, highly flammable. She pulled Blade down with amazing strength and sprawled atop him, dwarfed by his size, but pressing every inch of her tender golden flesh against his. Blade teetered on the brink of pleasure. Mitgu caressed and manipulated him intimately, not speaking but uttering little sounds of satisfaction as she kissed his body. She suckled him briefly but near to bursting point, then leaped astride him and impaled herself with a loud groan of pleasure. Blade dared not move lest he end it too soon. Mitgu rode him down the course with a delightful frenzy and when at last it was beyond bearing they both shuddered and cried aloud in cataclysmic orgasm. Then Mitgu, as was her custom, gave him one moist kiss and fell off to sleep.

Blade rested for a few moments, then left the pallet without rousing her. His head pained him slightly and he knew the signs. Lord L was searching again with the computer. He stood for a moment at the tent flap, looking back at the slumbering naked figure of his Golden Princess. He knew he would never see her again. After one last look he left the tent.

He went straight to his command tent and summoned all the captains into council. Then, with Gath at his right hand and Kaven at his left, he said what had to be said, told them what was to be. The council lasted for more than three hours and it was a sober and chastened group of captains that shook Blade's hand as they filed out. Only Gath remained, on Blade's request.

When they were alone Gath said at once, "I will go with you into the land of the Kropes, Sire. I have served you well and it is my right."

Blade went back to sit behind the field desk he had made. He pointed to a stool. Gath moved his swordbelt for comfort and sat down, scowling at his Sire.

"You will obey orders," Blade told him. "It is true that you have served me well. None better. So do not spoil it now. I have great need of you, Gath. As the little Empress will have when I am gone. I—"

Gath would have interrupted, but Blade hurried on. "It may be that I *will* return. I cannot know the truth of this. But I do not think so—and if I am right the Jedds, and most of all the Empress Mitgu, will need your wisdom and strength. You heard how I spoke to the council just now—you saw them all agree to follow you in my absence. You will be Regent, Gath, and of this moment you must begin to think like one."

The captain glowered and toyed with his swordhilt. "I would go with you, Sire. Let Kaven be Regent—or Crofta. Or Bucelus or Chardu or Holferne. Why must I be chosen?"

His temper flared for a moment and Blade leaned across the desk. "Because I say so! Because, damn it, I—"

Blade broke off and got himself under control. He smiled. "This is no time for friends to argue, Gath. Listen to me:

"One man, and one man only, has a chance to live beyond the Shining Gate. I am that man. I *know* that, Gath, and cannot explain how I know because there is no time. And even if I wasted a year in the explaining you would still not understand—"

"Am I so stupid, then?" Gath muttered and would not look at Blade.

"Not stupid," Blade soothed, "but you are a Jedd. And I am of another world, another place and another time. I tell you this now, at last, in all truth." Blade raised his right hand and closed his great fist. "In a sense, Gath, and for this purpose, I *am* the avatar!"

He thought that Gath shrunk a little away from him, but the blue eyes met his own with a steady gaze. After a moment Gath inclined his head.

"I will accept that, Sire. You are the avatar and it is not for me to question. I will obey you in all things, as best I can."

With that he drew his sword and laid it on the desk with the point toward his own heart. Blade did likewise. Gath placed his hand where the swords joined and Blade laid his hand atop it.

"I charge you," Blade said, "with the care of the Empress Mitgu. My wife. Not until I return, if I do, are you free of this charge. And if I do not return you must serve as Regent as long as she wishes it. In time, if the events serve and all goes well, it may be that she will take you for husband."

Gath looked shocked.

Blade chuckled. "It is not beyond belief, my friend. As you will see. And now enough of this—you know what to do?"

"I do, Sire."

Blade leaned back in his chair. "Repeat it to me then."

Gath told it off by rote. "If in two days you have not come back to us I am to drive the remaining Api to the Shining Gate and see what happens. If they are destroyed as before I know that you have failed, that you have been slain or made captive by the Kropes, and I am to turn

206

about and lead the Jedds back down the valley. I am to go as far south as possible, beyond the ruins of Jeddia, and found a new city among the ancient temples left there by my forefathers. I am to advise and aid the little Empress in ruling the Jedds."

Blade nodded. "And if the Api are not destroyed? If the ball of flame does not destroy them?"

"I will know that you have succeeded and I will lead my people beyond the shining wall, through the narrow passage of which you spoke, or find a way to open the gate, and so the Jedds will claim the land of the Kropes and live there and, in time—or so you say, Sire—we will come to know all the secrets of these Kropes."

It was well enough. Blade gave a few final orders and then took his leave of Gath. He felt suddenly very tired and much in need of sleep. And the pains in his head, though minor, were persistent.

As Blade sprawled on his cot he told a servant. "You will awaken me the moment the sun goes down."

He slept.

are very close to you...

Chapter 18

Blade was traveling light. For weapons he had only his short iron sword and a dagger. He carried neither food nor water. He waited for an hour after full darkness, then made his way through the narrow winze that had eroded past the end of the steel wall. The way was tortuous and he was scraped and bleeding from a dozen minor abrasions when he emerged on the Krope side of the wall. He sought safety in the shadows at the foot of the cliff and took a breather and his bearings. And knew at once that something was wrong—or, from his viewpoint, right.

Except for the shadows where he now lurked, the great wall was lighted clear across the valley. He could see no fixtures, no light standards, nothing physical, yet the light was there. A misty soft radiance lacking any glare, yet showing up every detail. Blade smiled a bit grimly. Transmission of power without wires. They were working on it now back in Home Dimension.

He studied the large metal building. It was well lit, but now stood in silence and with no movement of any sort. No sound, no sign of life, only the eerie, brooding loneliness. Blade began to understand. He waited another ten minutes, then stalked into the light, his outward mien bold enough and his spine cold. If the ball of fire rolled now, if he had guessed wrong—

Silence. Nothing. Blade approached the metal house and peered through a window. They were in there, the robots, and they were motionless, frozen, caught in strange attitudes when the power had failed.

Failed? Or had it been cut off deliberately? Blade thought it must be the latter. He had just bet his life on it. He was awaited.

There was a full moon. It shimmered up over the horizon, a great golden orb in a cloudless sky, and against it Blade saw the gleaming spear of the high-rearing tower he had glimpsed from the crag. He began walking toward it.

He trudged in a silence and a desolation he had never known before; not for a little time did he come to realize that the aching solitude was as much in his own heart as in the forsaken landscape. He thought of his dead Ooma and willed himself not to think of her. The golden image of Mitgu leaped to his mind and that he also banished. His head pained and he began to sweat copiously. On and on he stalked, past the soundless factories and the empty homes—though he could see robot figures motionless in them both—and at last he came to where the land moved away toward the horizon in an endless belt of slow motion.

Blade halted and wiped his face and neck. He was drowning in sweat. His vision was fuzzy. He stared at the moving earth, then laughed harshly at himself. It was a moving walk, a level escalator six feet wide, moving toward the shining tower over which the full moon now hung like a yellow lantern.

He did not step on the moving walk at once. New pain lanced his head and he doubled up with another pain in his belly. Sweat cascaded down his big body. When the gut pain had gone, Blade straightened and, with his fingers, explored his groin and armpits. They were there—the soft swell, the beginning mushy lumps. Buboes. He had mistaken the headaches! It was not the computer searching for him.

Blade had the plague.

His nostrils tickled and he put a finger to his nose. It came away slightly stained with blood. The Yellow Death.

For one moment he knew terror as he had never known it before. Fear scourged him until his knees trembled and

210

he could not breathe; and his throat and chest were stuffed with a noisome mist that choked him. For that instant he was a beaten man—then he breathed deep, stared at the tower and stepped on the moving sidewalk. He was not yet dead and there remained a task to complete. And there was, for him, a trifle of hope. Hope the Jedds could not know. Blade had a chance. A bare chance.

As soon as he stepped on the walk it speeded up. Now it carried him toward the looming tower at a great rate. He was right. He was awaited.

It was a quarter of an hour before he reached the foot of the tower. As he rode toward it Blade studied it with appreciation and awe. It was of the same shining metal as the wall across the valley, but here mere utilitarianism had been forsaken for beauty. As an aesthetic concept it had the just-rightness of perfection, in that Blade could not have imagined it any different. It stair-stepped up in massive beauty and was lost in small, moist clouds newly formed about the spire. The tower was, he reflected, very nearly a mile high.

The moving walk slowed and stopped opposite a tall arched entrance. Blade left the walk and went into the tower, past robot guards and attendants, past men and women and children, all robots, all frozen into workaday attitudes. There could have been no warning, Blade thought. These robots had been cut off in the midst of life. And yet they were not dead in the real sense. They waited.

He crossed a vast lobby to where a bank of elevators hung motionless, their machinery as dead as the robots. Blade began to search for a stair, wondering if he had the strength to climb a mile into the sky, when he heard a faint whirring sound. He found the source at the far end of the elevator bank. One small lift, nothing but a series of barren cages, was in operation. Like empty boxes on a chain the little cages constantly ascended and descended on the far side.

Blade hesitated, still wary, and for the first time the voice spoke to him. Spoke in his brain. There was no outward sound, no echo in the great lobby, nothing but the neutral and unshaded voice—pure sound—speaking clear in his mind. Wearily he wiped his sweat away again and prepared to obey. Sound telepathy.

In his brain the voice said: "Step into one of the cages, Richard Blade. Ascend to me. Fear nothing. When you have reached my level I will speak again."

Blade stepped into a moving box and was carried upward. The journey was slow and seemed endless. There were no doors, no windows, apparently no floor stops, and when the lobby vanished from sight he was in a tube of steel being borne upward. And up and up and up—

The voice spoke to him again: "Soon you will come to a light. Step off the cage there."

Up and up. He saw the light sliding down to meet him. As the box slid past, Blade stepped off and was in a narrow, upward-slanting tunnel of steel. A light glowed at the top of the tunnel. Blade made for it. He passed under it and through an open door and into a vast open rotunda. It was open to the sky on all sides and guarded only by a railing. Moonlight drenched it and Blade caught his breath. To the south, far off beyond the wall, he could see the fires of the Jedd camp.

The voice came back. "There is a ladder near where you now stand. Find it and climb to the next level."

Blade ascended the ladder. He was weak now, still drenched in sweat, and the head pains came with ever-increasing frequency. He could feel the tumors growing in his armpits and groin. How soon would the crazy laughter begin?

He was halfway up the ladder when the voice spoke to him: "You are dying of plague, Richard Blade. You know it and I know it. But you will live yet a time. Long enough to do something for me—the one thing I cannot do for myself."

Blade stared up, his big hands white-knuckled on the rungs of the steel ladder. "How do you know my name?"

"I have followed your every move, and known your every thought, since you arrived in my dimension."

Blade halted just beneath a square opening that led to

212

the level above. "You understand that? You know of computers and X Dimensions?"

Laughter in his brain. "I understand the concepts. But do not waste time. Climb. I am in need of you."

Blade climbed up through the aperture and found himself in a high-walled room of steel. A gleaming square room with no openings. In the exact center of the room was a high tank on stilts of metal. It too was square, about forty by forty feet and twenty feet in depth. A ladder led up the side to a runway atop the tank.

In his brain the voice spoke again: "Stop now. Try to understand what I say. I depend on you."

Blade put his hands on his hips and scowled around him. He might be dying of plague—as indeed he was—but the calm assurance, the superiority, of the bodiless voice was beginning to irk him.

"Where are you?" he asked.

Voice: "I am in the tank. As you will see presently. But now that you are here and cannot leave, and must do as I ask, I will take some little time for explanation. The plague will not kill you immediately and I—I have stood my pain for ages. I can bear it a little longer. I would have you understand, Blade."

Blade put a hand on his sword. "Understand what?"

Voice: "About the Jedds. When they were a great people and ruled the world. Our world. You have seen the robots?"

"I have seen them."

Voice: "They are part of the joke. A great cosmic joke. It was the old Jedds who invented the robots. But they did their work too well—the robots soon surpassed the Jedds and took over and sent them into exile. Far back in the beginning of time, this was, and ever since the Jedds, the humans, have been trying to find their way back here to the land of the Kropes. For so the robots called themselves. Kropes."

Blade frowned. He was sick, very sick, yet found himself with the will and strength to grow angry with this voice. Why the anger he could not understand. But it was

213

there. He was beginning to hate.

Blade said: "Why do you tell me all this?"

Voice: "It amuses me. And can do no harm. And I would strike a bargain with you."

"What sort of bargain?"

"In time—in time. Listen—it was the custom of the Jedds to destroy all their robots when they reached a certain age. They were junked, cannibalized, and new robots made from the parts saved. I, who speak to you now, was a robot and I was in turn discarded and torn apart. But that one time they were careless, the Jedds. My brain was not destroyed as usually was done, the thousands of parts not beaten into a fine powder as was the custom. Instead, a lazy Jedd flung my brain into a pond. I lay in that ooze for centuries and somehow, someway, life came to me. Real life and real intelligence. My own. And I began to grow. I was cunning and I learned how to hide myself. And all the time, over all the long eons, I grew. And at last I had my revenge on the Jedds. I ruled. I invented the Kropes. I built the marvels you have seen. The wall and this tower and all the rest. I built it with my brain. With my *will*. Are you familiar with the theory of telekinesis, Blade?"

Blade's head was spinning. Fever flamed in him and things began to shift slightly out of focus. He took a firmer grip on himself and answered, "I know the theory. I have never seen it work. To create actual physical things by sheer power of will—by *willing* them into existence."

Laughter in his brain. For a moment Blade feared it was his own, the dying manic laughter of plague, then shook it off. He had yet a little time—and in spite of all he still hoped.

Voice: "You *have* seen it, Blade. Look around you and see it again. But enough—to our bargain!"

"I am sick. Ill. I have a great tumor that is killing me. Even *my* will cannot cure it. But you, Blade, you with your sword can cut the tumor out and destroy it and I will be well again. You will do this?"

Blade stared defiantly up at the tank. "Why should I?

214

You are no friend to me. Why should I, who am myself dying, help you to escape death? On the contrary—I would rather have you die. Then the Jedds can come into this land and build it anew for themselves and their children. No. I refuse. You get no help from me."

A different kind of laughter in his brain now.

Voice: "I said a bargain, Blade. If you help me I will permit the Jedds entrance into my land of Kropes. I will aid them in any manner I can. I will put my robots at their disposal, to do all manner of work, and though I shall rule I will do it with kindness and understanding and the Jedds will remain a free people under their young Empress."

Mitgu. The Golden Princess. Blade shook his head to clear it. His temples were pounding now, the fever flaring higher, the loathsome buboes growing like vile toads in his groin and armpits. He would never see her again.

He stared at the shining tank. Moisture gleamed and dripped on the metal, a reddish exudation he had not noticed before. Then his own sweat blinded him again.

"And if I do not make this bargain?"

Voice: "I will die in time. But that will be long coming and before I die I will destroy the Jedds. I know your plans, Blade. When two days have passed I will remain quiet and keep my robots immobilized. The Jedds, as agreed, will come into my land. I will permit them beyond the Shining Gate. I will wait. Then I will send the flame and destroy them every one. To the last Jedd child. What do you say to that, Blade?"

Blade wiped sweat from his eyes with trembling fingers and did not answer. The tank was spinning now, before his eyes, like a great centrifuge. He was so damned weak!

Voice: "Do not underestimate my powers, Blade. It was I who sent the plague upon the Jedds, time and again, to keep them weak. It was either that or destroy them utterly, and I am not cruel for cruelty's sake."

Blade walked to the ladder at the side of the tank. "I will do as you wish." Fast, now. Quickly. Do not think lest the voice divine those thoughts. Act. Now.

He reached the top of the ladder and stood on the runway surrounding the tank. In the tank, all but submerged in a red liquid that gave off a faint smell of brine, floated the brain. It was the size of a small whale. Blade began to walk around the runway, loosening his sword in its sheath.

The enormous brain nearly filled the tank. The lobes were well demarcated and the convolutions writhed in complex whorls of pink and blue-gray tissue.

Voice: "You see the tumor, Blade?"

He saw it. Springing from the right frontal lobe, rooted deep through the dura mater and into the tender arachnoid and pia mater, was a monstrous and sickly white growth. The tumor was nearly as large as Blade himself. He went farther up the runway to examine it. He had a decision to make and he would get only one chance. Frantically, pushing everything else out of his mind, he strove to remember his anatomy, cursing himself for the many times he had dozed through class at Oxford.

He said, "I see the tumor. It is large and goes deep. Shall I begin now?"

Silence. It drew out. Then the voice said, "Begin."

Blade drew his sword and leaped from the runway to land on the floating brain. His feet sank a bit into the spongy cortex and he slipped and nearly fell, then regained his footing. He began to make his way slowly toward the ugly mushroom of the tumor, stepping carefully over the deep sulci that separated the convolutions. Suddenly, out of his own memory file, came remembrance of one of Lord Leighton's droning lectures.

Disrupt the axons of the granule cells in the molecular layer.

Blade reached the tumor and stopped. He raised his sword—and hesitated. There was a new flare of pain in his own skull. A different, but familiar pain. Lord L was reaching for him again.

The voice shrieked: "Get on with it. Cut out the tumor, Blade. Cut it out!"

Whatever their barbarities, Blade thought, the Jedds were human. They deserved their chance. This thing, this monstrous pure brain had outgrown all humanity and was, in essence, evil. It deserved to die. It must die.

Blade leaped over the spreading white tumor. With both hands he raised his sword and plunged it deep into soft pink-blue tissue. He cut and slashed and tore, using all his strength, summoning his last energies, and his iron blade ravaged the brain like a wolf might a tender lamb. Sweat poured from him and Blade heard himself cursing. He was knee deep in reddish fluid. He fell and nearly slipped down the lobe into the tank, but recovered by seizing a mass of tissue and digging in with his nails. All the time he was slashing with his sword.

A scream filled the mile-high tower. It shook on its foundations, trembling like a reed as a vast black wind blew through it. Blade hacked grimly away.

The tower spire was in darkness now. Dense black clouds enveloped it. Lightning drove golden forks into the gloom. The brain moved and heaved beneath Blade. He kept on cutting away in a frenzy of hate and fear. He was gouging out huge gobbets of brainstuff and flinging them aside. The brain lunged upward in the tank, like a fish leaping, and Blade clung for his life. In his ears, in *his* brain, was one long ascending scream of terror and death.

Then new pain. Blade was stricken, paralyzed. He dropped his sword and it slid down the brain and into the tank. Blade sank to his knees as the pain ripped him into shreds. His head left his body, torn away by lightning, and the top of the tower parted and Blade's head was propelled up and out into the night sky. He hurtled toward the moon, full and splendid, a mammoth gold piece in the sky. And suddenly, writ large across the moon in Gothic script, in Lord Leighton's crabbed hand, he saw the words—*Welcome Home, Richard*.

Chapter 19

Police Constable William Higgins was within six months of taking his pension and retiring. He was a big man with a comfortable girth, one of the old school of London bobbies, and what he lacked in formal education he more than made up in tact and patience. Thirty years on the force taught a man something. If it didn't there was no hope for him.

So many years on the force also taught a PC to recognize a gentleman when he saw one. A toff, a nob, boffin—call them what you would, there was always something indefinable, and definitely recognizable, about them.

PC Higgins' beat led him down Whitehall into Parliament Street and thence, by a left turn, into Bridge Street and onto Westminister Bridge. On this night, with Big Ben just gone ten and a raw mist drifting up from the Thames, Higgins huddled into his uniform greatcoat, settled his helmet more firmly against the wind and paused to look down the nearly deserted bridge. It was not a night for pleasure strolls.

PC Higgins made a deep sound in his throat that sounded like, "Oh, ar— Lord lumme! Looks like a bloody jumper."

Cautiously, walking as softly as his large and heavily-shod feet would permit, he began to approach the tall, elderly man who stood, both hands on the bridge parapet,

219

gazing down at the tide sliding muddily down to Gravesend.

As the constable drew near he heard the man talking to himself. The accents were well bred, definitely upperclass, and PC Higgins knew he had a gentleman to deal with. He continued his stealthy approach, hoping to get an arm around the man before he could rouse himself and jump. Careful, Higgins warned himself. Some of these leapers were pretty spry and determined, once they made up their minds to do the Dutch.

One last step and he closed a big hand around the man's arm and sighed with inward relief. Had the blighter now.

The man was indeed a toff. Elderly and distinguished in appearance, but with his Homburg at a rakish slant and his tie loose at the collar. From him, as he turned quietly enough to face Higgins, came a strong waft of whiskey that made Higgins wince. Drunk. Drunk as Billy-be-damned.

"Here now," said PC Higgins. "What's all this, sir? Won't do, you know. A gentleman like you must have a better place to loiter than this cold and blasty bridge. Eh, sir? Shall we be getting along to it, then? I'll walk a way with you and find a taxi."

"We saved him."

PC Higgins released his grip on the man's arm and stared. "Saved who, sir?" He cast a look over the parapet at the turgid river gurgling beneath the arches. What in bloody hell? Was there somebody down there after all?

"We saved Blade," said the tall gentleman. "He came back to us dying of plague, you know, but we saved him. Narrow thing, though. If it hadn't been for the drugs we had flown in from the States we would have lost him. Goddamn his Lordship to hell!"

PC Higgins tapped him on the shoulder in a kindly manner. "I'm sure you did, sir, and I'm glad it came out all right. Now, how about a little walk with me? It's after ten, and cold, and home is a cozy place to be."

"I have been walking," the man said. "Walking and

220

walking and walking. I must have walked over half of London. And I have been drinking."

PC Higgins had his moments. He smiled now and said, "Do tell me, sir. It's the last thing I would have thought."

"I have, though," the man said. He fell in step with the constable, who still held him lightly by the arm. PC Higgins breathed easier. It was going to be all right. No trouble of arrest. Now if he could find one of those sodding cabs that always disappeared when you needed them most.

A gust of Scotch blew into his wind-reddened face. The tall old man said, "I suppose you want some identification, officer. My name is J." He made no effort to produce his wallet or cardcase.

Higgins let it pass. J was good enough. Drunks came up with some mighty queer answers.

"I've been drinking all night," the man said. "Drinking and drinking and drinking. Making a fool of myself. Don't care. Couldn't help it. Glad I did. Because they saved him, you see. Saved Blade."

PC Higgins nodded. "You told me, sir. Now if we could step along a bit livelier, sir? I've still my patrol to finish."

"He came back raving and near dead," said the man. "Took the fools forever to diagnose plague. Can't really blame them, I suppose. Like bubonic and yet not bubonic. Couldn't find the bacillus pestis, you see."

"I'm sure," said PC Higgins and rolled his eyes skyward. You got all kinds. He thought of the snug cottage in the country, just purchased with his savings, and of the roses he meant to grow. Five months to go. Only five months. Lord gimme strength, he prayed.

They left the bridge and the constable cast around for a taxi. Not an effing cab in sight. Naturally. He took the man's arm again and led him gently down Bridge Street. There was an all-night stand down Whitehall a way.

"He was yellow," said the man. He pulled his arm away from the constable and pointed to a traffic stripe glinting in the street lights. "As yellow as that divider strip."

PC Higgins made comforting sounds. "Now, now, sir.

221

No need to dwell on it. I'm sure the gentleman is going to be all right."

"He will. He is going to get well. But no thanks to them, to those fools of doctors. They thought he had simple jaundice. I had to do it! I had to insist that they make a culture and find a growth media, search for some sort of bug. You'd have thought I was the doctor. And it was his Lordship, damn him to hell; but give credit where it is due, it was Lord L who got the drugs in from the States."

PC Higgins turned his face away from the blast of Scotch breath. Enough to make a man drunk just smelling it.

"I am very drunk," said the man.

The constable nodded heavily, gravely. "That you are, sir. Bed is where you belong. Just as soon as we find you a taxi."

"I am drunk, drunk, drunk," said the man. He skipped a few steps, whirled, leaped into the air and clicked his heels, then faced the constable. "Haven't been this drunk in forty years. Since I came down from Cambridge. Did I tell you my name was J? Are you going to arrest me?"

PC Higgins tipped back his helmet and scratched his balding brow. Lumme! This gent really had his load on. Where in the blinking hell was a taxi? The cabstand, now looming into view, was deserted.

"No need to arrest you, sir. Unless you become disorderly, and I'm sure a gentleman like you—"

The man called J leaned toward the constable, supporting himself by clinging to a lamp standard. His eyes were glazed and owlish. He said, "A gentleman like me does some very queer things, constable. Things you wouldn't dream of—things you wouldn't *want* to dream of!"

Ignoring the cold wind, PC Higgins took off his helmet and wiped his brow with a huge colored handkerchief. "I'm sure you do, sir. And I'm sure I wouldn't—Oho, there is a taxi now! Just pulling up."

PC Higgins put his whistle to his mouth and puffed out a mighty blast. The taxi made a U-turn and came back to

222

them. The constable bundled his charge into the back seat. "There you are, sir. You'll be fine, you will. Now just go home and have a nice sleep."

The man leaned out the window. For a moment his eyes cleared and there was concern on his face. His face was steady. "Thank you, constable. And I would appreciate it if you would just forget this—forget everything I said, whatever it may have been." He fell back into the seat and gave the driver an address in Belgravia.

PC Higgins spoke as the taxi pulled away. "I'll forget it, sir. With pleasure."

PC Higgins turned and started back toward Westminster Bridge. Five months until he took his pension. He grinned. Five months wasn't so long. Then he could grow roses— and rest his feet.